BORN TO THE BADGE

BORN TO THE BADGE

MARK WARREN

FIVE STAR
A part of Gale, a Cengage Company

Farmington Hills, Mich • San Francisco • New York • Waterville, Maine
Meriden, Conn • Mason, Ohio • Chicago

Copyright © 2018 by Mark Warren
Map: Travels of Wyatt Earp Copyright © 2018 by Mark Warren
Stuart N. Lake Papers courtesy of the Huntington Library, San Marino, California.
Five Star Publishing, a part of Gale, a Cengage Company

LIBRARY OF CONGRESS CATALOGING-IN-PUBLICATION DATA

Names: Warren, Mark, 1947– author.
Title: Born to the badge / Mark Warren.
Description: Farmington Hills, Mich. : Five Star, 2018. | Series: Wyatt Earp, an American odyssey ; book 2
Identifiers: LCCN 2018014291 (print) | LCCN 2018018063 (ebook) | ISBN 9781432848866 (ebook) | ISBN 9781432848859 (ebook) | ISBN 9781432848842 (hardcover)
Subjects: LCSH: Earp, Wyatt, 1848-1929—Fiction. | Holliday, John Henry, 1851-1887—Fiction. | United States marshals—Fiction. | Frontier and pioneer life—West (U.S.)—Fiction. | Dodge City (Kan.)—Fiction. | GSAFD: Western stories. | Biographical fiction.
Classification: LCC PS3623.A86465 (ebook) | LCC PS3623.A86465 B67 2018 (print) | DDC 813/.6—dc23
LC record available at https://lccn.loc.gov/2018014291

First Edition. First Printing: November 2018
Find us on Facebook—https://www.facebook.com/FiveStarCengage
Visit our website—http://www.gale.cengage.com/fivestar/
Contact Five Star Publishing at FiveStar@cengage.com

Printed in Mexico
1 2 3 4 5 6 7 22 21 20 19 18

For Susan
and all the days to come

Travels

1873 – 1879

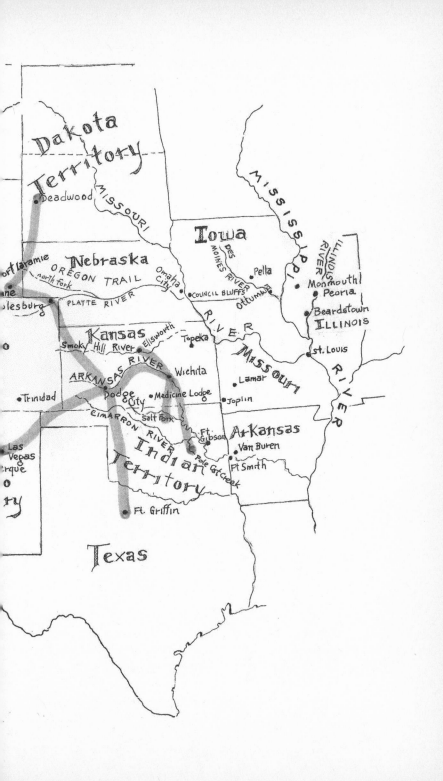

"They were in the vanguard of law and order in the early days of Kansas . . . God bless old Wyatt Earp and men of his kind. They shot their way to heaven."

~John Madden, Attorney, Dodge City, Kansas, 1928

CHAPTER 1

Spring, 1874: Wichita, Kansas

Wichita, Kansas, was hell in the making. With the Wichita and South Western rail tracks now connected to the Santa Fe's main line, commerce had been pumped into the town like a stick thrust into a hornets' nest. The tent phase of the business district had passed. Every building on the main street was built of wood with a flashy façade intended to show off wares and lure in customers. Soon the longhorns would be driven here from Texas to be shipped east by rail. The men who herded these cattle north brought with them old Southern grievances into the more prosperous land of the Yankees. That festering wound of the war and the God-given right to blow off steam at the end of the trail drive made for a volatile mix.

In addition to the drovers came a steady stream of bull whackers, mule skinners, buffalo runners, gamblers, and con men. Soldiers on leave from Fort Larned frequented the town and clashed with civilians in the saloons and houses of prostitution. Guns, alcohol, and hot-headed frontiersmen . . . all with something to prove. It had been the same in Ellsworth. Every railroad town on the plains had faced this double-edged sword of an economic boom. Some towns survived it; some did not. Only time would tell.

Without a settled personality, the town reminded Wyatt Earp of his first glimpse of Omaha City, where, as a boy of sixteen crossing the country, he had been witness to two men settling an argument by the sudden explosion of revolvers not ten feet apart. The remembrance of that fight had stayed with him as a vivid image. It reminded him that—regardless of the law—the ultimate tool of survival on the frontier came down to what a man did or did not do.

Now at twenty-five, Wyatt considered that such a budding center of commerce as this might supply the venue where his aspirations could take root. They were alike in ways, Wyatt and Wichita—both just getting their legs and wide open to possibilities. All he needed was the right deal with the right people. He had no real definition for that business opportunity, yet he knew that, whatever it was, he had the grit and lasting power to make it succeed.

He dismounted and stretched his legs as he walked his horses down Douglas Avenue to the river. The broad, muddy Arkansas cut through the settlement like a curved saber slash from God's judgmental hand. On the west bank it was called "Delano." There, outnumbering all other businesses, were the brothels and saloons, bawdy and flirtatious, their ambient music tinkling carefree across the slow glide of the brown water.

The east side, where he now stood, was showing signs of organization, sprouting from a seed of respectability. Connecting the two halves of the dichotomous community was a substantial wooden bridge that seemed appropriately long for the metaphoric crossover to sin or salvation, depending on a man's direction of travel . . . or his particular need at a given time of the day.

Here Wyatt sensed the same delicate balance of tensions he had witnessed in half a dozen other cow towns: the money brought in by cattlemen weighed against the politics of tolerating the sins of the drovers. When the herds came in, big money would change hands in the stockyards, but it would be Delano that would hold the drovers here long enough to support the merchants on either side of the river. At best, it was an awkward symbiosis, both delicate and dangerous. Every cattle town soaked one foot in a lukewarm bath of compromise, always trying to douse whatever spark inevitably flew loose, a pragmatic balancing of interests that Wyatt found distasteful. At the same time, it was a lively place to be, with plenty of cash flow to feed the gaming tables.

Wyatt had begun to consider himself a professional gambler, at least until he settled on a proper vocation with a promising future. Come late spring, when the herds came in, he might position himself as a cattle buyer. The right poker game with the right people could provide that kind of capital in a single night.

He led his saddle horse and pack horse down a ramp to the water's edge to let them drink their fill. In the privacy below the bridge, he wet his hair in the river and combed it by raking his fingers over his scalp. Then he changed into a clean shirt and wiped his boots to a dull shine with the oil-stained, gun-cleaning rag he carried in his saddlebag.

Only when he started up the ramp did he see someone watching him from the shadows under the bridge. A man lay sprawled out on a torn straw mattress, where the structural beams rested upon a levee of heavy wooden ties. The man was unshaven and shirtless, his suspender straps running over the bare skin and bone of his narrow shoulders. He propped on an elbow to be better seen.

"I could use some money if you think you can spare some," the man said in an offhand manner. "Ain't got no kinda work at the present."

Wyatt looked at the hard-luck story before him, embarrassed by the utter loss of dignity in the man's asking. "Know where I can find James Earp?" he said, nodding across the river.

"He's on this side." The man raised an arm and pointed

through the bridge. "You're 'bout standin' 'neath 'im."

Wyatt dug a coin from his trouser pocket and tossed it. Snatching it out of the air, the man showed surprising agility. He touched a finger to his brow in a poor man's salute, as Wyatt led his horses up the ramp back to the street.

The one-story clapboard house had been slapped together from rough-sawn lumber with no attempt at adornment. Wyatt tied his horses to the gate of a spring wagon parked beside the house and picked a path through various items of trash to the front stoop. On his fourth series of knocks, the door cracked open, and the timid face of a plain-featured, dark-haired female floated into view. With homely, close-set eyes and a pouting mouth, she peered out mutely and clasped the collar of her nightgown. Behind her someone snored in the front room. A cloying mix of powdered talcum, rose water, and unwashed flesh poured past her out of the doorway.

"I'm looking for James Earp," Wyatt said.

The young woman pulled in her lips, lowered her eyes, and drew back, her gauzy nightgown billowing around her. The door all but shut. When she reappeared, there was something different about her hair, and she now clasped the lapels of a faded robe to her throat.

"He's still asleep," she mumbled. "And Bessie's not up yet."

"I'm his brother."

Before she could react to this news, the girl turned to the sound of someone treading heavily across the room behind her. "We're not open, Sally. Tell him to come back." It was the husky voice of a woman in charge. "We got to catch our breath *sometime.*"

Sally lowered her head and started to speak, but the woman cut her off by swinging the door open wider. "We're not open, mister. Come back around dark."

She was imposing, with a strong, heart-shaped face that

clearly brooked no debate. Her jaded eyes bore into him without any tempering of courtesy.

"It's Jim's brother," Sally whispered from behind the door.

Bessie studied the visitor up and down. "Which one?" she said, her hardened face now a challenge.

"Wyatt."

"Well, good Lord!" She stepped forward, grabbed his sleeve, and pulled him into the room. "Sally, go wake up Jim." Bessie stepped back and propped her fists on her hips. "So how'd you turn out so tall? And handsome!"

Wyatt had no answer for that.

Still examining him, Bessie fussed with the back of her hair. "Well, get yourself comfortable," she offered. "He'll drag out of bed eventually." And then, chuckling to herself, she disappeared into a back room, shaking her head.

Still standing, Wyatt looked around. On a floral-print divan halfway across the room, a fair-haired woman lay snoring beneath a tattered quilt, half her face pressed into the cushion. Even so, he recognized her as the whore James had brought from Ellsworth. The perfumed warmth of the room pushed Wyatt back toward the opening in the door.

Within a minute the girl named Sally tapped mouse-like from the back of the house and stopped at the divan, her hands clasped together beneath her small breasts and pressed into the folds of her robe. When Wyatt caught her staring at him, she quickly turned her attention to the floor.

Then a much younger girl appeared from a back hallway and attached herself to Sally's waist. Sally leaned and whispered into her ear, and the girl nodded. Arms wrapped around each other, they stared at Wyatt as if peering through a peephole from a secret hiding place.

"Does James *live* here?" Wyatt asked.

Sally nodded. "This is his house," she said meekly. "Him and Bessie's."

Other than the snoring coming at intervals from the tangle of blond hair on the divan, there was not another sound in the house. A bead of sweat ran down Wyatt's back. The younger girl sucked in her lips, making her mouth thin as an incision. Wyatt wondered if she could speak.

"You sure he knows I'm here?" Wyatt said.

After a whispery conference with Sally, the little girl disengaged and bolted deeper into the house. "That's Bessie's girl, Hattie," Sally offered. "She'll get him up."

He nodded toward the back of the house. "Exactly who is Bessie?"

They heard the kitchen sounds of a cooking pot and china-ware clanging and rattling in the back, and Sally lowered her eyes again. "Bessie is Jim's . . . his wife."

The girl named "Hattie" reappeared, tiptoeing across the room, where she resumed pressing her cheek into Sally's ribs, her eyes soaking up their visitor. Wyatt plucked at the back of his damp shirt and began sidling through the open door.

"Have to go and see to my horses," he said. "Tell James I'm just outside."

Standing by the wagon where the horses were tied, Wyatt heard the door unlatch and saw Sally peering at him through the crack. He patted the mare's long neck muscles, then turned to the gelding to pick at seeds tangled in the bay's mane.

Within a minute the door scraped wide open. "Well, look what's washed up out o' the river," James laughed as he picked his way through the garbage in his yard. He pulled each suspender strap over his shoulders with the hand of his good arm. "You get rich yet?"

Wyatt took his brother's outstretched hand and nodded back toward the house. "Didn't tell me you got married?"

"Hell, yes. Married to the bone. You meet Bessie?"

Wyatt nodded and let his gaze rove over the rough carpentry of the brothel. "She in this business with you?"

"Hell, yes," James laughed. "She owns it."

Still inspecting the house, Wyatt pursed his lips and did not speak for a time.

"That girl . . ." he finally said, "she's little young for a whore, ain't she?"

"Hattie?" James coughed up a laugh. "She ain't no whore. That's Bessie's daughter." He made a grandiose sweep of his arm. "Bessie and me *run* this fine establishment. And I'm pourin' drinks at a few of the better saloons," he added, pointing east into the proper side of town. James smiled and poked a thumb over his shoulder at the house. "But this here's where the money is."

The building did little to advertise its profit. No paint. No trim work. The window shutters closed on leather hinges nailed into the frame. It appeared to be two shacks, one added to the back of the other.

"How is it you're on this side of the river?" Wyatt asked.

James snorted a laugh, and the skin around his eyes fanned with lines just like brother Morgan's. "Special arrangement, you might say. Over here, Wichita requires a license for brothels. It's like a tax, except it ain't on paper 'cause it ain't really legal." James squinted across the silvery surface of the Arkansas toward Delano. "Over yonder's the hell-town, where there ain't no fee, but . . ." He shrugged with his good shoulder. "I'm willin' to pay. Puts us up a notch bein' over here, so we can charge more." James turned quickly to Wyatt. "Hey, you planning on stayin'?"

"Not sure yet. I'm considering buyin' some cattle."

"Hell, you can work for me right here. I could use an enforcer."

Wyatt hesitated so as not to insult his brother. Again he

studied the building's crude exterior and thought back to his days in Peoria when he, too, had lived in such a place, using his fists to keep the clientele in line.

Bessie leaned out the door and called for James in a dull voice that carried the ring of insult. James's eyes flicked her way for an instant, but he only smiled and pretended to ignore her.

"So tell me 'bout bein' a cattle king," he said, leading Wyatt back to the house.

Bessie was waiting in the doorway, her face set for battle. "We got a lingerer in the back—that hairy-ape hotel man, Black. Says he'll leave when he damn well pleases."

"Who's he with?" James said, letting a little irritation surface in his voice.

"Kate," Bessie snapped, as though the whore were somehow complicit in the breach of procedure.

James led the way inside, followed by Bessie, and then Wyatt. "Hattie," James instructed in a calm voice, "I need you to step out to the front porch for a spell. Will you do that, darlin'?" He moved to a cupboard against the wall and rose up on his toes to reach the top shelf. "Sally," he said, checking the loads on a new Colt's revolver, "get dressed and run down to the marshal's office. See if Cairns is on duty. Get him down here quick as you can."

Sally appeared stricken to be assigned such a chore. "What if he's not there?" she whispered.

James snapped the loading gate shut and fixed his eyes on the back hallway. "Then he ain't," he said simply. "Just get on back here and stay with Hattie. We might have to handle it ourselves."

"You got no enforcer?" Wyatt asked.

James made his wry smile. "I'm it," he quipped, tapping his bad shoulder with the barrel of the pistol. "Half of it anyway." He raised the gun barrel up between them. "This here's the other half."

Wyatt looked past his brother at the back of the house. "Which room is it?"

A look of gratitude crept into James's face. "Second one on the right. He's a mean one, Wyatt. Strong as a bull. Used to be a blacksmith. Kate's the only one feisty enough to bed him."

"The door locked?" Wyatt inquired.

"None of 'em lock," James said.

"There a window in that room?"

James's brow furrowed. "Well, sure, but—"

Wyatt started toward the hall. "Go move your wagon away from the house and wait on me outside."

Holding out the Colt's as an offer, James stopped his brother. "Like I said . . . he's a strong sonovabitch."

Wyatt ignored the weapon. "Take that shooter with you," he said and walked into the dark of the hallway.

Stepping through the second door, Wyatt moved past the mound of flesh under the sheets and crossed the dingy room to the window. The stink of rancid flesh hung heavily in the still air. He unhooked the clasp and swung the windows open. Turning back to the room, he found the brawny customer peeling out of the sheets. The disheveled whore looked defiantly at Wyatt, though he could not be sure whether her anger was directed toward him or her customer.

"Who the hell're you!" the man growled. He stood in the bottom half of his union suit with the top hanging off his backside at half-mast. His belly was rounded and hard, his chest and arms matted with dark, curly hair. His arms were flaccid but thick as hitching rails.

"Your time is up. You can leave on your own, or I can help you. Which'll it be?"

The burly man gave Wyatt an expression of incredulity. "You can go fuck your—"

Wyatt's fist caught the man in the mouth mid-speech, sending him stumbling backward to sit on the bed. A stream of blood poured from his burst lip. As the hairy man bowed his head to probe the damage done, Wyatt grabbed a handful of hair and a knot of drawers at his lower back and heaved him clear out the window.

By the time Wyatt had joined James in the yard the hairy outcast had recovered from the fall enough to sit up. Craning his neck, he outstretched an arm, trying to assess the damage to an elbow.

James stood to one side, the Colt's revolver gripped firmly in his good hand. Wide-eyed, Bessie peered at Wyatt from around her husband's shoulder. From the open window, boots, clothes, and a hat began to rain down onto the side yard. They all turned to see the whore, Kate, leaning on the windowsill, half her naked body exposed to the world. When she let loose a string of profanity, James chuckled and waved her back inside with the pistol.

Sally came up from the avenue in a stiff-legged trot. Behind her a tall, lean man walked in a long stride that made the leather of his pistol scabbard squeak with a steady rhythm. On his shirt a silver badge flashed in the morning light. When Sally stopped at the corner of the house and wrapped her arms around herself, Hattie ran from the front porch and attached to her. The deputy stepped beside James, splayed his hands on his hips, and contemplated the scene.

The disgruntled customer pushed to his feet and squirmed into the top of his union suit, all the while his eyes fixed on Wyatt. "Think I don't know how to use a goddamned door?" he growled.

"Maybe so, Harvey," James said, "but you might not know *when* to use it."

"Charge dat ape double," Kate called from the window. "I

20

haff to wash deez sheets two times. He smell like da foul end uff a goat."

The man straightened and took a step toward Wyatt. "You sonovabitch. I was half asleep. I got a mind to take some o' that cock out o' your walk."

"You'd best be on your way," Wyatt said.

The man leveled a finger at James. "I paid for a night with that Hungarian she-devil."

James wagged the pistol barrel like a scolding finger. "You paid for a poke, Harvey. This ain't your hotel." He bobbed the gun toward the house. "We got other customers to service."

Then, with a dexterity that belied the man's bulk, Black turned and took a wild swing at Wyatt's head. But Wyatt was not standing where he had been. Off balance, the man attempted to redirect his blow, stumbled, and stretched his arms forward to catch himself. Stepping in quickly, Wyatt felled him with a hard-knuckled blow just behind the ear. Black lay dazed for a moment, staring at the pool of blood and saliva in the dirt that drooled from his open mouth. Pushing himself up, he managed to sit and seemed to accept his situation as the natural course of events that had started his day.

The deputy laughed quietly as he stepped forward to stand before the disgruntled customer. "Mornin', Mr. Black." Then he turned his head to James. "Any complaints here from either party?"

James put on a mischievous grin. "We were just trying out my new customer emergency exit . . . in the event of a fire."

The deputy cocked his head toward the ousted customer. "How's that workin' out, Mr. Black?"

Black looked up at the window, where the smirking whore still leaned on the frame. Then, inflating his cheeks, he spewed a stream of air through his swollen lips and pushed himself to his feet. After picking up his clothes and boots, he stuffed his hat on his head and limped toward the street.

Cairns turned to Wyatt. "You're the brother?" He extended a hand, and Wyatt accepted.

"He's *one* of 'em," James said. "This here's Wyatt."

"Jimmy Cairns," the deputy said and nodded in the direction that Black had gone. "Looks like you might save me some trips down here in the future. You here for long?"

"Don't know for sure." Wyatt kept his eyes on Cairns but spoke for James's benefit. "But I don't aim to work as an enforcer. Might like to try something else."

"Ever do police work?"

"Some."

"Where 'bouts?"

Wyatt hesitated only a moment. "Missouri. I was constable there."

"And Ellsworth," James butted in. "You hear about that? He wore a badge less than an hour and put it over on Ben Thompson and his crowd."

Cairns paused a moment, pushed his lower lip forward, and studied Wyatt. "We got us a marshal likes to hire on temporary help when the situation calls for it. Think that might interest you?"

"Might," Wyatt said. "Only I reckon I'll be anglin' for something more permanent."

"Well . . ." Cairns leaned and spat a dollop of tobacco into the dirt. "Truth is, 'tween the permanent and the temporary, you'd have the better end of the stick . . . leastwise when the cattle comes in."

"How's that?" Wyatt said.

Cairns spat again. "There's three of us deputies and the assistant marshal. We're the ones got to toe the mark, treat the drovers like they was our damn sisters." He shook his head. "*That* don't work, Marshal Smith calls up the specials on stand-by, encourages *them* to crack some heads. Then, to keep the drovers from grumbling too much, he can dismiss the specials like it's a favor to the Texas boys . . . 'til there's need for 'em again."

"Pay any good?" Wyatt asked.

As James began herding the women back to the front porch, Cairns turned and hitched his head for Wyatt to follow. "Two dollars a day," the deputy said as he ambled toward the street. "Supply your own artillery. Ammunition, too. You work five minutes as a special, you get the full day's pay." Cairns grinned. "Hell, *I* gotta work the whole damn day to make that." He shrugged. "Bonus on arrests. Every court fine you get on the books puts money in your pocket." The deputy smiled with the hint of a sneer. "Best part'll be watchin' you crack some skulls." He lost the smile and spat again. "I'm 'bout half-tired of coddling them damn Texas boys." He raised his eyebrows to Wyatt. "So . . . want me to tell Smith 'bout you?"

Wyatt looked down Douglas Avenue. It was a town big enough to suggest a number of possibilities, but until he narrowed those down, he would need to earn some money. A job with the marshal's office might give him both visibility and respectability in the community.

"Yeah," Wyatt said. "Tell him."

CHAPTER 2

Late spring, 1874: Wichita, Kansas

Two days after the first longhorns came in from Texas, Jimmy Cairns banged on Wyatt's door at the Sedgwick House and told him to get dressed and down to the bridge. "Consider yourself a special deputy for the day," Cairns said, turning to leave.

"What's going on?" Wyatt said, stopping him in the hall.

"You hear 'bout that nigger manhandled two Texans yesterday for badgerin' his wife? Well, they just shot him dead while he was carryin' mud up a ladder for a bricklayer. Some of those boys held a gun on Marshal Smith while the shooters hoofed it across to Delano. Smith's pullin' together ever' good man he can find. We're meetin' down at the bridge near your brother's place."

Wyatt dressed, checked the loads on his new revolver, and hurried to the livery to saddle the chestnut mare. As he rode up to the crowd at the river, he was surprised to see Cairns and the others on foot bunched at the end of the bridge.

"Where're your horses?" Wyatt asked.

Cairns spat tobacco over the handrail and stepped away from the others. "Smith wants us to stand guard here," he muttered, his tone full of embarrassment. He looked away and shook his head. " 'Case the Texans make a run at us," he added wryly and turned back to Wyatt to show his disgust for the plan.

Still sitting his horse, Wyatt scanned the crowd of armed men milling about on the road. "Where's Smith?"

"Last time I saw him," said a short, compactly built man carrying a carbine, "he was in his office writing up a report." His voice hummed with sarcasm.

Wyatt checked Cairns for confirmation. "Sounds 'bout right," the deputy said and spat again.

The shorter man approached Wyatt. "Earp? I'm John Behrens." He pointed to a blue-black gelding tethered to the bridge post. "Looks like you and me are the only ones serious about a man gettin' killed around here . . . nigger or not."

Wyatt looked across the river. "Those boys got no reason to come back over here."

"Hell, no," Behrens huffed. "I think I'll just go home and write me up a report or something." He walked to his horse.

Jimmy Cairns chewed aggressively on his wad of tobacco and glared across the river. Wyatt stared across the quiet glide of the current a few moments, then wheeled his horse around and returned to his hotel.

Over the next few weeks the drovers took every opportunity to mock the police over their useless display at the bridge. Wyatt, glad not to be wearing a badge that would advertise him as one of the do-nothings, concentrated on taking the Texans' money in the gambling halls. When he wasn't sitting in on a poker game, he watched the faro dealer's layout to learn the fine points of that game. With the use of a box to hold the cards hidden, there were new opportunities for a skilled player to turn the odds in his favor. No one was going to teach him these tricks, Wyatt knew. A man learned them on his own, or simply became a member of the fleeced flock.

On the day he went to pick up his two dollars for showing up at the bridge, Wyatt stepped into the marshal's office and leaned against a wall while a short, bug-eyed man with heavily pomaded hair and a suit too warm for the afternoon lectured

Marshal Billy Smith.

"It's a seven-hundred-and-fifty-dollar piano, Marshal. The second payment was due last month. I've gone down there three times and each time been turned back at gunpoint. Now I'm calling on you to either collect or foreclose. These papers are clear."

Smith showed soft features, as if he had never pulled a day's work that broke a sweat. His cheeks were rosy like a woman's. Leaning back in his chair, he tried to look serious without losing the practiced smile that seemed a permanent feature of his face.

"Mr. Chandler, if Ida doesn't have the money, all I can do is put her in jail. And as I'm not set up to accommodate a female, that would involve the added expense, puttin' her up at the hotel, see? If she's sitting in a hotel room, well . . . her business is going to slack off, and *that* won't help your problem much."

"Meanwhile my piano is sitting down there . . . unpaid for . . . and every time I go after it, one of the drunken patrons bangs on the keys with his pistol, while the rest threaten to kill me."

Tilting his head to one side, Smith let his smile widen. "Aw, they're just poking some fun at you, Mr. Chandler. We have to go a little easy on our visitors, you know." Smith, now occupied with the button on one of his shirt cuffs, would not meet the collector's eyes. Then he sat forward and began sorting through papers as though the interview had ended. "I'll talk to Ida, and we'll see if we can get some o' that money for you before too long. Just tell the folks in Kansas City it's early in the season. The city's income is just starting to roll in."

Welcoming a new order of business, Smith turned to Wyatt. "You're Earp, I believe."

Wyatt pushed away from the wall. "Come for my pay."

Smith held the same pleasant expression he had just used

with the collector, patient and self-satisfied, as though it was impossible to tell him something he did not already know. Smith leaned forward to extend his hand over the desk, and Wyatt took it.

"Billy Smith," the marshal said melodically. There was a proper turn to his words that, with a trace of English accent, reminded Wyatt of Ben Thompson. His grip was weak and the hand itself soft as a child's. Wyatt could find nothing of grit in the man. His eyes were like the open windows of an empty house, and the smile just part of the trim work.

The collector spun away with a peevish hiss of air and paced to the window. The marshal settled back into his chair and kept his eyes on a pencil that he tapped on the desk.

"I hear you didn't stay any too long at the bridge," he said through his fixed smile. "If you want to draw pay, you're going to have to do more than just make an appearance."

"Wasn't any reason to wait on something that wasn't going to happen," Wyatt said.

Smith shook his head at the pencil. " 'Fraid you got to do better than that."

"I was prepared to. Cairns said we weren't going into Delano. Your orders."

Smith glanced at Wyatt, opened a drawer, and dropped in the pencil. "Can't go starting a war with the Texans over a dead nigger."

"And now you're paying for it," Wyatt said, allowing an edge to his voice.

Smith looked up again, then he sniffed as if he hadn't heard the censure in Wyatt's voice.

Wyatt nodded toward Chandler. "How 'bout we start turning that around right now, and I go get this man's piano."

The collector perked up and approached the desk. "Marshal, if I go back without either the payment or the piano, I can assure you the state attorney general will have to get involved."

"We want to help you, Mr. Chandler; it's the ways and the means by which we do it that we have to live with here."

"I'll be the means," Wyatt said. "I'll need four men for lifting."

Smith stared out the window and pursed his lips. "I don't have four men to give you." He arched his eyebrows and smiled as if that were the end of the conversation.

"Then give me Cairns, and I'll choose the others. Am I a special?"

Smith fingered his smooth chin. "These other men," he said, "they'll have to come out of your pay." He studied Wyatt to see how this part of the verbal contract affected the proposal. Wyatt made no response. "And no gunplay," Smith ordered.

"Give me a badge. I want it official." Wyatt turned to Chandler. "You're going to need a wagon."

With his new Colt's "peacemaker" stuffed into his waistband, Wyatt walked into Ida May's brothel, followed by John Behrens, Jimmy Cairns, and two local men from the stockyards. Cairns and Behrens each carried a holstered revolver.

Five Texas cowmen sat at a table, their clothes rumpled but new. At the intrusion, they turned idly from their card game and watched the officers file into the room. Two others drank with a curly-haired woman on a long bench, no more impressed by the officers than a third man, who slept on the floor.

Wyatt crossed the room wordlessly, leaned his back into the bar, and hooked his right thumb in his waistband next to his revolver. At his nod, the four men he had brought with him walked over to the piano and squared off at the corners. One of the drovers, sensing the coming of trouble, called for Ida May, who flounced out of an adjoining room and stopped cold, frowning at the men gripping her piano.

"What in hell d'you think you're doing?" she barked. Her outraged face turned quickly to a wagon that rattled to a stop outside the door. There the collecting agent sat next to a driver and, frowning, peered back at her.

"Ida," Wyatt said, keeping his eyes on the men at the table. "Pay up now or the piano goes."

She marched toward the piano but stopped when Wyatt stepped in her way. Standing stiffly, she stared into Wyatt's eyes as her face reddened a shade beneath the powder caked on her cheeks.

"I paid *two* hundred and *fifty* dollars for that claptrap box of noise," she yelled, her voice high-pitched and grating like the grind of unoiled machinery.

"Yes," Wyatt said, "and you were due to pay that again last month." Without taking his eyes off Ida, he raised his voice. "Take it out, boys."

The two yard-hands crouched but hesitated when Cairns and Behrens remained upright. With a hand on the butt of his holstered gun, John Behrens faced the Texans at the table, while Cairns turned to the two on the bench. Ida tried to maneuver around Wyatt, but he took her by the arm and swung her around.

"You interfere, Ida, I'll have to arrest you."

Her face turned savage now, and she tried to jerk free. "Get your fucking hand off me, you pious sonova—!"

Wyatt sat Ida on the bench. "I reckon these Texas boys here are the reason you got the piano in the first place."

Ida looked at the customers clustered around the room. All the men in the card game held hard looks on their faces, their hands motionless on the tabletop.

Wyatt nodded toward the stalled poker game. "Probably got enough money right there on the table to pay for your music," he said.

One rangy Texan opened his mouth to speak but said nothing.

"Were you about to offer to pay?" Wyatt said and stepped behind the man. "Take off your hat."

As the surly Texan twisted around to glare at him, Wyatt knocked the hat off his head. It fell with a light *chink* as it tumbled a stack of coins on the table. The Texan tried to stand, but Wyatt kicked the chair into the back of his knees and pushed him back down.

"Pass the hat around till there's two hundred and fifty in it," Wyatt said. Every Texan's face went to stone. When no one made a move to comply, Wyatt spoke in the same even voice. "Make it five hundred. I don't want to have to come down here and go through this again."

"Easy to push when you got a gun," said the man holding his hat.

Wyatt stepped to the man's side. "Like how you run the collection man outta here?" Wyatt, his eyes now hard with challenge, pulled the Colt's from his waist and tossed it to Cairns, who almost dropped the gun, as surprised as he was.

The long-limbed Texan eyed the gun in Behrens's hand. "Still don't mean I won't get shot."

"That all you Texans do?" Wyatt said, ". . . is talk?" He kicked a chair leg, and the man visibly jumped. The room went so quiet that when Wyatt spoke, it was barely over a whisper. "Cairns, no gunplay. Unless one of these whiskey-pissers pulls on us."

Wyatt knew how it would play out. In front of his friends the man had no choice. The Texan stood. Man to man they were equal in size, but Wyatt's fierce will was like a locomotive about to roar out of a tunnel. The Texan swung at him, but Wyatt stepped inside the blocked arm and knocked the drover across the room. The man stumbled into the wall and slid to the floor.

He did not try to get up.

Wyatt walked to the next man. "Your turn, Texas. Pass the hat or stand up."

The cowman held his look of defiance for only a moment before his face melted into an ugly sulk. Ida May looked with interest at the money on the table. Wyatt kicked this chair harder, and the drover's hand moved reflexively toward his stack of coins. He dropped a cascade of silver eagles into the hat and passed it to the next man.

When the hat was full, Wyatt called in Chandler, who counted out the proper sum of cash, wrote a receipt, and walked briskly from the saloon. When the wagon pulled away, Wyatt took his revolver from Cairns and walked out with his four companions following on his heels.

On the street Wyatt paid Behrens and the yard-hands a half-dollar each. "This squares it," he said, "two dollars split four ways. Jimmy, you're already gettin' paid. Tell Smith what happened. You can tell him there's likely to be trouble."

"He ain't gonna like it, Wyatt."

Wyatt snugged the Colt's back into his waistband. "I don't expect he will."

Within an hour, word had come from Delano that the Clements outfit was preparing to ride into Wichita and run the law into their holes. Thirty armed citizens assembled at the bridge, with Wyatt, Cairns, and Behrens among them. Unarmed, Marshal Smith approached on foot, snapping orders to anyone who got in his way. When he saw Wyatt, he stopped, his usually rosy face now dark, his facile smile replaced by a nervous frown.

"I don't like the way you handled this, Earp. This is trouble we don't need."

Wyatt regarded the marshal. "Best decide right now whose town it is," he advised.

Smith exhaled sharply and squinted down the bridge. "There

could be fifty men coming."

Wyatt looked across the gentle brown glide of the river, its current a quiet testament to the natural order of the world. The man-made bridge spanning the water was sturdy and well-built, but only wide enough for a single coach and team of horses.

"Can't be fifty men coming across all at once," he said. "Too narrow."

Smith said nothing to that. He would be no help, Wyatt knew, but there were men there to be counted upon. He recognized their reliability in the way they waited, their hands relaxed, their eyes vigilant without betraying useless anxiety.

The sound of horses' hooves struck the far end of the bridge, setting up a steady rumble in the distance. Every man on the Wichita end went still, watching the oncoming army of drovers. The sound escalated with the horses' progress across the wood planks, like a long roll of thunder telegraphing the length of the bridge. Cairns stepped beside Wyatt, even as Smith drew back.

"That's Mannen Clements up front," Jimmy said. "The one in the short, gray coat."

Wyatt made note of the man leading the small army. Several of the riders behind him had slipped rifles from their scabbards and carried them barrel-up with the stocks propped upon their thighs. Every rider he could see wore a pistol in a holster at his hip.

Behrens appeared beside Cairns. "Best not let 'em get over here and spread out." He looked at the marshal. "You wanna select who you want to walk out there to parley?"

Smith stared across the bridge and swallowed. "Hell, I don't care," he said angrily. "Anyone with a badge . . . one of you get out there!"

"Who's to do the talking?" Cairns said. "Shouldn't that be you?"

When Smith did not respond, Wyatt nodded to a man with a

shotgun. "We'll need that scattergun. That'll do most of our talking."

Marshal Smith cursed, snatched the double-barrel ten-gauge away from the surprised man and shouldered his way up front. "Come on," he snapped. "And stay close, goddammit!"

Halfway across the span of the bridge the cattlemen slowed their horses to a brisk walk. The bounce of the riders in the saddle made them appear like a single unstoppable force, agitated and bristling for a fight.

Smith brusquely led the way, but when he unexpectedly stopped, Wyatt, Behrens, and Cairns found themselves standing in front of him. Far behind them, several citizens broke from the cluster at Douglas Avenue and wandered out onto the bridge to hear the exchange.

Clements reined up ten feet away. One of the men from Ida Mae's eased his horse forward, leaned to Clements, and spoke in a low monotone that could not be heard above the clatter of hooves on the boards behind them. The drover's hand came up to point at Wyatt. Clements noted the deputy scroll pinned to Wyatt's shirt, and then his eyes fixed on Wyatt's like two bright nails.

"Get the hell out of our way!" Clements ordered. "We're comin' over!"

Smith inverted the shotgun and lowered it to the bridge planking like a walking cane, the sound of it tapping on the wood an embarrassment to the men standing with him. "Mannen," Smith said, clearing his throat, "we'll need to talk this out."

Clements pointed to Wyatt. "This'n here manhandled some of my crew and took money off 'em."

"You can settle up with Ida Mae," Wyatt said. "*She* owes you boys now."

Clements surveyed the guns in front of him. Screwing his

mouth into a tight smile, he jerked his thumb over his shoulder.

"I got better'n fifty men behind me."

Smith started to respond, but Wyatt cut him off by taking a step forward. "We ain't got that many, but right here, it's just the few of us. I'd say we're the ones that count."

"We ain't afraid to die," Clements said, his raspy whisper a taunt. "How 'bout you town boys?"

Marshal Smith shifted his weight as though he might step backward. "Now wait, Mannen," he began, but he said no more, only running his tongue across his lips.

" 'Fraid to die?" Behrens laughed and raised the stock of his rifle to his shoulder. The skin on his face went as taut as stretched canvas. "You want . . . we can turn this bridge red right now," he growled. "But you're not fuckin' crossing over."

Clements leaned on his pommel a moment and then straightened, taking the weight off his arms. His eyes ticked back and forth between Behrens's carbine and Wyatt's undrawn revolver.

"Cairns," Wyatt said without taking his eyes off the cattleman, "take hold of that scattergun." When he heard the transfer, Wyatt watched Clements's eyes lock on Cairns. The Texas leader sat his horse stiffly, as Wyatt slid his Colt's easily from his waistband. He could see in Clements's face the worrisome calibration of what that shotgun could do. "Cock it, Jimmy," Wyatt ordered.

Against the shearing sounds of the water parting around the bridge pilings, the shotgun's hammers made a crisp, metallic *click-click*. The light in the sky seemed to open wider over the narrow stage of the bridge. The random rhythm of the horses idly shifting their weights on the timbers and the creak of saddle leather were clear and punctuated, as though these random sounds were meant to fill in the wordless vacuum.

Wyatt pivoted his body, turning his right side to the front, the barrel of his gun poised at an angle toward the planking like a man about to engage in pistol practice. "I want you to understand something, Mannen," Wyatt said loud enough to be heard by the men immediately flanked behind Clements. "If one of your men throws down on us—it don't matter which one—you die first. So this is really about you. You can turn around . . . or you can go to hell from this bridge right now."

Clements again eyed Cairns's steady hold on the shotgun. Then he studied Wyatt and Behrens. Finally he looked past them at Wichita, spat on the bridge, and curled his mouth into a scowl.

"There'll be other days," he said and raised his arm in a circling motion as he reined his horse around. Like a sleeve pulled inside out, the front horses folded back into the crowd, the slatted muscles in their hindquarters shifting with the syncopated clap of their hooves on the boards.

Smith bustled forward, teeth bared. "You really think that's the last of that, Earp?" he hissed.

Wyatt would not look at him. "More like a start," he replied.

Smith exhaled loudly. "You could have gotten us all killed with that stupid bluff!" He glared across the river, as if uncertain what to say next. "Goddammit," he muttered under his breath.

Wyatt and Behrens looked at one another, and then, shaking his head, Behrens walked back up the bridge toward town. Wyatt slipped his gun into his waistband and stepped in front of the marshal.

"I reckon we're done here," he said. "I'll come by later for my pay."

Before he had reached his horse, Wyatt heard Smith light into Cairns in a muffled tirade of exasperation. Wyatt mounted and watched the deputy lower the hammers of the shotgun.

"It weren't no bluff, Billy," Cairns said flatly and pushed the shotgun into the hands of its owner. Smith frowned at Cairns's back as the deputy walked up Douglas Avenue. Wyatt met Smith's eyes briefly before reining the chestnut around and heading for the livery.

CHAPTER 3

Summer, 1874: Wichita, Kansas

After the incident on the bridge, Marshal Billy Smith showed no inclination to use either Behrens or Wyatt for police work. Instead, to back his deputies, he agreed to an armed committee of citizens that could be summoned at a moment's notice by ringing a triangle hung from the rafters of the courthouse porch. But the standoff at the bridge had served Wyatt's interests. Word of how he had handled Mannen Clements spread quickly, and two gaming houses took him on as a dealer, his very presence ensuring order.

On the first night the alarm sounded, Wyatt was working at the Gold Room. Gunshots had echoed across town for several minutes before Wyatt closed his faro game, stood, and removed his new coat. After draping the coat over the back of his chair, he rolled his sleeves midway up each forearm. Borrowing the manager's pistol, he walked toward the gunfire and found the vigilance group gathering on the corner near Friar's Saloon. Keeping to the boardwalk, he paralleled the armed citizens as they walked toward the front of the saloon, where a rowdy group of Texans had formed a ring around two men—one a deputy of Smith's, the other a lanky, long-haired drover who raised his pistol above his head. The shot he fired echoed loudly between the buildings before the report was swallowed by the night sky.

The drunken shooter staggered and threw back his head to laugh. "Ah-roooooh!" he sang, howling like a coyote. "I'm Hurricane Bill, goddammit!" He raised his gun again and fired straight up into the darkness, then he weaved his way over to the boardwalk, where he flopped down heavily into a chair. From there he aimed unsteadily, and the Texas crowd parted just before he fired off a round into the street. The bullet kicked up dust beside the helpless deputy and whanged off the hard-packed dirt to smack into a storefront on the opposite side of the street.

"You want help with this, Botts?" Wyatt called out to the deputy.

Relief flooded the officer's face. "I damned sure do!"

"I'll take that as official," Wyatt replied and walked directly to the seated Texan.

Confident in their numbers and fogged with liquor, the Texans paid Wyatt no mind. Pushing one man out of his way Wyatt stepped quickly to Hurricane Bill and kicked his wrist with the toe of his boot. The Texan's gun clattered to the boards, and he grabbed his wrist and wailed like a petulant child. Wyatt jerked up on the arm of the chair, and the drunkard crashed onto the boards and into the light of the open door of Friar's. Wyatt picked up the gun and straightened to see a familiar face. George Peshaur walked out of the saloon. When the scar-faced Texan recognized Wyatt, his whiskered face tightened like a wrung-out rag.

Inside Friar's the music stopped, and the customers crowded the door and windows, vying for a vantage to see the loud-mouthed Bill sprawled across the boardwalk. Peshaur flung an empty bottle onto the walkway, where it clanked off the boards and rolled into the street with a hollow ring.

"Well, shit! It's the goddamn California boy," he roared. "Ain't there anywhere in this fuckin' world I can go without trippin' over your sorry ass? What . . . are you the errand boy in this piss-pot town now?"

Wyatt ignored Peshaur's taunt and, gesturing toward the man laid out on the walkway, called over to the deputy. "Botts, are you taking this man to the jail?"

Botts, who had been content in the anonymity of the crowd, now approached and drew his revolver. His sinewy hand tensed with a stranglehold on the gun's grips.

"Hell, yeah, I'm takin' the sonovabitch to jail. And anybody else that wants to go with 'im."

Wyatt waved the gun at the Texans standing mutely in the street. "Then go over there and pick out a few. Anybody carrying a gun'll do."

Wyatt handed the confiscated pistol to the deputy. When he saw that the citizens' group had leveled their guns at the mob in the street, he stuffed the barrel of his borrowed revolver back into his waistband. Botts jerked Hurricane Bill to his feet and pulled him into a reeling walk down the street. Wyatt turned back to Peshaur.

"Well, ain't you a pushy little piece of town shit!" Peshaur snarled. "Always stickin' your nose where it don't belong!"

"You're drunk," Wyatt said. "Get off the street."

"Damn right I'm drunk, but 'at don't mean I can't handle you."

Wyatt had begun rolling his shirtsleeves back to his wrists, but now he stopped and let his left arm hang loosely by his side. His right hand thumb hooked in his waistband next to the butt of the revolver. Two drovers pulled at Peshaur, coaxing him back toward Friar's.

"Come on, Georgie, 'fore he d'cides to shoot ya."

Muttering a few choice words about the law in Wichita, Peshaur allowed his friends to pull him inside. Wyatt turned to face the remaining Texans, who now began to disperse and scuff their way to other saloons on the thoroughfare. Across the street the citizens' group eased from the walkway out into the street and milled around as if deciding whether or not they should stand guard in the business district. Wyatt unrolled his sleeves, turned on his heel, and started back for the Gold Room.

When he stepped inside the saloon, he found his faro table vacated, his coat still perched stiffly on the chair where he had left it. In one corner of the room, James and cigar merchant Dick Cogswell played poker with two others at a back table. James waved his brother over. Wyatt started to return the borrowed gun, thought better of it, and walked to his layout, where he donned the coat. When he had settled the garment comfortably on his shoulders he moved to the rear of the room.

James laughed. "Well, your customers gave up on you, little brother," he said, nodding at the idle faro layout sprawled across Wyatt's table. "Come sit in with us." James hooked a chair with his boot and slid it from another table. Wyatt opened the front of his coat, slipped the borrowed revolver from his waistband, and set it upon the table. Then he sat.

James frowned at the revolver and then carried the frown to Wyatt. "Where the hell've you been with that, son? Are the cards not giving you enough excitement?"

Before Wyatt could answer, Jimmy Cairns strode into the room and dragged another chair to the table. "I hear you were down at Friar's," Cairns said. He spun the chair around backward, straddled it, and sat, stacking his forearms before him on the curve of the chair back. "Smith sent me to tell you he don't want you thinkin' you were on duty as a special."

"I reckon Botts is satisfied I was there," Wyatt said dryly.

"What happened?" James asked, looking from Cairns to Wyatt.

"Texans," Cairns said, as though the single word were explanation enough. "Discharging weapons on the street, resisting arrest. Wyatt here put it over on 'em. We got five o' them jaybirds in a cell right now."

James smiled and raised his whiskey glass to his brother. "Well, Wyatt . . . here's to volunteering to do the marshal's job for him . . . without pay."

No one joined his toast, so James downed the drink and poured another. After he drank this one, he gave Wyatt his deadpan stare and began shaking his head.

"Not much future there, brother, long as you make Smith look inept."

Dick Cogswell snorted as he gathered the loose cards from the last play. "Smith doesn't need much help with that now, does he?" he mumbled.

As the others laughed, James leaned and thumbed the sleeve of Wyatt's black coat.

"This is new, ain't it?" When Wyatt nodded, James squinted. "Guessin' that's a new shirt, too." James smiled. "Hell, son, you're startin' to look like a professional of the green cloth."

"Every occupation's got its tools," Wyatt said and took the deck from Cogswell. "A well-dressed man might look like he's got a wad o' money to lose."

Cairns laughed quietly to himself. "That's why you backed that big Texan off with your gun, ain't it? Didn't wanna soil that shirt."

As his hands deftly shuffled the cards, Wyatt held Cairns's eyes with his own. Then, when he glanced toward the door, both James and Cairns turned to see what had claimed Wyatt's attention. Big George Peshaur stood at the bat-wing doors, his eyes scouring the room and settling on Wyatt. The Texan pushed through with three other men following in his wake. Unarmed, the Texans moved toward the bar, the rowels of their spurs jangling collectively like a sack of loose nails. When they bellied up to the bar, Wyatt ignored them and finished dealing the cards.

James turned back to his brother. "Ain't that the big'un was

41

with that Texas crowd in Ellsworth when you backed down Ben Thompson?"

Wyatt said nothing. Slowly he dealt cards to the players and set the deck aside. In his peripheral vision he saw Peshaur slap an empty glass to the bar and then do the same with his hat. The Texan turned from his friends and approached Wyatt's table, where he stood behind Cogswell. Leaning forward, he splayed his hands on the table to glare at Wyatt. Beneath the man's bulk, Cogswell was forced to hunch forward, his nose just inches from the table.

"Last time I saw you in Ellsworth, you were runnin' errands for that piss-ant mayor . . . deliverin' that gutless message to Ben Thompson." Peshaur coughed up a rough laugh and leaned more heavily on Cogswell. "You got any messages for *me*, errand boy? 'Cause if you do, you won't find me quite so easy as Thompson was. I don't lay over for nobody."

Wyatt contemplated his cards for a few seconds, then closed them, looked back at the big Texan, and let his eyes go to ice. Peshaur's smile was profane, some of his teeth recessed like the sunken keys of a cast-off piano.

"You're crowdin' my friend," Wyatt said evenly. "If you got something to say, step back and say it."

The room went deathly quiet. Every man in the saloon had turned to spectate. The legs of Dick Cogswell's chair began to scrape the floor as he tried to work his way out from under the Texan's overbearing weight.

Peshaur leaned closer and sneered. "Yeah, I got a message for you, California boy. Without a gun and a piece of tin pinned to your shirt . . . you ain't nothing." With that, Peshaur pushed at Cogswell and rose to his full height. He stepped around the table, bumping James's chair as he approached Wyatt. When he stopped, he spread his boots and showed his teeth again. "Get up! I'm gonna take that strut out o' your walk."

Every man in the room watched Wyatt as he carefully set his cards facedown on the table. The gun lay just inches from his right hand. From down the street the jaunty notes of a piano drifted to them, the sound as alien and inappropriate to the moment as the voices of children laughing at a funeral.

Peshaur huffed a profane laugh. "What's the matter, Earp, you—?"

Wyatt came out of the chair and hit him under the chin with such speed that Peshaur's teeth snapped shut in mid-sentence, the sound like a pick axe cracking into ice. Before the Texan could recover, Wyatt drove a fist into the man's abdomen, forcing a rush of air to expel from the braggart's lungs. Peshaur went down heavily and lay still, his eyes bulging and his mouth forming a soundless rictus as he worked at sucking in air from the room.

"Goddamn, Wyatt," James breathed. "Don't kill the son of a bitch."

No one moved to help Peshaur. Slowly, the gasping Texan rolled to his side and propped up on an elbow to concentrate on his breathing. With unsure fingers, he gingerly probed the angle of his jaw.

"You goddamn bastard," he rasped. "A straight-up fight ain't good enough for you, is it? You always got to have a edge."

Picking up the gun Wyatt waved it at the three Texans still standing at the bar. "Get him out of here . . . now!"

When the bartender leveled a shotgun over the bar, the trio went into motion and lifted Peshaur by his armpits. When the big Texan finally got his feet under him and regained balance, he jerked free from his friends.

"You goddamned yellow piece o' Yankee town-shit," he growled.

Wyatt stuffed the revolver into his waistband and looked at

the men behind Peshaur. "I ain't gonna tell you again."

One of the Texans pulled at Peshaur but kept his eyes on Wyatt. "Come on, Georgie. It's all stacked against you."

"Hell, yeah," Peshaur yelled as he was led away. "That's the way the fuckin' law works in this shit-hole town." He made to spit across the floor at Wyatt, but the best he could do was a dry airy sound. Even after he stumbled backward through the doorway and passed out of sight, Wyatt re-gripped the handle of the gun and kept his eyes trained on the empty door frame, where he could hear the Texans arguing in hoarse whispers. Then Peshaur's booming voice filled the street.

"The law in this town's nothin' but a bunch o' sheep-fuckers!"

Wyatt walked across the room and out the door, the gun hanging by his leg now. James and Jimmy Cairns followed behind him, and the other patrons followed in a cautious line.

Out on the boardwalk, Peshaur thrust a finger at Wyatt. "You're a yellow bastard! Always stackin' the odds your way." One of the Texans watching Wyatt's face tugged on Peshaur's sleeve, but the big man's momentum was set. "I'd give a month's pay to have you alone in an empty room."

With his eyes on Peshaur, Wyatt spoke up so sharply that the Texan standing closest to him jumped. "Dick?"

Cogswell shouldered through the small crowd of onlookers. "Right here, Wyatt."

"That back room in your store . . . is it empty?"

Cogswell's face paled. "Well . . . yeah," he said uneasily. "Pretty much, I guess."

"Can I use it?" Wyatt said.

"Wyatt, I . . ." Cogswell licked his lips. When Wyatt turned to face him, the merchant looked startled. "Well, sure . . . I s'pose you can if you need to."

Wyatt looked hard at Peshaur and hitched his head toward

the door where Dick Cogswell stood. "Give him your month's pay . . . unless that was just more talk."

Peshaur frowned a moment, until his lust for violence brightened his face. He dug into a pocket for a roll of bills, peeled off several, and tossed them at the door. The paper money flew apart and fluttered to the boardwalk. No one made a move for it.

Wyatt pointed. "Next block. Move!"

No fewer than a dozen men clattered down the boardwalk following them. But for the rumble of boots on the tread boards, the walk to Cogswell's cigar store was as quiet as a cortege. Cogswell unlocked the front door, went in alone, and lighted an oil lamp. Then everyone else filed inside. The sweet pungency of tobacco gave the impression of an exotic land—a place exempt from the laws of Kansas. Cogswell pushed open the door to the back room and stood aside. With a flick of his gun barrel Wyatt motioned Peshaur into the dark room.

"We'll need the lamp, Dick," Wyatt said. He handed the revolver to James, removed his coat, and laid it on the counter.

"Well, wait a minute, Wyatt," Cogswell protested, "what if you start a fire?"

Wyatt pulled his shirt over his head and laid it on top of the coat. "We won't," he said and took the lamp from Cogswell. He entered the room and set the lamp on the floor. When he straightened, his elongated shadow spread across the far wall and engulfed Peshaur. The men in the front room watched the door close, the slice of light narrowing until there was only a slit beneath the door.

Those gathered in the dark of the store listened to a light scuffing of boots that soon became a steady shuffle. The dull smacks of fist against flesh ran a gauntlet of rhythms, until a loud crash shook the near wall, making the cigar jars rattle on the shelves. Then a crash to the floor jarred the building, and a muted groan—eerily melodic—trailed off, like a train whistle fading into the distance across the plains.

No more than three minutes had elapsed when the door opened again. Wyatt's dirty-blond hair fell damp over his forehead. His color was high, and a rime of sweat gave his face and torso the sheen of alabaster. No one spoke to him as he approached the Texans.

"Take him outta town, and tell him he ain't to come back."

The Texans tried for a surly look as they sauntered into the back room. There they took a grip on Peshaur's inert body and began dragging him through the doorway.

James stepped before his brother and squinted. "Well, you look like you'll live."

"I need some air," Wyatt said and picked up his clothes to lead the way outside.

Standing in the cool night air, Wyatt handed his coat to James, and then he donned the new white blouse. Tucking the shirttails into his waistband, he watched Peshaur's friends help the groggy Texan down the boardwalk.

"All right, Wyatt," James said, "would you tell me where in hell you learned to fight like that?"

Wyatt bent to inspect the knee of his trousers. The smooth new fabric showed a two-inch tear.

"Can any of those girls at your place sew?" he asked.

"That mousy one, Sally, she'd fall all over herself to do that for you. Good at it, too. Makes her own clothes." He slapped Wyatt's shoulder and laughed. "Why don't you go over to the house and bed her. I think she likes you. Or, if you're up for it, that Hungarian hell-cat, Kate."

"My shift at the Gold Room runs till two," Wyatt said and took back his coat.

James cocked his head with an impish smile. "You know, brother, for all that talk about making a fortune in the cattle business"—he nodded toward the cigar store—"maybe the truth is you're just cut out for lawin'. Virgil always said you'd wear a badge."

"This had nothin' to do with a badge," Wyatt said, giving James a look.

"Just keep tellin' yourself that, brother." James chuckled. He extended the revolver, butt first.

"That belongs behind the bar at the Gold Room," Wyatt said. "Would you return it for me?"

"Where're *you* going?"

Wyatt examined the knee of his trousers again. "Got to change clothes."

James dropped the pistol into a coat pocket. "We ain't all bound to get rich, Wyatt . . . but most men never even get the respect for being good at what they *can* do."

Wyatt looked up the street. "Respect is good, but I want to make some money, too."

James squeezed Wyatt's upper arm. "Well, hell. We all want that, Wyatt," he said and laughed again as he started up the street.

Cairns stepped beside Wyatt, and together they watched James walk away in his off-kilter gait up the middle of the road, his bad arm swinging out of sync with his stride. "I don't reckon Smith'll be payin' you for this either," Cairns said dryly. "But, hell . . . I'd'a paid five dollars for a front-row seat in that back room." He turned and looked at the stillness in Wyatt's profile.

"I got to go change clothes," Wyatt said again and turned to cross the street.

"I'll keep an eye on the Gold Room till you get there," Cairns called to his back.

When Wyatt came out of the alley, the gibbous moon hung above the buildings to the east—an imperfect circle of stained and yellowed parchment held before a candle flame. The amber color was like a burning memory returning to the forefront of his mind. He thought back to a New Year's Eve celebration in San Bernardino, just after his family had come west. There he had met the Mexican girl who had ushered him into manhood with her experienced hands. At the same time she had spoken words that had haunted him almost a decade later. Words that were meant to remind him that most men never fulfill their dreams. It was only human to wish for things, she had said, but in the end a man is lucky to fill his belly with food each day.

The orb of moon held him as it floated above the rooftops, its damning eye come to bear witness to the truth that the victory over Peshaur had been an empty one. He had known it from the moment he had arranged the fight. There was no money in it.

He looked down at the torn knee of his new trousers and hummed a low growl that served to sum up his evening spent with a few Texans hell-bent on making life hard for anyone who would suffer their bravado. The sound from his throat was reminiscent of his father's gruff voice. Picking up his pace again, he strode across the street toward the silhouette of the Sedgwick House. Keeping his eyes straight ahead on the building, he decided to purge everything from his mind that did not involve making more money for himself. With his gait so deliberate, he began to loosen up from the tension of the fight. Still, he was careful not to look again at the judgmental eye of the moon.

CHAPTER 4

October, 1874: Wichita and south to Indian Territory

Autumn had swept across the Kansas plains, marking the end of the cattle drives for the season and ushering out most of the men who had driven stock from Texas. With all of their wages squandered on gambling, liquor, and women, these drovers had exited Wichita more humbly than they had entered. The town seemed to settle into a more respectable version of itself, but the merchants were already planning inventories and strategies to be employed come the next spring when the cowmen would return to stoke the economic fire on which the town depended.

Wyatt had little use for these men who broke the law for sport, but he would miss their contributions at his faro table. With so many unskilled card players gone south, his income at the Gold Room and the Custom House would take a steep decline. There was little chance that he could make up the difference by working for the law. Marshal Billy Smith showed no inclination to associate with the men who had handled Mannen Clements on the bridge. It was his way of saving face, Wyatt supposed. And, besides, there was little need for a special officer in the off-season. Like an old she-bear, Wichita was easing into its wintering den for the cold months, and Wyatt decided to settle in with her.

Sitting in the kitchen at Bessie's house, James and Wyatt sipped their respective drinks by the wood stove as James regaled his brother with reminiscences of the war. These stories had

49

been locked inside the crippled Earp for a decade; but now, in the quiet of his home and with his tongue loosened by an excess of whiskey, James confided in Wyatt, baring all the privations, worry, and gore that comprised a soldier's life.

"Prob'ly a damned good thing Pa caught you when you tried to run off to the war," James summed up, rotating his glass on the table as he gazed into the amber liquid that tried to turn in a slow eddy. His mouth tightened to a crooked smile as he looked up. "Bein' so young as you were, they'd 'a prob'ly had you carryin' a flag, and every last one o' them damned Rebs woulda been wantin' to take a potshot at you." He nodded once. "I seen it happen twice to two young'ns barely big enough to boot into a stirrup." James's smile slackened, and he glanced at his bad shoulder. "Them damn Southern boys could shoot, too," he added and allowed a quiet alcoholic sigh to escape his lips.

Wyatt tested his coffee and set it back on the wood stove. "Least you made it back," he said.

Sally appeared in the doorway and stood quietly until James looked at her.

"There's a man at the door," she announced in her mousy voice.

James laughed. "Well, darlin', I think you know how to handle that, don't you?" He leaned toward her and spoke slowly, as though mouthing the words for a deaf-mute. "That's why you're here, Sally. Go get Bessie to collect the money, and then get to it."

Her cautious eyes seemed to hold a question. "He wants to see your brother," she whispered and allowed herself only a guarded glance at Wyatt.

James pulled his pocket watch from his vest and opened the cover. "Who comes lookin' for Wyatt at three o'clock in the morning?"

Sally stared at James with three lines cut across her pinched forehead. "Said his name was 'Burns' or 'Barnes.' I'm not sure which." She pulled in her lower lip with her upper teeth, and her eyes darted from side to side like she was watching an insect fly in a tight circle. "Kinda short and stout," she said and wrinkled her nose. "He smells like tar."

Wyatt smiled. "John Behrens. Why don't you ask him to join us?"

When Behrens entered the warm room, Wyatt was pouring coffee into a new cup. James started to rise but thought better of it and offered his hand from his chair.

"How you doin', John?" James said, coming alive now like an actor given his cue. "We don't usually have men show up here at night looking for an ugly ox like my brother. Mostly our late visitors are after the milk cows." He smiled and pointed down the dark hallway toward the cribs.

Behrens shook hands and nodded a greeting to Wyatt. When Wyatt offered the coffee, Behrens took it. Wyatt retrieved his cup and both men sat. Sally hovered in the doorway, staring at Wyatt, until James shooed her back toward the front room.

Behrens tried the coffee, set it down, and looked directly at Wyatt. "How'd you like to help me recover a stolen wagon?"

Wyatt narrowed his eyes. "I didn't expect any more work comin' from Smith's office."

"Won't be workin' for Smith. We'll be workin' for Moser . . . that fruit farmer who opened the wagon shop on Main Street. Pay's good. You and I can split it right down the middle."

"How much?" Wyatt said.

"Seventy-two dollars, fifty cents . . . each." For several seconds Behrens watched Wyatt weigh the fee against the trouble. Then he laughed quietly. "The wagon costs a hun'erd forty-six. Moser's keepin' a dollar for himself 'cause, he says, he's a businessman." Behrens's smile disappeared as quickly as it had come. "Burns him up that these boys skinned out on 'im like they did." He leaned his forearms on the table and narrowed his dark eyes. "But we might stand to make a lot more out o' this. These same skunks put it over on some of the other merchants, too." His face went hard with the possibilities. "Could add up to a handsome re-ward, so says Moser."

When Wyatt did not answer, James leaned closer to Behrens and frowned. "How is it you smell like tar?"

Behrens shrugged. "I been doin' some roofin' to pick up some cash." He carried his embarrassed look to Wyatt. "That's why I wanna go after this wagon. My back is 'bout broke in half from bendin' over on a damned sloped roof."

"Who did the stealin'?" Wyatt asked.

"Who else? Texans. That outfit workin' for Higgenbottom." Behrens sat back and smirked as he shook his head. "I'd say Texas credit is gone to hell in Wichita."

"Why doesn't Smith go after 'em?"

John Behrens's mouth curled in disgust. "They're out o' town limits now. He says it falls to the sheriff." Behrens snorted a whispery laugh through his nose. "Sheriff figures they're out o' the county. Meagher is the only federal deputy in town. Hell, I know he'd go after 'em, but he's in Topeka. It's why I wanna go now . . . before Meagher can get wind of it."

Behrens pushed his coffee aside as if he were done socializing. He flopped a forearm on the table and waited for an answer.

Wyatt looked toward the window, the only one in the house with glass, where the dark of night had transformed the panes into mirrors that reflected the spare décor of the room. Slowly he began to nod.

"If we're not carrying a badge, what kind of authority will we have?"

Behrens tilted his head to deliver a tight smile. "The kind

that speaks the loudest." Leaning to one side, he pulled a revolver from under his coat and laid it down on the table. The loud tap of metal on wood filled the room like the bang of a judge's gavel.

James poured himself another glass and laughed. "That looks as convincing as a badge to me."

"I can't go after 'em alone," Behrens said to Wyatt. "Are you in?"

Wyatt nodded. "I'm in. When did they pull out?"

"Looks like early afternoon. They were camped below Delano. Moser went down there an hour before sunset, and the whole lot of 'em had pulled up stakes and headed south. We leave now and maybe we can catch 'em before they reach the Nations."

Wyatt stood and set his cup by the basin. "Give me an hour. I'll meet you out front o' here at the bridge."

Behrens took a last pull on his coffee and stood. Holstering his gun, he looked around the kitchen as though he were inventorying the accoutrements of the makeshift home.

"Oh, Wyatt," Behrens called. "Better pack along a shotgun. I ain't real sure how many o' these jaspers we're after, but Moser says to expect a crowd."

They pulled out before dawn following the well-used drovers' route that ran along the west bank of the Arkansas. Where the trail forked southwest toward Caldwell, fresh wagon ruts provided an easy sign. Riding through the day they entered the Indian Nations by late afternoon. An hour before dusk, after crossing a creek and topping the rise on the far side, Wyatt looked out over the ocean of yellowing prairie grass cut by a long, straight stretch of the well-used cattle path. At a distance he spotted a wagon and five men on horseback.

"That's them!" Behrens said. "Moser said to look for a flat

canvas stretched over the wagon bed."

"Back up," Wyatt advised, and the two detectives eased back down the gentle slope out of sight.

"We can tail 'em," Behrens suggested, "then we could take 'em tonight."

Wyatt shook his head. "Not with six or more men. Too many things can go wrong in the dark."

"What're you thinkin', Wyatt?" Behrens said.

"Those boys are bound to be watching their back-trail. We just ride up on 'em, they might open up on us." Wyatt dismounted and pointed over the rise. "We got no cover down there. We need to go around, set up, wait, and let 'em come to us."

John Behrens pushed his lips forward and began nodding. "Yeah. That sounds good to me."

Wyatt led his horse into the scant shade of the willows growing by the creek. Behrens took his horse at a walk and followed.

"We'll rest up here, where the horses have got water," Wyatt said. "Then we'll ride through the night and get ahead of 'em. Tomorrow they'll walk right into it."

Behrens grunted his approval and dismounted. Wyatt began unsaddling his mare.

Behrens lighted a cigar and smiled back toward the rise. "Sleep tight, you jokers," he said through clamped teeth. "There'll be hell to pay tomorrow."

CHAPTER 5

October, 1874: Chikaskia River near the Salt Fork, Indian Territory
At dusk the trackers geared up and took a bearing west of southwest into the dark. It was a trackless expanse of desiccated grass that slithered across the chests of their mounts like water parting around the prows of two small ships. Using the experience of his days hunting buffalo on the flats of the Salt Fork, Wyatt navigated the vastness of the plains using the stars and the sparse landmarks available. The two men never talked as their horses kept up a steady rhythm, Wyatt in front, John Behrens behind, cutting a single path across the prairie. The chill of the autumn night made the white points of light in the sky appear like tiny shards of ice clinging to the black pelt of a buffalo robe.

A little before dawn they cut the Chikaskia River ten miles deep into the Nations. Moving downstream, they reached the shallow ford on the trail where the Higgenbottom crew would cross the stream on their way back to Texas. After setting up a dry camp a hundred yards upstream, Wyatt and Behrens spread their bedrolls and stretched out to let the aches of the long ride leach out of their bones.

At first light they broke camp and went by foot to the ford. There they separated, taking up positions on either side of the trail, Wyatt kneeling beside an oak in the brush and Behrens lying inside a stand of dried switchgrass and bluestem. They had waited less than an hour when they heard the jangling of harnesses and the rattle of a wagon in the distance.

Five horsemen came into view, the wagon trailing just behind. In addition to the saddle mounts and the team pulling the wagon, an eighth horse was tied to the tailgate. Every horseman wore a revolver in a leather holster at his hip. Rifle stocks jutted from each saddle scabbard. The driver of the wagon appeared unarmed, but any kind of weapon could be stowed in the driver's box next to his boots.

As the crew approached the river, the lead rider dismounted and let his horse drink as he wet a neckerchief and used it to scrub his face. He was a short, thick man with rough whiskers blackening the lower half of his face. When the others arrived, the driver tied the reins around the brake handle and climbed down from the wagon, where he began checking the tie ropes on the canvas covering the bed. Finally the other four men unlimbered from their mounts and ambled toward the water, each man twisting off the cap of a canteen. With the Texans' hands so engaged, Wyatt knew there would be no better moment to throw down on them.

"When we get back to Texas," one man said, "I'm gonna spring for a room in a hotel and sleep in a real bed for a week. Might even convince a cheap whore to throw in with me."

When all had clustered at the edge of the river to watch their horses drink, Wyatt stepped onto the trail behind them. The constant shattering sound of the water threading through the rocks filled the air and covered his approach as he leveled his shotgun at the three men on the right. Behrens appeared from the other side and covered the other three.

"Keep your hands empty, and you might live through this," Wyatt said, his voice deep and full so as to be heard by all. "Drop those reins, and turn around slow."

Every Texan released his hold on his horse and turned, each face slack with surprise. One drover's eyes were like bright coins reflecting light from a campfire as they cut back and forth from one shotgun to the other. One by one their hands floated upward above their heads, the movements automatic and syncopated, as though an unpracticed puppeteer were tugging at strings from somewhere above them.

"What the hell is this?" said the stocky man, putting a rough growl into his words.

"We're after some men robbed the bank up in Salina," Behrens said, his voice flat and his expression as dead as a seasoned poker player.

The man eyed Behrens carefully. "We're just drovers headin' home."

"Who do you ride for?" Wyatt said.

The man started to answer but then closed his mouth.

"For Higgenbottom," said the driver of the wagon. "You can ask anybody. Look at our brands," he suggested, nodding toward the horses. "We ain't been to Salina. We come from Wichita."

Behrens smiled at the shorter man. "Ain't too smart, is he?" Then widening that smile he showed his teeth to the driver. "The Higgenbottom crew is who we're after, jackass."

"You men are going back with us," Wyatt informed them and cocked his head toward their back trail. "You left some unpaid debts in Wichita."

"We don't know what you're talkin' 'bout, mister." This came from the youngest of the group, a raw-boned kid with sparse, wiry, blond hairs curling over his lip. "And we don't like being waylaid out here in the Nations." He conjured up a sneer and began lowering his hands. "B'sides . . . there's six of us here . . . and only two o' you."

Behrens stepped forward and pressed the muzzle of his shotgun into the soft flesh beneath the boy's chin. When he cocked the hammers, the quiet *click-click* of the gun cut through the sound of the shoals with an authority that seemed to stop time. The young drover stretched his head so high that the tendons in his neck stood out like the roots of a sapling.

"Way I see it," Behrens said, his voice humming with the pent-up violence that sometimes seemed to rise off his skin like heat, "two men with two loads o' buckshot is plenty enough to put it over on a crowd o' thievin' assholes from Texas. You wanna test my judgment on that, young'n?"

The boy tried to lick his lips, but his teeth were locked together by the extreme tilt of his head. "Well, what was took?" he managed to say, mumbling lockjawed from his awkward pose.

Behrens pointed back to the wagon. "That rattle-box you been rollin' 'cross the prairie, for one thing. Cost a hun'erd forty-six dollars. That ain't even countin' the team o' draft horses you rented from the livery." Behrens coughed up a short laugh. "I'd be willing to bet most everything stacked inside that wagon bed ain't yet paid for neither."

"You ain't the law!" the kid challenged.

Behrens laughed. "Don't matter who we are, boy. We're the ones holdin' shotguns, and you're the ones with your elbows up around your ears."

The lanky boy tried to rekindle some anger. "You can't just pull your damned guns on us and—"

"Kid!" interrupted the oldest of the Texans. He was a tired-eyed, balding man wearing a tattered wool vest over his union suit top. This was the first word he had uttered since dismounting. Now he glared at the youngest of the crew, and his eyes went hard in his flaccid face. "I don't wanna die for a hun'erd forty-six dollars, do you?"

When the kid began to sulk, Behrens backed away. For several seconds no one spoke. The horses stood fetlock-deep in the river, their muzzles dipping into the water and then rising with droplets of water raining down from their chins without sound. There was only the sizzling whisper of the shoals as the reality of the arrest settled over the Texans. Each of the six men stared into the dark muzzles of the shotguns as though trying to catch a glimpse of a future that might still be possible.

"We're gonna do this one at a time," Wyatt said and nodded to the man standing closest to him. "You first . . . lower your left hand, take out your pistol with two fingers on the grips, and throw it over here in the dirt next to me."

The Texan moved slowly, reached across his belly to his holster, and pinched the butt of his revolver with thumb and forefinger. With an easy toss, he dropped the gun next to Wyatt's boots. When all six men had submitted, Wyatt collected the Texans' guns and horses, and Behrens walked the prisoners to the back of the wagon, where he forced them belly down in the dirt to make a flank.

As Wyatt stood guard, Behrens searched the prisoners one at a time. After checking their boots and turning every pocket inside out, he told them to flip onto their backs.

"Count yourselves lucky I don't cuff your hands behind your back," Behrens barked. "But I don't wanna hear you complainin' about pissin' yourselves."

Moving down the line of bodies, he locked on wrist-irons with each man's arms crossed at his belly. When he finished, he stood back and hissed a laugh.

"You Texas boys ain't got the sense God give to a wall-eyed jackrabbit. If you're gonna steal something, you ought'a at least be able to hide the damn thing in your pocket. But a wagon . . . ?"

Wyatt finished dumping out the cartridges from the pistols he had collected. Then he poured the hardware into a burlap bag and stowed it in the wagon box.

"Let's get started," Wyatt ordered quietly. "We got a long road back to Wichita."

Behrens squinted at the sun still low in the east. "I'll fetch our horses, Wyatt." After a last look at the prisoners, he started upstream, where the two mounts were tethered in the brush.

"Hey, mister," the young drover said, glaring at Wyatt from his place on the ground. "You think your friend really woulda blowed my head off over a stole wagon?"

"Wasn't about a wagon," Wyatt said and turned to the boy's impudent face. "It was about you knowin' who had a hold of you."

The kid attempted a sarcastic laugh. "You mean . . . some crazy sonovabitch wantin' to take my head off?"

Wyatt held the boy's angry eyes. "You ask me . . . you were the crazy sonovabitch, tryin' to argue with a scattergun."

The kid's face closed down with insult. "Only thing we did was come up a little late on our payment. Don't mean we weren't gonna send the money soon's we got back to Texas."

Wyatt's expression remained unchanged. "You boys know the rules. You broke 'em. Now you're gonna pay."

Every man raised his head and looked at Wyatt, but no one had anything to say. One by one the Texans settled their heads back into the dirt. All but the kid, whose eyes could not convey enough disdain for the men who had captured him.

"You didn' never steal nothin' before?" he challenged.

Wyatt took in a deep breath and let it seep out slowly. This boy was about the age Wyatt had been when, as town constable, he had skimmed money from the school taxes back in Missouri. And that had been less than a year before he had been locked in a filthy jail for horse theft.

"This ain't about me," he said plainly.

"Well, if it ain't anything about you, why're you out here in the middle o' the God-forsaken Indian Nations huntin' us down?"

Wyatt plucked a dried stem from the grasses and inserted it in his mouth. "Just business."

"So you're a damned bounty hunter?"

"Don't matter what you call me. It don't change what you boys done."

Behrens walked up the embankment leading the horses. Tying them off to the wagon, he surveyed the prisoners and saw the color in the boy's hardened face.

"What's the little shit-kicker bellyaching about now?"

The boy turned away, giving Behrens the back of his head.

"Thinks you went a little hard on 'im," Wyatt said.

Behrens smiled broadly and then raised his voice like a stage actor. "You know, Wyatt, I think this Texas boy would cry if his mama showed up."

The boy's head whipped back around. "Yeah, well you didn't have to—"

"Kid!" snapped the driver of the wagon. "Shut the fuck up!"

Behrens took a coil of rope from his horse, walked to where the boy lay, and knelt. "You dealt these cards, son. Now you got to play the game out." He played out the rope and ran it through each man's cuffs with a double turn so that they were linked together like a chain gang.

As the Texans lay prone, Wyatt unlashed the canvas over the wagon and inspected the contents in the bed. The majority of the freight matched the unpaid items on the list of goods that Moser had given to Behrens.

"Aw-right . . . everybody git up!" Behrens ordered. He backed away and balanced the shotgun in the crook of his arm.

"How the hell're we gonna mount our horses if we're all tied together like this?" the wagon driver said.

"Won't need to," Wyatt replied. "You're walkin'."

"Walkin'!" This from the kid. "Hell, it's more'n seventy miles back to Wichita!"

Wyatt climbed up into the box and unwrapped the reins from the brake handle. "You boys stole so much merchandise, there's no room for you in the wagon."

"We got our damned horses!" the driver said. "Why can't we ride?"

"Too many of you," Wyatt said. "Can't trust you on a horse . . . hand-cuffed or not."

The scowl on the driver's face cut deep furrows into the flesh around his eyes. "You sonovabitch . . . you can't make us walk seventy miles!"

Wyatt waited as Behrens stepped into the stirrup and mounted his horse. Once in the saddle, Behrens balanced the shotgun crosswise on the pommel, the muzzles of the gun pointing toward the prisoners.

"You can walk or be dragged," Behrens said. "Your choice."

The Texans frowned but said nothing.

"I figure we can carry two at a time in the wagon," Wyatt suggested. He pointed to the two men standing at the head of the line. "Get in."

The other four men watched their two friends squirm their way backward over the tailgate and into the wagon bed. Behrens positioned himself at the end with a view of all the prisoners.

"We'll switch off every five miles or so," Wyatt said, looking back at the men still standing. "Dependin' on how you behave."

The driver's neck stiffened as he craned his head forward. " 'Behave'? What's that s'posed to mean?"

Wyatt raised the reins in his hands. "You'll figure it out," he said. "Right now I want you boys to walk and be quiet." He snapped the reins over the haunches of the draft horses. As the wagon turned a wide arc, the grumbling prisoners stumbled in the clumps of dead grass as they tried to keep up with the pace. When the train had moved past him, Behrens tapped his heels into his horse's flanks and followed.

"Well, what if we ain't quiet!" the driver barked.

"Like I said," Wyatt remarked over his shoulder, "you'll figure it out."

CHAPTER 6

Three days later, October, 1874: Wichita, Kansas

When the entourage of ex-officers Earp and Behrens and six Texas prisoners marched into Wichita on a late afternoon, the retrieval of stolen goods was the talk of the town. Nobody told the story better than John Behrens. Unless it was M. R. Moser himself, who had claimed the lion's share of the recovered goods.

A crowd gathered in Rupp's Saloon, where Moser insisted on treating Wyatt and Behrens to a round of drinks. The onlookers watched as the wagon craftsman counted out two stacks of bills on the counter. Wyatt pocketed his share as John Behrens shuffled through his bills to tally up the total for himself.

"These boys fear nothing and nobody," Moser announced, raising his glass. "Too bad we don't have a police force up to these boys' standards." He motioned for the bartender to pour drinks for his hired detectives, but Wyatt waved away the offer and moved the glass to the far side of the counter.

"I'll take some coffee if you have it," he said.

The bartender nodded, poured a glass for Behrens, and then started for the back of the room where a blackened kettle sat upon the wood heater.

"Well," Moser laughed, "tell me what Smith's face looked like when you boys delivered those scoundrels to his jail."

Behrens snorted. "Pleased as punch, I'd say, that he didn't have to get off his ass and do some work." John leaned in closer to Moser. "But he did look a little bare-assed." Behrens winked.

"Smith knows when his feathers have been trimmed."

Moser shook his head. "Oh, he'll find some way to make the credit slide over to his side." He turned to Wyatt. "He's a fool not to use you boys on the force."

The bartender set down a cup of coffee on the counter, and Wyatt picked it up and sipped off the top. It was not fresh, but it was hot, and the warming liquid was welcome to cut the October chill from the last stretch of the ride.

Wyatt tilted his head toward Behrens. "John and I don't much agree with the way Smith handles things . . . and Smith knows it. It ain't likely he'll hire us unless he gets desperate."

Moser made a crooked smile and leaned in closer to Wyatt. "Come April, some of us businessmen are going to see to it that Smith doesn't hold an office."

Wyatt tried his coffee again and began preparing what he would say if the merchant offered to back him in the elections. Being marshal of Wichita would be a step up. It was a job he knew he could handle well. After a term or two, he might be better positioned to ascend to a higher aspiration—some business that did not involve chasing after out-of-luck drovers across a thankless prairie.

"Wyatt, you boys be patient, and I think you'll find you'll have jobs next spring . . . with a marshal who knows how to get things done."

Wyatt's expression did not change. He took another swallow of coffee and set the mug on the bar.

"That so?" he said in a flat voice. Around him the crowd began to break up at the bar.

Moser flashed a knowing smile, leaned in, and lowered his voice. "We're going to make a push for Meager, the federal deputy. He was a good marshal once before. We like his cut."

Wyatt fitted his hat to his head and nodded. " 'Preciate the pay . . . and the coffee, Mr. Moser."

The farmer reached down for Wyatt's hand and pumped it four times. Wyatt tolerated the man's enthusiasm, nodded to Behrens, and started out. As soon as he had pushed through the doors into the cool of the evening, he felt the anger that he had pent up inside his chest now course through his veins like heat rising through a stove flue. Walking the middle of the street in long strides, he tried to purge the flame burning at the center of him. When he neared the bridge and made out the silhouette of the claptrap house where James and Bessie ran their whoring business, it struck him why Moser would never consider him for the marshal's post. The respectable businessmen of the town could never support a man whose brother managed a brothel.

On the bridge, he walked a few yards over the river and leaned on his forearms against the railing to think things through. The dark water slid beneath him like a giant serpent intent on some immutable destination that lay somewhere out in the night. The lights from the saloons in Delano reflected off the water like candle flames wavering gently in a breeze. Wyatt listened to the water part around the pilings and then fold together again on the downstream side.

It shouldn't matter what a man's brother does, he reasoned. It's what the man is . . . what he does . . . that's what counts. Anybody who judges a man by studying his brother is a fool. He straightened and looked back into the business district.

"Damned fools," he muttered. "To hell with them."

As he walked toward James's house, he smoothed out his pace and felt the heat in his chest dissipate. Already he was convinced the people of the town would come around to his way of thinking. They would have to. It would only take some time. He had five months before the election.

"Plenty of time," Wyatt said, and, hearing the rough certainty in his voice, he was reminded of the times he had heard his father ordain a future he demanded from the world. For old

Nicholas those imperatives had seldom panned out. Everywhere the elder Earp had dragged his family along the smolder-line of the frontier, he had run up against the same failed dreams.

Stopping in James's front yard, he turned to look at the moon. The pale orb glowed behind a stratum of clouds like a solitary lamp seen across a smoky room. Its luminescence was muted by the overcast sky, but its color was a clear and pure white. Nothing like the mud-dappled moon the Mexican girl had prophesied for him in California.

Valenzuela Cos. He had not thought of her for months. Where was she now, he wondered. If he ran into her on the streets of Wichita, what would she think of his ambitions? His lot was not much improved since he had last seen her. Outside of gambling, he had no real job. He had acquired no fortune. Beyond a handful of Texas cattle pushers, his name was not well known.

Pivoting around, he studied the front of James's ramshackle establishment. Here was the Earp legacy, it seemed. This whorehouse was the Earp landmark in Wichita, and Wyatt was connected to it by blood, no matter what his aspirations might be. There were some things that could not be changed, and this was one of them.

Though he did not look up again, he felt the moon now like a condemning eye, peering down at him through the haze and making its own judgment as if by the sanction of God. Turning away from the brothel, Wyatt started down Douglas Avenue for the Sedgwick House. As he walked, the cloud cover thickened until the glow of the moon was lost altogether. His boots in the dirt set up a steady rhythm—a confident sound full of industry and endurance. He decided to never again think of Valenzuela Cos. Or that damned moon made of mud.

CHAPTER 7

Winter, 1874-75: Pole Cat Creek, Indian Territory

When the first snows came to the plains, Wyatt and John Behrens were hired again over a private concern—this time to guard a herd of cattle whose ownership was under dispute by two livestock buyers. To avoid legal confrontations, they drove the beasts into the Nations and nestled them in a scrub valley where the shoulders of Pole Cat Creek widened to form a natural bowl in the land. Just upstream of the corral they set up a decoy tent where they prepared meals but never slept. After dinner they banked the main fire, and then each man retired to his distant blind on higher ground to pass the long winter night with what heat he could trap under a four-inch heap of blankets. Neither man had any wish to be gunned down in his sleep, though Behrens sometimes lamented in the morning that no one had put him out of his frozen misery.

On a bitterly cold afternoon, with Behrens having taken the wagon into Sapulpa for grain, Wyatt built a small pit fire on high ground that commanded a view of the herd and the main trails leading into camp. The cold crept into his bones, and he opened the blankets draped around his shoulders to gather heat from his fire. The sky promised more snow.

Two hours before sunset a lone rider approached on the trail from the north. Wyatt watched the interloper ride straight into the main camp, dismount, and look around as though searching for signs of inhabitants. The stranger wore a heavy overcoat and

68

wide-brimmed hat and walked with a stilted gait as though unsure of his footing.

When the intruder disappeared inside the tent, Wyatt waited until he was satisfied that no one else had accompanied the newcomer. Then he banked his fire and started down the hill.

Coming up on the back of the tent, he stopped thirty feet away and worked the lever of his rifle. The sound was like an axe splitting oak and sufficient warning for anyone inside that the upper hand had just been dealt.

"I got a full magazine of forty-four-forties that'll tear that canvas to hell," he called out. "Come out with your hands high and empty." After quietly changing his position, Wyatt crouched and braced the butt of his rifle against his shoulder as he looked down the barrel at the tent opening. In the cold quiet, a bawling calf mewled from the valley in the few seconds while Wyatt waited for something to happen.

The intruder emerged slowly—hatless, with slender white hands raised over her head. With her hair gathered above her ears, Wyatt barely recognized James's whore, the one who sat so still in the room whenever Wyatt visited. He relaxed his grip on the gun, and she lowered her arms.

"Sally? Something wrong at James's place?"

She pushed out a sudden sharp breath that steamed white in the air, but she would not answer. When she shifted her attention to the cattle and glared at them for too long, Wyatt knew that any trouble she had brought with her was of her own making.

"I'm leaving!" she finally said and pinned him with a defiant stare.

She looked altogether different in the daylight, though mainly as a result of some internal energy that rose up from deep inside her. Wyatt looked away from her determined gaze and recognized her gray horse as one from the pair that pulled James's wagon. Balancing the rifle in the crook of his arm, he walked toward her.

"James know about this?"

"He doesn't own me."

Wyatt nodded to the horse. "Prob'ly owns that mare, though."

"I don't want to work there anymore. I *never* wanted to."

"I reckon you can do what you want, Sally."

She laughed, but it was a bitter sound. "Sally *Earp*," she hissed. "We all had to be *'Earps,'* you know." Her nostrils flared when she spoke the name. "Otherwise, we might look like, you know, a *brothel.*" Her tight mouth loosened and began to quiver. "My name is Celia, not 'Sally.' But back home I was 'Mattie.' "

When tears formed in her eyes, Wyatt busied himself wiping at the ice forming on the rear sight of his Winchester. She would not continue talking until he looked at her again.

"When you run away," she continued, "you change your name if you don't want to be found."

She set her jaw, and her eyes seemed to blaze with white heat. The wind heaved against them and stirred the winter-dry grass into a frenzy. Small flecks of snow began to flutter diagonally through the air and cling to her hair. Clutching the overcoat tighter to her throat, she let go of some of her anger.

"I'm tired of being 'Sally.' I'm not a whore, Wyatt."

Hitching his head to one side he looked north toward Wichita. "Nothing wrong with being a whore." When he looked back at her, she was gazing out into the prairie at nothing . . . to a place that perhaps no man could see. A cold gust of wind strained the tent ropes into a tight, ticking sound.

"Can we get out of this?" she said, clutching the overcoat lapels against her pale throat.

Without waiting for an answer, she bent and slipped through the tent opening. After a few moments, Wyatt followed, tied down the door flaps, and turned to find her weeping in the half-light. Her misery seemed genuine enough.

"I could build a fire outside," he offered.

He watched her wipe at the silvery streaks that shone on her cheeks. Now she would not look at him.

"Where're you headed? Don't you know you can freeze out on the prairie on a night like this?"

"I came to find you," she whined in a mousy voice.

"Well . . . you done *that*. Now what?"

"I'm not a whore, Wyatt."

"All right," he said and nodded once to her. "But you might be a horse thief."

"Maybe I earned that horse," she replied, lifting her chin.

Wyatt stared at her for a time. She looked so serious about everything. Finally he nodded.

"Maybe you did earn it. I earned the title once myself . . . 'horse thief,' I mean."

"You stole a horse?"

"People said I did. I doubt anyone's above it if the situation's right."

"Or wrong," she said.

He propped his rifle against the crate of cooking pots and utensils. "I guess that's what I meant," he said.

Outside, the wind whipped the brittle grasses against the canvas, the sound like frantic birds scratching to get in from the weather. The windward side of the tent bowed taut and bulged inward, thrumming as though it had been pitched under a waterfall.

"Bad night for travelin'," Wyatt said.

"Can I stay here?"

"Nobody sleeps in here. Could be dangerous."

"Where do you sleep?"

He pointed. "Up on the rise. I set up under a piece of low canvas. Not too hospitable, I'm afraid. Only got a small pit fire, and I can't have *that* after dark."

"I'm going to stay with you," she declared.

Wyatt looked down at the dirt floor and moved his toes inside his cold boots. When he looked back at her, she was staring at him as though she could read his thoughts.

"Well," he allowed, "it'll be cold as hell out there."

"Only half as cold tonight," she said quietly.

She sat down on the card-playing crate. The grainy light was fading by the minute, but it settled around her without dampening her will. She was like a stone statue that could outwait any man.

"I'm gonna start a fire," he said. "Can you eat some salt pork and beans?"

She nodded. Wyatt waited, because it looked like she wanted to say more. When her gaze met his again, she seemed to have traded her look of desperation for a stab at certainty.

"People need each other, Wyatt."

He frowned and stared at the strain of the tent on the windward side. "Well," he said and narrowed his eyes, as though nothing could be so easily summed up. "Sometimes, I reckon."

He sorted through a crate and found a tin of beans. Then he pushed out through the flap and started tying it back in place, but she slipped out through the gap before he could stop her. She snatched the tin from his hand.

"You work on the fire," she said. "I'll handle the food."

CHAPTER 8

Spring, 1875: Wichita, Kansas

By the time the snow on the prairie began to melt, Wyatt knew he had made a mistake taking Mattie in with him at the hotel. There was not enough space in the room, but neither was there a place for her in the privacy of his thoughts. Quiet as she was, she was nonetheless a constant noise that had begun to chatter in one corner of his mind. Even when he stayed up all night gambling in the saloons, he felt her like a scent clinging to his clothes, hovering around him, making it harder to breathe.

He had not foreseen the tenacious grip of which she was capable—the way she had of making him feel that taking care of her was somehow owed her. Wyatt knew that James had not forced her into her line of work. Mattie was simply one of those people who found others to blame for her problems.

At the bottom of it all, he knew that she was like a wounded animal, hopeless on her own. When he wasn't bedding her or tolerating her, he felt sorry for her, and she had learned to thrive off his pity, taking it as a definition of his commitment. Whenever he tried to back away from her to give her room to stand on her own, she rededicated herself to his every need: washing and starching his shirts, cleaning his boots, and keeping their room dust-free. Wyatt began going to the gambling halls earlier and getting back later.

In April, when the citizens of Wichita expressed through ballot their discontent with Billy Smith, Mike Meagher took over as city marshal. He was a tough enforcer who had run the marshal's office for three years before Smith's glad-hand reign. In addition, he had been commissioned a deputy US marshal, a post he still held. Now Meagher appointed his old friend John Behrens as assistant marshal, and, at Behrens's suggestion, Wyatt and Cairns became full-time deputies. Because of Meagher's no-nonsense expectations, the four officers worked together well—each knowing exactly where he stood on the issue of enforcement: the law came first, politics a distant second.

With the steady income of his deputy's salary, and with a regular profit from his faro table, Wyatt was able to rent a small house to better accommodate Mattie and himself. The change was good for her, he reasoned, giving her more space for the sewing work that seemed to be her only natural talent. With that change he thought there might be a chance she could develop the fortitude to disengage from him and start over on her own.

He seldom took her out, hardly wishing to send her a message that he was settling with her. Whenever she asked to go with him into town, he begged off, saying he never got a chance to spend time at home. Before long, he didn't have to lie. Most nights, by the time he came home, she was drunk, sprawled out on the bed in her house clothes. To counter the stench of alcohol, he went through a nightly ritual of opening the bedroom window and covering her with a blanket. Then he lay down beside her, his back to her heavy breathing, his face to the rejuvenating night air and the sequins of stars hanging over the flat skillet of the plains.

Just as the spring wildflowers dappled the prairie with color, Morgan, Wyatt's younger brother, arrived from Montana. Footloose and ever quick to laugh, he divided his time between "enforcing" at Bessie's and running his luck in the gambling houses.

As James told Wyatt, "Morg wants nothing more than to be like his older brother, and I ain't talkin' 'bout me or Virgil." James laughed. "Hell, he even looks just like you . . . or at least he will in a few years when he fills out."

On a cool night in early May, Morgan accompanied Wyatt on the rounds, checking the closed-up stores and the alleyways. Morgan was a talker and one of the few people Wyatt liked to listen to. They touched on subjects Wyatt shared with no other man. Only one topic was taboo, and that was the memory of Wyatt's deceased wife, Aurilla, and the baby who had died with her. Morgan knew never to broach it.

"So tell me 'bout Mattie," Morgan prodded. "Are you two hitched . . . official?"

Wyatt tried the door at Dick Cogswell's store and then cupped his hand to the window to peer through the glass. "She lives with me for now . . . that's all."

Morgan nodded. "She's a quiet one, that's for damned sure. Hard to figure whores sometimes. Sarah Haspel was like that . . . when it was just the two of us, I mean."

Wyatt turned, surprised. "You lived with her?"

Morgan smiled. "Before you showed up in Peoria. She used my name for a while." He cocked his head at the memory. "That was one wild girl, but she got plumb wore out on life."

When the two Earp brothers stepped into the light from the Gold Room, Morgan was drawn to the swinging doors like a moth to a flame. "Think I'll sit in on a game. You mind?"

Wyatt almost smiled. "You're not makin' any money trailin' me around town."

Morgan's face turned as earnest and innocent as when he was a boy. "You think Meagher might hire me as a special when the cattle season starts?"

"Might if he needs you. You got my recommendation."

"Hell," Morgan laughed, "I'd better!" He pushed through the

doors, and Wyatt watched him for a time as he picked up an easy conversation with each man he encountered.

Moving along Douglas Avenue Wyatt passed the New York House and walked to the edge of town, where he saw the dark silhouette of a man standing outside the corral gate of Denison's livery. The man's face bloomed with light from a match he struck for a cigarette.

"You have business here?" Wyatt said as he approached the man.

"Just checkin' on my horse, Marshal," the man said in a relaxed manner. He pushed away from the fence and offered Wyatt a smoke. Wyatt shook his head and looked at the empty corral.

"What horse might that be?"

The man turned as if he had not noticed the lot was vacant. "Must be in a stall. I'll come back tomorrow." He started past Wyatt, but Wyatt's hand flattened on the man's chest.

"What's your name?"

"J-Johnson," he said with a stutter. "Wesley Johnson."

Wyatt turned the man until they stood face to face just inches apart. For a full fifteen seconds, Wyatt studied the man's build, face, and finally his hat with its braided band.

"Ever been to Coffey County, Mr. Johnson?"

Johnson narrowed his eyes and pursed his lips. "That's up northeast o' here, ain't it? On the Neosho River?"

Wyatt tolerated the performance and turned the man back toward the business district. "I want you to walk with me up the street, Mr. Johnson." He prodded the man into a shuffling walk, and together they moved up Douglas Avenue without any further conversation.

When they reached the Gold Room, Wyatt slowed and steered the disconcerted man toward the door. "Step inside here with me."

"What for?" Johnson said and stopped. Frowning, he nodded down the street. "I need to get back to my room."

Wyatt's manner remained relaxed, even as Johnson grew more agitated. "This won't take long."

Inside the saloon, they stood near the oil lamp perched behind the bar. After sizing the man up for weight and height, Wyatt stared deep into his nervous eyes.

"You going to stay with your story, Mr. 'Johnson'?" Wyatt said.

"I don't know what you mean, Marshal. What story?"

Wyatt looked around the room and saw Morgan trying his hand at a faro layout. "Let's walk down to the city offices," Wyatt said to the fidgety man. "I wanna have a look at some papers."

When they reached the intersection at the New York House, the man claiming to be "Johnson" gestured down Douglas toward the livery. "Let me just go get my personal papers. They're in my saddlebags."

They walked in silence at a steady pace until, ten yards out from the stables, the man bolted away from Wyatt and vaulted the gate as spry as a circus performer. As the stranger sprinted through the dark interior of the livery barn, Wyatt drew his Colt's and ran around the outside of the building down the alleyway. When he broke into the open area next to the corral, he saw the fugitive scamper over the fence and start through the yard of a neighboring house.

On the run Wyatt raised his gun and fired straight up into the air. At the report, Johnson looked back and in the next stride caught a clothesline in the crook of his neck. The line stretched taut and then thrummed a twanging note as it flipped the fugitive flat on his back. When the man hit the ground, Wyatt heard the air rush from his chest as if he'd been punched in the pit of his stomach.

"Goddamn!" he gasped. "Am I shot?" His voice was dry as sand.

Wyatt lifted the man by his coat collar. "You try and run off again and you might be."

At the marshal's office Wyatt sat the man on a cell bunk and, leaving the door open, retrieved a stack of circulars from a drawer in Meagher's desk. Reentering the cell, he shuffled through the papers until he found what he was looking for.

" 'W. W. Compton,' " he read. " 'Five feet, four inches . . . one hundred forty pounds . . . light-brown hair and moustaches . . . center-peaked campaign hat with four indentions and a braided leather band around the crown.' " Wyatt lowered the paper and watched his prisoner glare at the tattered hat sitting on the bed next to him. "Is that you?"

Leaning forward with his elbows on his thighs, the prisoner let his head sag between his shoulders. "Yeah, it's me," he mumbled.

Wyatt continued reading. " 'Wanted for the theft of two horses and a mule from Leroy in Coffey County, Kansas.' " Wyatt looked up. "All this sound about right?"

Surprised to be asked, Compton looked up quickly at his capturer. Then, trying to disguise his show of curiosity, he pretended to probe at the damage on the front of his neck. The clothesline had raked a broad, raw scrape mark under his chin. He nodded and flung a hand toward the stack of papers in Wyatt's hand.

"How the hell did you happen to remember me out of all those?"

Marshal Meagher came in from the night and stood for a moment looking at Wyatt and the prisoner. "Was that you fired off a round behind Denison's?"

Wyatt closed the cell door and locked it. "It was." He handed the Coffey County circular to Meagher, who read it and then stared through the cell bars to inspect the man. "I'll turn him over to the sheriff tomorrow," Wyatt said. Walking back into the office, he set the papers back on Meagher's desk.

"Mr. Compton," Marshal Meagher said, squinting to inspect the man's wound from a distance, "I'm the Wichita chief of police. Are you shot?"

The prisoner shook his head. "No, but I might be about half-hanged," he said, lightly dabbing at the wound on his neck. With a heavy sigh, he lay back on the bunk and covered his eyes with a bent arm.

Meagher turned to Wyatt. "Did you miss?"

Wyatt hung up the cell key on the peg by the cellblock door. "Fired off a warning shot into the air."

Meagher looked back into the cell at Compton. "What the hell happened to his neck?"

Wyatt opened the loading gate on his Colt's and ejected the spent cartridge. "Mr. Compton tried to run off but got tangled in a clothesline."

Meagher stared at his deputy, as though waiting to see if Wyatt would smile. John Behrens came into the office and looked from Wyatt to Meagher and then through the cellblock door at the prisoner.

"Who the hell fired off that shot down behind Denison's?"

Wyatt loaded a fresh round into the cylinder and put away his gun. Then, after slipping on his coat, he straightened the hang of the fabric over his gun.

"That was me." He nodded back toward the cells. "Horse thief from Coffee County." He crossed the office to the front door and opened it with a glance back at Meagher. "I'll go finish my rounds."

"Well, dammit, hold on a minute!" Meagher barked, stopping Wyatt. The marshal approached with a question narrowing his eyes. "How the hell did you know who he was?"

Wyatt stood in the doorway and fitted his hat to his head. He had never seen such curiosity on the marshal's face.

"Hat," Wyatt said.

Meagher frowned and seemed to wait for more. "Hat," he repeated, intoning the word as if it had insulted him.

Wyatt nodded.

Meagher coughed up a quiet laugh, lifted the stack of circulars only to slap them down on the desk again. "Well, hell, son, go out there and round up the rest of 'em. You need some more clothesline?"

When Wyatt did not respond, the marshal slapped his shoulder and turned him toward the boardwalk. Both men walked out into the cold, the marshal still in his shirtsleeves.

"You just keep doin' what you're doin'. You and me are gonna get along fine. Wish I had about three more like you."

Wyatt lingered on the tread boards and looked out over Wichita's main thoroughfare. "Got a younger brother in town. If you need a special come the cattle season, he would be a good one."

Meagher struck a match and lighted a cigar. Squinting through the smoke he tossed the match out into the road.

"We talkin' about James?"

Wyatt kept his eyes on the stores across the street as he shook his head. "Morgan."

The marshal studied his cigar as he rotated it between his finger and thumb. Then he turned to Wyatt and narrowed his eyes.

"This brother . . . he got any experience?"

Wyatt nodded. "He wore a badge in Montana."

John Behrens came out of the office buttoning his coat. Closing the door, he stepped beside Wyatt and jerked a thumb over his shoulder toward the jail.

"How'd you nail that jaybird? Has he been pickin' up

livestock around here?"

Wyatt shook his head. "Name's Compton. Got a circular on him a few weeks ago."

"And you read those?" Behrens asked, smiling.

Wyatt gave Behrens a look. "I read 'em."

Behrens's smile faded. He waited, squinting at Wyatt, his lips parted as though trying to minimize the sound of his breathing.

"So how'd you nail 'im?"

Meagher sucked on the cigar and spewed a spreading plume of smoke into the cold air. "Hat," the marshal offered, saying it much as he had before. Behrens turned to Meagher and frowned, but no more explanation was forthcoming.

The three officers stood in a flank at the edge of the boardwalk. Turning their heads slowly, they surveyed the street, the vigilance in their eyes reflecting light from the saloon across the street as brightly as the badges pinned to their vests.

"I'll keep your brother in mind," Meagher said to Wyatt. "Coupl'a months from now I might could use him." The marshal looked up at the stars dusted across the black blanket of the prairie sky. "Long as he's the kind that don't mind bangin' on a man's head if the situation calls for it. Can't have a man who'll let them wild-ass Texas boys walk over 'im."

Wyatt stepped down into the street and buttoned his coat against the chill of the night. "If there's any o' that to be done, we'll be the ones doing the walkin'."

Meagher grinned. "You got any more brothers like you we can call on?"

"There's six of us," Wyatt said.

The marshal whistled a low sliding note that trailed away to nothing. "If we stuffed that many Earps into the same town, there'd likely be a lot o' goddamn Texas boys tiptoein' around our fair city."

Behrens coughed up his raspy cackle of a laugh. "Maybe we

could get them Texas boys to just start their cattle north to us on the trail . . . while the goddamn drovers stay back in Texas and kill each other. Save us a lot o' trouble." He started to laugh again but caught himself. "Hell, what am I sayin'? If that happened . . . we'd be out of a job."

Meagher sniffed and flicked a brick of red cigar ash into the street. "You just now figurin' that out, John?" He took a last drag on the cigar and tossed the butt into the road. "Cold as hell out here," he said and walked back into the office.

The two deputies continued to stand as they watched three men shuffle out of the saloon just east of the city offices. As the trio began to stumble down the sidewalk, the shortest man began to sing in a high Irish tenor, but one of his friends clamped a hand over his mouth and looked back repeatedly at the two officers.

"So, what about this man you arrested?" Behrens asked Wyatt. "What's this about a hat?"

"It's on the poster," Wyatt said.

Behrens studied Wyatt's face for several seconds. "And that's how you knew him . . . this man Compton . . . by his hat?"

Wyatt nodded.

Behrens chuckled. "Well, damn, Wyatt. If I ever turn outlaw, remind me to change my hat ever' week or so."

Wyatt pulled his coat collar up around his neck. He turned and gave Behrens his poker face.

"If you ever turn outlaw, come on into town to the marshal's office and I'll remind you."

Behrens's eyes pinched, and his whiskered face sucked in at the cheeks. Wyatt started down the street to finish his rounds.

"Hey," Behrens called out, "was that a joke?"

Wyatt kept walking.

"Wyatt Earp just told a goddamned joke!" Behrens crowed and provided the sole laughter for the occasion.

CHAPTER 9

Summer, 1875: Wichita, Kansas

When the longhorns came north again, so came the Texas drovers who prodded the rangy beasts up the trail. This time the cowpunchers' entrance into Wichita was less celebrative, less grandiose than in previous years, when a rowdy hurrah of gunfire on the streets had announced the end of their trail obligations. Wyatt, Morgan, Jimmy Cairns, and John Behrens met the cattle crews outside the city limits and delivered a new set of official mandates: First, all beeves would be driven to the stockyards by skirting the south side of town and approaching from the east, not through the main streets of the business district, as had been the time-honored practice. Second, no firearms were to be worn, concealed, or carried within town limits.

"You want us to pay for your liquor and women and fancy restaurants, but we cain't carry our guns to defend ourselves?" one trail boss complained. "Might as well ask us to come into town naked as a newborn."

"Please, for God's sake, don't do that," Morgan said, holding a straight face. "My mare happens to be in heat right now, and she is not known to be choosy about her siring selection."

Wyatt turned to Behrens and pointed to a herd of cattle spread out by the river to the southwest. "Why don't you and Morg take the word over to that outfit? Jimmy and I'll finish up here with this brand."

When the two lawmen rode into the swale, Wyatt stepped closer to the Texan to deliver his message quietly. "Your men don't need a gun for drinkin' and whorin' and eatin'. We'll have a check-in station at the bridge." He thought of Morgan. "We'll have a man there to look after your possessions. You can drop your hardware there and then go into town. Nobody will be carryin' in Wichita, so your men will have nothin' to defend themselves against."

The drover cocked his head and cracked a sneering smile. "Nobody 'cept the law, you mean."

"That's right . . . except us."

The Texan's mouth tightened into a disagreeable knot. Shaking his head, he leaned and spat to one side.

"Shit!" he said and carried a doubtful look back to Wyatt. "And what if some tin-horn gambler pulls a belly gun on one o' us across a poker table? What then?"

"You just tell your boys to behave. We'll take care of any problems that come up. We're here to protect your trail hands just like we are everybody else."

The Texan rubbed at the whiskers on his face, the sound as dry as wind-blown sand. "Well, I can tell 'em. But they're gonna do whatever the hell they want."

Wyatt shook his head. "Not good enough. These men work for you. You tell 'em what you expect from them while they're in town. They'll stomach it better comin' from you." Wyatt held the man's gaze with his own. "If we have trouble with your crew, we might have to throw the lot of you into the calaboose."

The boss frowned and watched some of his men pester the cook at the gate of the chuck wagon. "I'll do what I can," he said, still clearly troubled by the proposition. Then he narrowed his eyes at Wyatt. "You the new marshal?"

Wyatt shook his head. "Deputy."

"But you're Earp, right?"

Wyatt nodded. "I am."

The Texan pursed his lips and looked back at his crew. "These boys've been talkin' about cuttin' loose in Wichita for the last two weeks. This'll go hard on 'em."

Wyatt booted into his stirrup and mounted his mare. He had three other cattle outfits to see before his work outside of town was done.

"Go harder on 'em if they don't stand by our rules," he said and reined his horse around and took her at a walk toward a crew camping farther downstream on the river.

By late afternoon the saloons began to fill with drovers, and more were coming in off the grassy flats below the river. Wyatt and Jimmy Cairns were checking for loose treads on the boardwalk on Main Street when Charles Hatton, a prominent attorney appointed to handle the city's legal affairs, came toward them at a brisk walk from across the street.

"There may be some trouble brewing down at the Keno Corner," Hatton announced. "Where is Marshal Meagher?"

Crouched over a board, Cairns looked up, set down a hammer, and removed a pair of ten-penny nails he had pinched between his lips. "He's at home."

Wyatt had been kneeling with a pry bar. Now he straightened and began unrolling the sleeves of his blouse to button them at his wrists.

"What kind of trouble?" Wyatt said.

Hatton looked back down the street as if he might have been followed. "Some loud-mouth . . . calls himself 'Sergeant King' . . . claims he is a soldier, but he's not wearing a uniform. Says our law on checking firearms is unnatural. Says he won't give up his gun to any man. He's daring someone on the police force to come try to take it from him."

"Sergeant King," Wyatt repeated, his voice resigned, as if

recalling the name from a list of miscreants.

"You know 'im, Wyatt?" Cairns said.

Wyatt nodded. "I heard of him. He alone?"

Hatton frowned and pushed both hands into his trouser pockets. "Hard to tell," he said. "He certainly has an audience, and he seems on good terms with the cattlemen."

"Drinking?" Wyatt asked.

"Oh, yes," the lawyer huffed. "Looks like he's trying to drain the barrels dry down there."

Wyatt pushed his shirttails deeper into the waistband of his trousers. "Thank you, Mr. Hatton," he said and picked up his holster and revolver from the bench under the awning. Buckling the belt, Wyatt turned to Cairns. "Jimmy, get a scattergun from the office and meet me at the Keno." Wyatt picked up his hat and fitted it to his head.

Cairns dropped the nails into his shirt pocket. "Shotgun? Inside a gamblin' house?" But Wyatt was already walking away with the portly lawyer hurrying behind him. Cairns snatched up his gun belt from the bench and broke into a run for the city offices.

Just before reaching the intersection of Douglas and Main, Wyatt could hear the laughter of an all-male crowd. When he rounded the corner, he saw two dozen men loitering on the boardwalk and street, all of them enjoying the one-man show out in the center of the thoroughfare. On the far side of the street, merchants and their customers crowded the doorways of sundry shops to observe from a safe distance.

The lone entertainer was a strutter, grunting and gesturing with his arms as he paced a circle in long strides and delivered his oration to any and all who would listen. His bright blue blouse was the color of the summer sky and still showed crease marks where recently it had been folded on the mercantile shelf. His canvas trousers were equally new, dyed a blue-black and unmarked by dirt or stain of any kind. A broad-brimmed hat matched the trousers. Only the boots showed wear—the same boots Wyatt had seen on every soldier he had met while gambling at Fort Larned. On his left hip the man in the street wore an Army Model Colt's stuffed into a military holster with its flap cut away. The gun sat at a diagonal angle on the belt with the butt forward.

"*Look* at you!" he barked, pointing at the crowd and pivoting the outstretched arm to include everyone in front of the gambling house. "You boys call yourselves '*Texans*'?" He thrust a thumb at his chest and leaned forward to drive home a point. "Well, I ain't gonna let some piece o' town shit wearin' a tin star take away my damned gun! Not in this Godforsaken dust hole in Kansas . . . not anywhere!"

A few of the bystanders caught sight of Wyatt's approach, and heads began to turn like a slow shuffle of cards. When Sergeant King saw the movement, he turned to face the oncoming deputy. King's right hand reached across his midsection and clamped down on the pistol butt.

"Pull that and I'll kill you," Wyatt said, his hand stopping its natural swing to take a grip on his own revolver. He kept walking steadily forward, never altering his stride, his right elbow cocked upward to accommodate the grip on his Colt's.

Behind him Wyatt heard the clomping of boots come to a halt in the street, but he could not afford to take his eyes off the showman before him.

"I'm right here, Wyatt," Cairns called out to his back. "I got the ten-gauge." By the sound of his voice, Cairns was sidling away from the Keno for a better angle.

Wyatt kept moving toward King. "Jimmy," he called over his shoulder, "check that crowd for weapons from where you are. You see anybody move a hand an inch, I want you to open up on 'em."

Several of the men on the boardwalk straightened and stared at the shotgun. Two metallic clicks from the shotgun's hammers stilled the group of Texans into the living likeness of a tintype. Wyatt kept walking.

"Who the hell're *you*?" King demanded. His quick, flinty eyes jumped to the dull, silver scroll pinned to Wyatt's blouse. His hand tensed on the pistol grips, his knuckles blanching like chips of white stone embedded beneath the skin.

Six yards away Wyatt kept coming, his stride smooth and deliberate. The sound of his boots in the street was like a clock ticking off the seconds that separated the here and now from eternity.

"I asked you a goddamned question!" King shouted. "Who *are* you?"

"I'm the man who's gonna take that pistol from you."

King tried to laugh, but the sound caught in his throat like the croak of a raven. "D'you know who I am? I been—"

"Don't matter who you are," Wyatt interrupted. He watched the tip of the man's tongue dart across his upper lip as his jittery gaze settled on Wyatt's grip on his gun. "You're breaking the law."

"Son," King bellowed, trying to conjure up some grit for his audience, "I chew up people like you for breakfast. You ever hear of Sergeant King?"

Wyatt stopped so close to King that he could smell the factory scent of his new blouse. "Take your right hand off that gun," he ordered, "and then you're going to hand it to me with your left . . . two fingers only."

King stiffened. His eyes flicked toward Jimmy Cairns's shotgun and then to the crowd that had backed toward the sidewalk. When he looked back at Wyatt, his upper lip curled, and his face wrinkled like the muzzle of a snarling dog.

"Nobody takes my goddamned gun . . . 'specially no

cocksure, sonovabitch lawman from Kansas."

Wyatt's face showed nothing. Under the brim of his hat, his blue eyes were like ice, unwavering and set with purpose.

"You got this one chance," he said so quietly that King had to cock his head to put one ear forward. "I ain't gonna ask you again."

King smiled and manufactured a dry, raspy laugh. "You think you can get that gun o' yours into—"

The stinging slap of Wyatt's open hand could be heard half a block away. The braggart's new hat flew off his head as if by a sudden gust of wind that affected no other person present. Wyatt had moved so fast, King's delayed reflex to cover himself appeared comical. The surprised troublemaker reeled and came close to losing his footing. When he recovered, he crouched and tightened like a coiled spring, his right hand still wrapped around the curve of the pistol handle. Then the hostile expression on his face dissolved when he saw the Colt's in Wyatt's hand leveled at his chest.

"Left hand," Wyatt reminded him.

As King glared back at him, Wyatt could see a strange twist of light turning in the man's eye. He had seen it before in Ellsworth, when Ben Thompson's little brother had killed Sheriff Whitney with a shotgun at point-blank range. There was no reasoning with people like these—half-cocked, unpredictable, well on their way to moon-howling drunk, and maybe a little crazy if the rumors about King were true. Any officer who tried using logic with men such as these, Wyatt knew, was himself a fool.

Stepping forward, Wyatt clamped his left hand on King's wrist and with his right swung the heavy barrel of the Colt's into the man's temple. King went down hard, crushing the new hat that had sailed to the dusty street, but his hand was still gripped to his holstered weapon. Wyatt swung the gun again, slashing at the wrist until the man released his hold on the revolver.

Lying on his back now, King screamed and cradled his damaged wrist in his left hand. His eyes squeezed so tightly shut, the skin pulled taut across the bones of his face. Cursing through gritted teeth, he opened his eyes to find Wyatt standing over him.

"Take the damn gun then, goddamn you . . . unless you wanna break s'more of my bones for me, you sneaky sonovabitch!"

Wyatt knelt. "No, you're gonna give it to me," he said quietly, "just like I said."

King's face went slack, and the crazy glimmer in his irises was replaced by a dull sheen of confusion. "What?" he whispered.

When Wyatt held out his free hand palm up, the prostrate man awkwardly shifted in the street, bent his left elbow, and pinched the pistol with the thumb and forefinger of his left hand. With the gun dangling so, he raised it high enough to drop into Wyatt's hand.

After checking the man's waist and boots for another weapon, Wyatt stood and faced the crowd standing on the boardwalk in front of the Keno. "Anybody else carryin', Jimmy?"

"Not that I can tell, Wyatt," Cairns reported.

Wyatt held his glare on the crowd. "How about it? Anybody else?"

The Texans' faces went hard and sullen, each man trying to salvage some pride with a show of insolence or resentment or indifference. Not one of them spoke.

"You obey our laws," Wyatt said plainly, "and you're welcome here in Wichita." He holstered his gun and jerked King to his feet. "Otherwise," he continued, "you'll be spending your celebration time inside the city jail and nursing a sore head."

"What kind o' law gives you the right to crack a man's skull like that?" said one of the drovers.

Wyatt recognized the complainer as one of the trail bosses he had met earlier in the day. "I figure a man would rather wake up with a sore head . . . instead of in a grave."

The foreman seemed to be at a loss for words. Finally, he pushed his palm in front of him as if waving away an irritating insect.

"Aw, hell . . . he wasn't one o' ours anyway." Turning on his heel he walked back into the gambling house. One by one the others followed.

Taking King by the scruff of his collar, Wyatt hauled him down the street toward the city jail. Still groggy from the blow to his head, King stumbled and did his best to keep up. All his venom was gone. An open gash on the side of his head poured a slick stream of blood down the left side of his whiskered face.

"You broke my damn arm . . . and pro'bly my head, too," King whimpered.

"You dealt the hand," Wyatt said. "I had a legal right to shoot you. Would you rather I'd done that?"

King thought about the question for a moment. "Well, I might've, goddamn you!"

When they came abreast of Cairns and Charles Hatton, the four men walked together with Cairns gripping the prisoner's other arm. Cairns leaned in close, narrowed his eyes, and studied King's wound.

"He's gonna need a doctor, Wyatt."

Wyatt nodded. "Jimmy, see can Doc Fabrique come down to the jail."

"You want me to run out to Meagher's house and tell 'im?"

Wyatt shook his head. "Just the doc."

Cairns took off at a run. Hatton hurried ahead to the city offices and opened the door for the deputy and his prisoner. Wyatt settled King into a cell and locked the door. When he returned to the marshal's office, Hatton was waiting.

"That may have been the nerviest thing I've ever seen a man do," the lawyer said.

Wyatt gave the man a questioning look.

"He could have made a fight of it," Hatton continued. "Could have shot you down."

Wyatt pursed his lips and began shaking his head. "Not likely," he said and stored King's revolver in a drawer of Meagher's desk.

"What makes you so sure?"

"He's mean, but he's not the kind who's ready to die to prove it," Wyatt said. "Probably the kind accustomed to bluffing other men down."

"And you were willing to stake your life on that?"

Wyatt sat on the edge of the desk and met Hatton's eyes. "What happened out there needed to happen. And everybody who witnessed it . . . they needed to see it."

"You mean . . . so the drovers will know we're serious about our new ban on firearms in the town limits." When Wyatt did not answer, the attorney pressed on. "But how did you know he wouldn't pull on you? You yourself said he was a killer."

Wyatt looked down at his hands, opened and closed them, and then met Hatton's earnest face again. "He's killed some. But not face to face, I'll wager. A man who has to convince ever'body else how brave he is . . . that's a man who ain't sure of himself. He knows he's afraid. That's why he's a back-shooter."

Hatton started to push his argument but closed his mouth when Wyatt continued.

"A coward like that can recognize a man who sees into 'im. Gives that man the upper hand."

Hatton lowered his eyebrows and frowned. He puckered his

lips in a thoughtful expression and began to nod.

"Well," the lawyer said, "I'm in no position to argue the matter with you. You seem to know what you're doing."

Wyatt pushed up from the desk as the door opened. Cairns and the doctor bustled in and moved straight to the cell block. Wyatt walked to the doorway to watch Cairns open the iron door. King was complaining about being manhandled even before the doctor could ask a question.

"Wyatt?" Hatton said from the front door. "I still think it was the nerviest thing I've ever seen."

Wyatt looked back into the dark of the cell block, where King bowed his head as the doctor probed at his wound. "I reckon it's part o' the job, Mr. Hatton," Wyatt said. When he turned back to the attorney, he raised his chin toward the window and the street beyond. "Now that it's done, I reckon things'll run smooth enough."

Deep in thought, Hatton stared into the middle distance and frowned. "Yes," he finally admitted. "I imagine they will."

CHAPTER 10

January, 1876: Wichita, Kansas

The demonstration of force exhibited in the King arrest served to set the precedent that Wyatt had intended. The cattle season ran its course, bringing in the revenue that the town had hoped for . . . without the rowdiness and gunplay that had been the norm in the past. For the lawmen there were fewer bonuses for arrests and court appearances, but the deficit was balanced somewhat by grateful merchants who afforded the police force discounts on their goods. Most of this was levied through liquor in the saloons . . . or, in Wyatt's case, coffee. A free cup awaited him in every establishment in both Wichita and Delano.

More importantly, Wyatt's reputation had sunk its roots into every layer of society. He was not invited to upper-crust gatherings or to meals with the councilmen and their families, but the deference he was paid by all the citizens was apparent in the respectful glances he received on the street.

Mike Meagher knew what he had in Deputy Earp and began to call on him more often, especially when a situation needed a quiet resolution. Behrens, the marshal knew, could handle any trouble that dragged into town, but Earp's demeanor in instances of conflict left a calmer wake in the current of town gossip that followed. Meagher saw this as a feather in his cap that might solidify votes for him when the elections came around again.

Wyatt thought otherwise.

When the summer burned out and the prairie began to yellow, Morgan, Cairns, and two other deputies were laid off, leaving only Wyatt and Behrens to serve on the force with Meagher. Trading on his gambling skills and his mastery over a billiards cue, Morg divided his time between half a dozen saloons on both sides of the river. His boyish humor had won him many a friend among the sporting crowd, and—because they were brothers—this popularity seemed to leaven Wyatt's way of handling all situations with his no-nonsense, taciturn manner.

As Behrens put it outside the Gold Room one night, "If you two Earps could join at the hip to become one package, you could probably be the mayor, police chief, and big boss gambler of Wichita all rolled into one."

Wyatt barely cracked a smile and looked down at his boots. He knew Morgan would provide a comeback for both of them.

"Well, John," Morg began, "as I see it, that would present a coupl'a problems. First of all . . . ever' time we walk into a saloon, we'd have to mix up a terrible concoction of cold beer and hot coffee to satisfy the both of us." Morg made a face. "Sort o' cancels out to lukewarm, don't it? I ain't sure I can handle that." He traded his sour expression for one of dead earnestness. "And second . . . there's a lot o' frisky women in this town dependin' on me to slake their urges, if you know what I mean." Morg lowered his eyebrows and pressed his mouth into a hard line of regret. "I ain't so sure I could perform with my big brother lookin' over my shoulder."

"Hell!" Behrens laughed. "It'd be his pecker, too, wouldn't it?"

Morg's face pinched with worry. "Well, damn . . . that won't work either. Sounds like I'd be havin' only half the fun."

Both men looked at Wyatt to see if he would laugh. Wyatt cut his eyes from one to the other and then settled on Behrens. "If I ever join at the hip with someone, it won't be this smiling moon-calf." He jabbed a thumb toward his brother, turned, and started slowly down the street. "I'm gonna make the rounds," he called over his shoulder.

Morgan smiled and winked at Behrens. "Hey, Wyatt," he called out. "We'd be a force to be reckoned with. I might be willin' to share some o' those frisky women with you."

Wyatt did not respond. He kept walking, his eyes already scanning the merchants' doors and windows, checking that they were secure. As soon as he finished his circuit through the business district, he had a faro game to open at Rupp's.

Just after the New Year, Wyatt sat in a four-hand poker game in the Custom House. The only other customers in the room were two railroad men downing beer as they argued over an unfurled map they had pinned to the table with empty mugs. The bartender slowly pushed a broom around the floor, trying to keep the stirred-up dust to a minimum.

"Henry," called one of the railroad men to the barman, "I been suckin' in coal dust and cinders for two days. I was hopin' to learn how to breathe again."

Without complaint Henry laid down his broom and walked behind the bar, where he upended a partially full whiskey bottle above a funnel inserted into another. When the upper bottle had drained, he corked the lower one and set it on the liquor-lined shelf behind him.

When the door opened, Wyatt glanced up to see Morgan push in from the night. Blowing against the cold and slapping flakes of snow off the sleeves of his dark overcoat, Morg spoke to Henry and nodded to every patron in the room. Wyatt watched his brother only long enough to deliver a silent message: *Business is in session.*

The three men at Wyatt's table studied their cards, one of them gnawing at his lower lip with a yellowed tooth, the other two trying to appear confident. Wyatt sipped his coffee and waited. At the gaming table he was imperturbable, his professional demeanor as fixed as the North Star. Setting down his coffee, he folded both hands over his closed cards and continued to wait.

"Raise thirty," he finally said, his voice clear and without inflection. From his wallet he counted out the proper bills and stacked them at the center of the table, where a few modest denominations marked the beginnings of the pot. The oil lamp sitting on the table gave the paper money a yellowish cast.

The players frowned at him but got no reaction. Returning their attention to their own hands, they stared at their cards like would-be alchemists attempting to divine gold out of lesser metals. Wyatt leaned and set his coffee cup on the wood heater.

Morgan hung his coat on a wall peg and moved to the stove, where he splayed the fingers of both hands to the heat and then rubbed his palms together briskly. "Cold enough out there to put out a lit cigar!" he declared. "I think maybe the river has froze solid."

When no one replied, Morg ambled over to the table to watch the game. Half a minute ticked by without a word or movement.

Morg laughed. "Holdin' a prayer session here, boys?"

Wyatt kept his eyes on the players. One of the gamblers—a thickset man with tufts of hair spilling out from under his shirtsleeves—added a fan of bills to the loose stack. "I'll see your thirty and . . . raise you ten."

The other two men folded, one gracefully and the other with an irritated slap of his cards. Both players sat back as spectators and appeared relieved to be out of the running.

Wyatt added a ten . . . and then he counted out three additional bills. "How 'bout we take it up thirty more," he said quietly.

The remaining player flashed a crooked smile on his meaty face. "I believe you're tryin' to buy the pot, Earp."

Wyatt nodded at the possibility. "Cost you thirty to find out, Mr. Black," he said.

Black privately fanned open his cards again and held his smirk. He took in a fill of air through his nose and purged it quickly. Several seconds passed, and no one spoke or moved. Finally a log tumbled inside the stove, and a spray of sparks shot out of the vent and crackled in the air like a flurry of distant gunshots.

"Aw, hell!" Black grumbled and threw his cards face down on the table. "I go home empty handed and my wife will tack my hide to the hotel door." He curled his lip at the money on the table. "Take it, goddammit, but don't tell me whether or not you got what I think you got. I'd rather not know if you skinned me." He pushed both hands at the air toward Wyatt. "I'm done." He looked at the men at either side. "How 'bout you boys?"

The three men rose as a party, the same way they had come in. Wyatt nodded to each of them. Only when they moved to the bar did he begin to sort through the money, stacking the bills by denomination.

Smiling, Morgan sat and folded his arms over his chest. Then he tilted his head to one side and widened his smile at the pile of money.

"Well, ain't you the fluff on the ki-yote's tail? How much?"

Wyatt checked the bar. The three men were deep into their shared condolences and talking over mugs of beer.

"Little under two hundred," Wyatt said quietly.

Morg reached across the table to turn up the cards his brother had set down. Wyatt let him.

Morg's eyebrows lifted, and he hummed a sliding note of approval. "Weren't bluffin', were you?"

Continuing with his count, Wyatt cut his eyes to Morgan, letting his silence be answer enough.

Morg turned in his chair to watch the men at the bar work on their drinks. When he turned back to Wyatt, he wrinkled his nose so that his front teeth showed beneath the sandy wisp of moustaches he was grooming.

"Ain't that the Black who James said you threw out o' his whore's window?"

Wyatt nodded. "It is."

Morg smiled. "Well, how the hell d'you get 'im to play poker with you?"

Wyatt put away his money, tapped the cards together, and held up the deck next to his face as he stared at his brother. "Cards are business. When you sit down at the table, it's all about the money. You leave everything else out of it." He laid the deck on the table next to his watch. He could have been a parson, finished with his reading and setting down a Bible.

Black and his two friends scuffed out of the saloon, leaving the room to the two Earps and the two railroad workers . . . and the bartender, who now cleaned the countertop with a damp rag. After the door slammed and the bar settled into a new silence, the barman began to hum a tune.

Wyatt lifted his Colt's revolver from his lap and set it on the table, the gun making a decisive tap on the varnished wood. Morgan frowned and stared at his brother.

"What the hell? You had that sittin' there all along?"

Wyatt let his eyebrows float up a quarter inch. It was as close as he ever came to shrugging.

"If ever I'm wrong about a man like Black," he said, "it don't hurt to be careful."

Smiling, Morg shook his head and picked up the gun. "I got to get me one o' these. I might be the last man in Kansas slavin' over a cap and ball."

"That German down at the gun shop can convert it for you,"

Wyatt advised. "B'fore long, you won't be able to buy cap and ball supplies."

Morgan hefted the weight of the gun and tested its balance in his hand. "Feels good, don't it?" When Wyatt did not answer, Morg's face turned serious as he laid the gun back down on the table. "Reckon you'll run for the marshal's post come spring?" he asked Wyatt.

Wyatt pushed his fingers through his hair and rubbed at his eyes with the heels of his hands in a grinding motion. "I been thinkin' on it." When his hands came down, he blinked to clear his eyes until the blur of the room returned into sharp resolution. "I guess maybe the time is right."

"Will Meagher run?" Morg asked.

Wyatt thought about the question and then nodded. "Prob'ly."

"Will that be a problem . . . between the two o' you, I mean."

Wyatt wrapped his hand with a white handkerchief and reached for his coffee. He shook his head.

"It's like the cards," he explained. "It's business. If I was to win, I'd want to have him on the force. I 'spect he'd do the same for me." He sipped from the cup with an airy sputter, careful to avoid the burn on his lips.

The door opened again, and John Behrens brought in a gust of wind and snow. He kicked the door shut with his boot and walked straight for the heater. His nose was ruddy red and his eyes watery. Snow clung to his hat and shoulders. When he saw the gun next to Morgan's hand, his face pinched, and his beady eyes narrowed to slits.

"You need help over there, Wyatt? Looks like you come up against a honest-to-God desperado."

Morgan laughed. "Ain't me he's worried 'bout. He's been sittin' here through a poker game keepin' his pecker warm with this." He picked up the pistol and waggled it in the air.

"Hell, I'd wear it there, too, if I thought it would keep me warm tonight," Behrens said. He hitched his thumb toward the oppressive cold of the night waiting outside the door. "You been cuttin' the cards with Black again?"

Wyatt nodded and reached for his gun. "Let me have that, Morg, before you shoot someone." Dropping the Colt's in the side pocket of his coat, he pushed back his chair, stretched his legs beneath the table, arched his back, and flexed both arms, bending them until his fists were beside his ears. He took in a lot of air and exhaled in a rush. "Sittin' too long," he said and let his hands drop to the arms of the chair.

"Hey, John," Morg said, winking at Wyatt, "are you thinkin' on runnin' for marshal in April?"

Behrens looked surprised. "Truth be told, I'm just hopin' to still be the assistant marshal. Why?"

Morgan couldn't keep the smile off his face. "What would you think about Wyatt runnin'?"

Behrens stared open-mouthed, his eyes cutting from one Earp to the other before settling on Wyatt. "You're runnin' against Meagher?"

"Just thinkin'," Wyatt said and pushed himself upright in the chair. As he started to stand, he felt the Colt's tumble free from his coat. Before he could lower himself, the gun clattered off the seat of the chair and struck the floor.

The gunshot filled the room. It was as if a bolt of lightning had cracked through the roof and split the floorboards into splinters. Morgan dodged partway under the table, and Behrens belatedly crouched behind the stove. The bartender stood slack-jawed staring at Wyatt, but the two rail workers had lunged for the door in tandem as if they had been shackled together. Now the two stood like statues peering toward the back of the room.

"What the hell!" Behrens coughed dryly.

Wyatt looked down at the gun still smoking on the plank floor. Then lifting the skirt of his coat and fanning it out to his side, he discovered a new hole where the bullet had ripped through the material just above the side pocket and below the breast.

"Everybody all right?" the bartender volunteered.

One of the men by the door straightened up but kept a hand on the door knob. "I ain't sure till I know who the hell is shootin' at who?" he said.

"It's all right," Behrens announced to the room. "Just an accident."

Wyatt's face was hard, his eyes like pale-blue stones set in white marble. He stood, walked to the gun, picked it up, and held it in the flat of his hand as though considering its weight. He returned Behrens's gaze, but neither man spoke. Stuffing the pistol into his waistband, Wyatt returned to the table and picked up his coffee, his movements stiff and self-conscious. His cheeks were tinged with a rufous glow. The coffee had cooled, so he set it back down on the table.

Smiling now, Morgan looked at the gouge in the wall where the bullet had ricocheted off the paneling and then punched a hole in the ceiling. Wyatt waited for his brother to meet his eyes.

"Morgan," Wyatt said in a low, firm monotone, "just shut up."

Morg's face opened with youthful innocence. His shoulders rose up around his ears as he lifted both hands palms up. As he posed like that, his eyes began to twinkle with a devilish light. Then, just as quickly, he took on a solemn expression and turned to Behrens.

"Hell, I'll still vote for 'im, won't you, John?"

Before Behrens could answer, the door opened, and Marshal Meagher bustled in from the cold. He appeared at once curious and angry, his right hand clasping the butt of his holstered revolver. There was enough snow layered on the brim of his hat that he reached outside to slap it against the building before slamming the door. Even as he questioned the men at the front of the room, his eyes locked on the three men in the back.

"Ever'thing's dandy, Mike," Behrens called out, rocking his hat forward and back on the top of his head. "Gun went off, is all."

Meagher strode to the back of the room, spread his boots, and tossed his hat on the table. Looking from one man to the next he waited for an explanation.

"I got two deputies on the payroll," he began in his gravelly voice, "but I couldn't find neither one to see about a gunshot. Now it turns out you're both down here and prob'ly the goddamn cause of it."

"Well, Wyatt ain't on duty," Behrens offered. "I am."

The marshal sucked something from his teeth and spat it toward the floor with a little popping sound. "Do one o' you wanna tell me what the hell happened here?"

Behrens took off his hat and tapped it against his leg as he studied the toes of his boots. Morgan filled his cheeks with air and let his breath slowly seep out.

"Gun slipped out o' my pocket," Wyatt said, his voice even and clear. He offered nothing more.

The wind outside rattled some loose roofing somewhere, and the vibration seemed to suck all other sounds out of the room. Meagher eyed the side of Wyatt's coat.

"You've got a damned rip in the back of your pocket." Flashing Wyatt an impatient scowl, Meagher pushed back his coat to prop his hands on his hips. His marshal's badge caught light from the table lamp and reflected it back like quicksilver. "You're makin' steady wages . . . why don't you buy yourself a holster?"

"Already got one," Wyatt said. "Like John said, I'm off-duty."

Meagher looked away toward the men settling back at their table. The cartilage in his jaw pulsed like a heartbeat.

"Happened to me one time, Mike," Behrens volunteered. "In the coach from Topeka. Almost killed a shoe salesman."

A little twinkle showed in Morgan's eyes, and he opened his mouth to add his story, but the look he got from Wyatt changed his mind.

Meagher relaxed his stance, and one corner of his mouth twitched with what might have been the beginning of a smile. He slipped his hands into his coat pockets and slowly began to rock on the balls of his feet.

"Well, hell," he said, "I done it once, too." Then he looked around the room at the bartender and two patrons. Turning back to Wyatt, he lowered his rough voice to a mumble. "But I weren't wearin' a badge at the time and didn' have me an audience."

No one spoke for the time that Meagher studied the walls and the ceiling. He looked like he was searching for damage, but Wyatt knew the marshal was just going through the motions of being in charge.

"Nobody got hurt, Mike," Behrens said. "Forget it."

The marshal gave Behrens a dead-eyed stare. "Come spring, when somebody runs against me for this badge . . ." He tapped a finger to the metal shield on his chest. "I don't wanna hear my opponent talkin' about how one o' my deputies let loose with a stray shot in a place of business." He swept a hand through the air as if erasing all the plans he had made for himself. "That's all it takes, you know. One damned little thing like that . . . and it's over."

Wyatt kept his attention on Meagher, but in his peripheral vision he saw Behrens and Morgan cut their eyes to him.

Ignoring Wyatt's warning, Morgan smiled at the marshal with the crinkle in his eyes that endeared him to everyone. "Hell, Mike, this is the most excitement we've had since the cattle crews dragged out o' Wichita. With all this shootin' goin' on durin' the off-season, maybe you oughta open up another deputy slot." Morg's face turned thoughtful and then quickly brightened. "Hey, how 'bout me? I'm free!"

Meagher smiled down at the floor for several seconds and nodded as though actually considering the question. When his head came back up, he was all business.

"Come next season," he said, "if I'm still marshal, you'll be on my list." Then his face softened, and he allowed a fleeting glance in Wyatt's direction. "Just the same, check with me in a few days, and I'll see if any of my present staff have shot theirselves by then."

Meagher turned and walked to the bar. "Any damages, Henry?"

The bartender looked around as though he had not considered the possibility. "Nothing to speak of, Marshal Meagher." He started up with the rag again, polishing the bar in big overlapping circles.

When Meagher walked out, the railroad men followed him into the night. Wyatt marched to the coat rack, knifed his arms into the sleeves of his overcoat, and settled his hat on his head. As he started for the door, Morg called his name. Wyatt turned and waited.

"Wyatt, we'll still vote for you," Morg said. His expression was virtuous but for his sparkling eyes. He had more ways to show mischief in those eyes than a schoolyard prankster. "Gettin' two votes out o' the whole town . . . that won't be so bad." Turning quickly to the bartender, Morg added, "Hell, you'll vote for 'im, wouldn' you, Henry?"

Henry stopped his work and frowned at Wyatt. "Vote for you for what?"

Wyatt shook his head at the bartender and then fixed his eyes on his brother. "Don't pay no attention to my brother, Henry. He talks too much."

Morgan's eyes widened with contrived umbrage. Bringing his hand up to his face, he pinched his lips together between his thumb and forefinger.

Wyatt opened the door. "Let me know if I owe you for any repairs, Henry."

Shutting the door behind him, Wyatt stood in the bracing wind, the snow swirling around him like feathers from a burst down pillow. He watched through the door glass as Morgan and Behrens sat and leaned toward one another in conversation.

"Goddamn it," Wyatt mumbled beneath the whip of the wind.

Heading for home, he kept close to the buildings and turned up his coat collar, gathering it tightly under his chin against his throat. When the heat of anger began to flow through his veins again, he released the collar and squared his shoulders, walking into the wind now as though it were his adversary. Six people knew about his gun going off. Word was bound to get around.

"Goddamn it," he murmured again, the sound of his voice barely rising above the wind.

Over the next two days Wyatt heard nothing about the incident, not from Meagher or Behrens or any other citizen. Even Morgan knew not to press the issue. On the third day, in the late afternoon, Wyatt started his rounds at the east end of Douglas and worked his way toward the bridge. The wind was still pushy, and dust blew up from the street in big gusts that scoured the storefronts. The snow had reduced to a sparse shining glitter of sunlight as it spat through the air.

Approaching the bridge Wyatt heard his name called from James's house. Turning, he spotted his brother leaning out of the same window through which he had expelled the hotelier, Black. James was waving him over, so Wyatt turned into the side yard and stopped by the spring wagon.

"I hear you 'bout shot your fool head off the other night,"

James yelled over the wind.

Wyatt frowned at his brother. "You been talkin' to Morg?"

James laughed. "I ain't seen 'im." He disappeared inside the room for a few moments. When he returned, he held out a rolled newspaper. Wyatt moved to the window and took the new edition of the *Wichita Beacon*. "Second page!" James instructed, trading his amused smile for one of brotherly concern.

Fighting the wind, Wyatt opened the paper and folded it by sections until he found the article. It was all there: the Custom House, the accidental discharge of his pistol, even a quote from one of the patrons, who thought the saloon was under siege. As he read, Wyatt felt the heat of anger rise in his blood. At the same time, some of his half-made plans began sinking in his gut, like a piece of bad food that would take its toll on him no matter what else he did.

When he finished reading, he looked up to see the window closed on its crude leather hinges. He slapped the paper against his leg and walked through the sparse weeds and desiccated grass of the front yard to stand on the bluff above the semi-frozen river. There he stood for a while, just listening to the water break around the bridge pilings beneath the erratic fluctuations of the wind. At the center of the current the water flowed swiftly, indifferent to the fringe of ice working its way from the shorelines. Across the wide swath of the river Delano spewed narrow flumes of smoke from the scattered chimneys and stovepipes of its sundry businesses—a barrage of white streams that angled sharply on the wind and spread into gauzy plumes that were eventually lost in the gray of the sky.

He looked back at the house, where James now stood on his front porch with a blanket wrapped around his shoulders. Unwrapping an arm free James cupped a hand to his mouth.

"To hell with 'em," he yelled to Wyatt. "They ain't got nothin' else to write about, I reckon." James stood for a while, flexing his knees and shivering. Finally he turned around and went back inside. When the door shut, Wyatt turned back to the water.

In time his blood cooled, and he settled his mind to accept what had happened. Some things could not be helped, he knew. Everything in the past was set in stone. There was nothing that could change it. But this was a mistake he would not revisit again in his lifetime. Even then, as he stood on the bridge, the hammer of his Colt's rested upon an empty chamber.

"Well," he said to no one and glanced at the article again. "They finally spelled my name right."

CHAPTER 11

Spring, 1876: Wichita, Kansas

By the time city elections came around again, Billy Smith had repositioned himself into the public eye, fanning the hope of regaining his old post as city marshal. On a night with a cold wind blowing down from the north, Wyatt walked into the warmth of the Gold Room to find Smith loudly espousing his own virtues, asking the listeners to consider the prudence of having a police chief who was literate and adept at diplomacy when it came to negotiating with cattlemen and the city council.

Waving a beer mug before him, Smith drove home his points like a seasoned politician. Every man standing before him held an identical mug on the ex-marshal's tab. Wyatt walked to the bar, propped a foot on the boot rail, and listened. Smith did not acknowledge him, but most eyes in the room cut to Wyatt, whose silent stare served as effectively as half of an impromptu debate. One by one the men shuffled off to the tables to drink among themselves.

Finally noticing Wyatt's presence, Smith managed a congenial wrap-up of his speech, paid his bill, and walked out. Wyatt followed him to Rupp's and waited outside as the politician bought drinks all around and began his oration again, at which time Wyatt repeated his silent interruption. Just like at the Gold Room, the audience retired to card games and private conversations. Not once did Smith look at Wyatt as he walked out of the establishment and headed for his home.

The next morning, on the eve of the election, when Wyatt checked in at the office, Meagher was waiting for him. "Don't do me any good at the polls if people think we're intimidatin' my opponent. I want you to lay off Smith, you hear me? Let him dig his own hole."

"You don't mind being called 'illiterate' in front of the town?"

Meagher didn't look up from the warrants he sorted. "D'pends on what it means."

"Means you don't read or write."

"I don't care if people think I don't spend my day gawkin' at a goddamned book. What I care about is doing my job. Let it go, understand? Finish collecting the taxes in the business district."

That night in front of the post office Behrens passed Wyatt on his rounds. "Smith's over at Rupp's flapping his jaw. Best not go over there."

"Got him a crowd?"

"Oh, yeah. As many as he can buy a beer for. Your brother's over there."

"Well, he works there."

"No, I mean Morgan."

Wyatt went very still for a few seconds and then started down the street, already imagining the catcalls Morg might contribute to the meeting. He stopped just inside Rupp's doors and looked over the crowd. Morgan sat in a card game, none of whose participants were listening to Smith's discourse at the bar. Still, Wyatt saw the prudence of removing his brother from the room, so he stepped through the door and walked past Smith to his brother's table.

"Morg," Wyatt said leaning to Morgan's ear, "I need to talk with you . . . outside."

Morgan looked up and feigned surprise, his deputy badge flashing on his vest. "What! And miss this pretty speech?" He said it loud enough that Smith faltered for a moment. "B'sides," Morg went on, keeping up a performance, "be hard to throw in a hand like this." He turned his cards for Wyatt to read: a pair of fours, a six of spades, a ten of hearts, and a diamond queen. But for the twinkle in his eye, Morgan's face was as somber as a preacher's.

"I'll be outside," Wyatt said. "Come on out after this hand."

On the boardwalk Wyatt leaned against the wall and lipped a fresh cigar. Billy Smith's ardor seemed to intensify after Wyatt's exit. Morgan walked out, laughing.

"I don't know who's the bigger bluff: me with a pair of fours or Smith and his silver-tongued lies." He frisked Wyatt's coat and copped a cigar. Wyatt cupped a match for both of them.

"Meagher wants me to steer clear of Smith until after the election. I reckon that extends to you, too. Smith has a way of saying things that get under my skin. Probably go the same with you."

Morgan struck a pose of mock surprise and flattened a hand to his chest. "You're saying I need more restraint as a lawman?"

Wyatt ignored the theatrics and watched the wind whip up wisps of snow from the edge of the street. "Why don't you make the rounds with me?"

Before Morgan could answer, both brothers heard the name "Earp" ring clearly from the nimble lips of Billy Smith. In unison, they turned their heads and stood very still.

"Seems we got a lot of these Earps on the city payroll," Smith continued. "Then there's the one who runs the brothel down near the river on *our* side of the bridge. It would seem this Earp family has charmed our present police chief." So captive did Smith's charismatic gift of oratory hold the room that Wyatt could hear every nuance of the man's dainty speech. "If Meagher wins this election, who do you think will be his deputies? Which whorehouse will be exempt from the laws on this side of the river? Say, maybe we should just start over here . . . and rename our town 'Earp City.' ”

As the theme veered into the moral uplifting of a growing Wichita, Wyatt re-entered the room and walked straight to Smith, who was leaning toward his listeners, chopping both hands in the air like cleavers to emphasize a point. When he noticed Wyatt, his hands lowered, and he straightened. The silence in the room was a sound unto itself.

“You're mighty damned loose with the names of my brothers and me.”

Smith pasted on his congenial smile. “Do you deny, Wyatt, that Meagher would hire your whole clan full-time if re-elected?”

“I can't speak for him, but if he did re-hire us, in my estimation, it would be to the benefit of Wichita.” Wyatt's deep, sandy voice was unruffled, but his ice-blue eyes were cold as the night.

“Well, that might be a matter up for debate,” Smith countered with an irritating chuckle, “unless Wichita is planning to expand its whore market. Your brother James is in violation of the law as we speak.”

Wyatt held his hard stare on Billy Smith's know-it-all smirk. “Same thing he was doing when you were marshal.”

Smith's smile broadened, and he cocked his head toward the floor as though the statement amused him. “Well,” he purred, “at least he's supplying some of the town with *respectable* wives.” He grinned and winked at someone in the front row.

Smith might as well have used Mattie's name. Wyatt slapped him across the face, and Smith stumbled back into the bar, where he steadied himself and touched the back of a hand to his lip.

“Is this some of Meagher's campaign plan, Earp? To quiet me with your roughshod ways?” His voice trembled beneath an attempt at laughter. “You couldn't have made my point for me any better, now, could you?"

"You speak of my personal life again, and I'll make your points even clearer."

"Are you threatening me in front of these men?"

"You're goddamned right I am."

Smith swallowed and lifted his chin. "This is about you living with a whore, isn't it?"

The air in the room seemed to crack when Wyatt slapped him again. The sting of this blow purged Smith of all rational thought, and he lunged at Wyatt. Wyatt brushed aside the oncoming arms and drove his fist into Smith's face before someone grabbed him from behind.

"That's enough, Wyatt! Goddammit! Back off!" Marshal Meagher's commands carried the iron ring of authority. Wyatt glared at the bleeding Smith, who managed a look of vindication. Meagher turned his deputy to face him. "Get down to my office and wait on me."

Wyatt ran his fingers through his hair, picked up his hat, and walked out the door, not speaking to his brother on the boardwalk. Morgan grinned and watched his brother march down the street.

"Don't you worry, Wyatt," Morg called to his back, "I'm gonna work on that self-restraint."

When Meagher entered the city offices, Wyatt stood with one boot on the bench and stared out the window as he sipped from a cup of coffee. The marshal hung up his coat, racked his gun belt, and sat down at his desk, never once looking at his deputy.

"You don't leave a man much choice, Wyatt. You and Behrens are the best I got, but there's a hellava lot more to lawin' than being a hard-ass." He swiped a newspaper off his desk, and the paper fell to the floor. The tendons in Meagher's jaw stood out like pulsing chunks of stone. "I'd like to slap the silly son of a bitch around myself, but now if I don't come down on you, this won't go right for me." The marshal punched a finger down on his desk. "Lay down your badge."

Wyatt's face remained impassive. He crossed the room, unpinned his deputy's badge from his vest, and set it down on the desk. Meagher jerked open a drawer, threw the metal shield inside, and slammed the drawer shut. The two men stared at one another for a time, before Meagher took a cigar from the jar on his desk and bit off the tapered point. The matches sat right in front of him, but he only chewed on the cigar and glared at the desktop. Finally he removed the cigar and stuffed it into his shirt pocket.

"Shit," he said, stood, and walked to the coat rack. "Now I got to go tell somebody with a loose tongue that I suspended you." He stabbed his arms through his coat sleeves and marched back out into the night.

Meagher won the election handily. After a time he deemed appropriate, he put Wyatt back on the police force. But after Wyatt's thirty-dollar court fine for slapping Billy Smith and lost pay over the last weeks, there was a palpable tension in the office. While Behrens and Jimmy Cairns tiptoed around it, Meagher ignored it. Wyatt did his work, and that was all Meagher cared about. As long as there was the trust to be backed up if he got into a corner, Meagher could cohabitate with a rattlesnake. This had been the defining nature of their tacit pact from the beginning. Both were men of business.

The city council was not so forgiving. In their meetings, the names of cattle barons like Mannen Clements took on the resonance of financial saviors of the town. Anticipation of the coming season's commerce was high; the city fathers put out of mind the downside of being taken over by the rowdy cattle crews that spread their money all over Wichita. When a council majority vote declared that Earp must go, Meagher sat down with Wyatt and told it straight.

"I don't think you should write it off completely," the marshal explained. "They voted three times, and each time the vote was more to your favor. I'm going to do what I can for you. The force needs you, Wyatt. If you can hang loose a little while, we might can get you reappointed."

Wyatt's face betrayed no emotion. He had expected this. When he laid down his badge this second time, Meagher looked him in the eye.

"You understand this has got nothing to do with you and me. This is all about city business . . . and those fat jaspers that pay our salaries."

"I know that," Wyatt said.

Meagher sat and picked up a sheaf of papers. "I got to get a telegraph off," he said, but he remained at his desk. It was the first time Wyatt had seen him tap papers on their edges to straighten them. Meagher did it three times on three different edges, and then he stood and walked out.

For a time Wyatt stared at the badge lying on the desk. Then he donned his coat and walked out into the growing dark, where John Behrens stood on the boardwalk as if he had been waiting for him.

"Got a minute, Wyatt?" John asked.

When Behrens turned, Wyatt followed him across the street into the dark alley beside the billiards parlor. There they stopped just past the lighted window and faced one another, Behrens leaning against the clapboard wall and Wyatt standing before him straight as an awning post. Behrens pushed his hands into his coat pockets and stiffened his arms so that his shoulders shrugged up near his ears.

"I know what Meagher told you, Wyatt. But the town ain't gonna renew your appointment. Not ever. Billy Smith's got too many friends in the council. I'm just tellin' you this 'cause we're friends."

Wyatt looked deeper into the alley where the darkness was as complete as the bottom of a well. "So I ain't got much future here . . . not in lawin' anyway."

Behrens's eyes widened like an apology. "Maybe not in *any* business. Smith ain't much at runnin' a town, but he's got his fingers pretty deep in the big pie. Merchants listen to what he has to say."

Wyatt nodded and kept staring into the boxed end of the alley.

"There's more, Wyatt," Behrens said and stepped in front of him. "The mayor of Dodge City put out word through a friend of mine that any time I wanted a job there on the force, it's mine." Behrens's words poured out faster now, carrying a new energy that held Wyatt's attention. "Word is, he likes his lawmen tough. Hell, most o' what I done here worth talking about, I done it with you. We made a damned good team. So, if Dodge wants *me*, it's the same as sayin' they want *you*. The fact is, I don't care to leave Wichita right now. I got other prospects here. But if you're interested, I figure I can write a letter for you."

"I was in Dodge a while back. Mostly just a hangout for buffalo hunters and sharpers in the gambling houses."

Behrens snorted. "Well, it's the mother of all hell now, is what I hear. With the Santa Fe rail runnin' right through its main street, Dodge will draw more Texas longhorns this season than Wichita ever did. You want to bang some heads, Dodge City is your place. Half the state of Texas will be there come a coupl'a months from now."

"What's the pay?"

Behrens snorted again. "Ain't nobody gonna get rich wearin' a city badge, Wyatt, you know that. Meager only makes half again what us deputies do. Only lawman pullin' in any money is

the fat-cat sheriff, collectin' taxes from all over the county"—
John raised his right hand between them and rubbed the pad of
his thumb against his fingertips—"and keepin' a good goddam
percentage of it. But you got to get elected to *that* post. To get
elected, you got to put in the time, let people get to know you,
shake a lotta hands, and take a lotta guff off the city fathers."
Behrens made a sour face. "But that ain't *you*, Wyatt . . .
'specially here in Wichita with people like Billy Smith to poke a
stick into your wheel spokes."

Wyatt listened to the click of billiard balls through the wall
and thought about a town still wild and wide open, a place he
could start fresh again. After putting in so much time trying to
establish himself in Wichita, he was mildly surprised at the ap-
peal of a new town and a new start in lawing.

"I'll think on it, John."

"There's one more thing," Behrens said and dug a hand into
his trouser pocket. Bringing out a wrinkled envelope, he opened
the seal and peered down at its contents. "Town council's with-
holding your pay for the time when Meagher brought you back
on the force. This should cover it."

Wyatt took the envelope and inside it found a half-inch stack
of bills. "Where'd this come from?"

"That includes the thirty dollars you had to pay for slappin'
Smith around," John added with a smirk.

Wyatt stared at his friend until Behrens's smile dissolved.
"You didn't answer my question, John."

Behrens ran his tongue over his teeth. "It's from the city
taxes we collected." He pushed back the brim of his hat and
frowned at Wyatt. "Don't git righteous on me, now. If you don't
take it, it'll prob'ly go toward a new spittoon for the mayor's office . . . that or line some damn councilman's bottomless
pocket."

Wyatt felt his past wash over him like the stench of a dug-up carcass. "It ain't a matter of righteous. I ain't nearly above it. It didn't sit well once before though, and I don't care to slide back into it."

"Wyatt, this ain't the first time I milked off the city's teat. Remember the time you found that drunk passed out in an alley with five hun'rd dollars on 'im? Hell, I'd a kept the damn money and slept like a baby."

They locked eyes until Behrens had to look away. When Wyatt pushed the money back into Behrens's hand, John scowled at the envelope and exhaled a long sigh.

"I'll take the letter," Wyatt said, "on the chance I go to Dodge."

Behrens nodded and curled the envelope in his fist. They strolled back to the street and stood together in the gap of the boardwalk. It was a cool night, and now the stars were strewn to eternity. Probably looked the same over Dodge, Wyatt thought.

"If you go to Dodge, are you taking the woman?" Behrens asked.

A team of mules pulled a freight wagon past them and turned north on Main toward the depot. Wyatt watched it until it disappeared around the corner and only the clinking of the traces could be heard.

"Don't figure on slippin' that money to her, John, if that's why you're askin'. I'd never see it. It'd go for whiskey."

Behrens lowered his eyes and nodded. "All right, I'll shut up about it." He stuffed the envelope of money inside his shirt. "What about Morgan? He goin' with you?"

Wyatt shook his head. "I reckon he'll take over my faro tables here . . . see what he can squeeze out o' the drovers this season."

"Well," Behrens said and blushed as he offered his hand. "You take care o' yourself, you hear?" They clasped hands and shook, Behrens's grip like steel. "I'll write that letter for you tonight." He snorted an airy laugh through his nose. "I ain't really sure if I'm doin' you a favor or buying you a one-way ticket to hell. But . . . it's a job."

Behrens turned to walk to the front of the billiards parlor, but he stopped in the light of the window and faced Wyatt again. "One more thing . . . it's about your brother James. If Smith gets his way with the council, word is he'll move your brother's whorin' business across the river and up his tax to collect back fines."

Wyatt felt a ball of heat spreading in his chest, just as it had before he'd slapped Smith in Rupp's saloon. He stared into the darkness down Douglas Avenue toward the bridge where James's and Bessie's brothel stood as the last stop before Delano.

"Hell, yeah," Behrens said, reading Wyatt's expression. "James stands to lose everything on this side of the river."

Wyatt closed the distance between them and thrust his hand out toward Behrens. "Give me the damned envelope."

With a vindictive smile, Behrens slapped the money into Wyatt's hand. "To hell with all of 'em, Wyatt," John said and went inside the parlor. Wyatt stuffed the envelope into the pocket of his coat and strode off for the Gold Room and his faro table. If he had no future in Wichita, at the very least he planned to take some more of the town's money with him when he left.

CHAPTER 12

Spring, 1876: Dodge City, Kansas

Dodge had blossomed like a cluster of soiled flowers trying to rise out of a crowded buffalo wallow. From his perch on the wagon box, Wyatt saw it like the scores of other prairie towns he had seen—an assorted jumble of boxy buildings and canvas tents clustered together, all hastily erected monuments to sundry enterprises. The spring rains had softened the soil, which in turn had been churned to mud by hoof and wheel. This dark halo bled out into the grazing fields south of town, where herds of longhorns already nosed the flats along the river for patches of new grass.

Along the grid of streets and avenues, saloons and false-front stores stood like mismatched gravestones erected so close together as to deny elbow room for the departed. People and wagons and horses were in constant motion, especially near the railroad depot. The town sat on a bluff over the muddy Arkansas with the Atchison, Topeka, and Santa Fe Rail Line slicing through the south end just above the old Santa Fe Trail. Skirting the southeast side of town, the river was narrower here than at Wichita, spanned by a railroad trestle to the east and a public bridge to the south, both leading to wide expanses of prairie that rolled uninterrupted to the horizons.

Knowing that Wyatt had been charitable in bringing her, Mattie had been careful of her words on the trip. Now as their destination became something measurable to the eye, her reticence shifted to restrained anticipation. She sat a little straighter, and her eyes sharpened at the sight of civilization. She put away the knit work that had kept her hands busy for the last miles as the wagon had rumbled across the desolate prairie.

Considering the moment as one of some import, Wyatt pulled up on the ribbons and hummed a low command to the draft horses. When the wagon came to rest from its ceaseless pitch and bump across the grasslands, he removed his hat, leaned forward, and rested his forearms on his knees.

"That's it," he said simply.

They sat there on the rise for a time looking down on the burgeoning village, neither traveler turning to face the other. Wyatt quietly cleared his throat.

"Sometimes," he began, and nodded toward the town, "a new place gives you a chance for another start."

The rattle of the buckboard had been a constant shield against conversation for these last days. Now as they sat inside the quieter swirl of wind and dust, he could almost feel Mattie trying to compose a proper thing to say to him.

"I know all about that," she said and turned to face him. Wyatt kept his eyes on the horses as they shifted their weights in the harnesses and trembled an isolated muscle each time a horsefly tried to land on their sweat-slick pelts.

Mattie pasted on the crooked smile that had become her standard reaction to the disappointments in her life. She laid aside the half-finished shawl and ball of yarn and continued to stare at Wyatt.

"Only it's not so easy for a woman as it is for a man," she volunteered.

Wyatt made no response. He couldn't help it that Mattie had not been born a man. There was nothing he could do about that. Relaxing the reins, he stared at the town. Dodge would show more promise, he knew, when the big cattle herds would arrive. His first time here—when he had outfitted for a buffalo hunt—he had felt the undefined excitement of seeing a new town put down roots to get its start. He had been alone in those days, and he supposed his aloneness had played some part in that anticipation. With Mattie beside him now, he knew it would be easy to pick up with the same dreary existence they had learned to live with in Wichita. He sat straighter in the wagon box and made a conscious effort to look for something positive in both their futures.

"Might be something promising here for you," he said, trying to put some kindness into his voice.

When she turned to him, he kept his attention on the distant hodgepodge of buildings. "I've got what I want," Mattie whispered. "I can do everything you need . . . and maybe sew for extra money."

He shook his head. "That ain't what I was talking about." He tried to contrive some means of converging their two separate conversations into the one they needed, but he didn't know how. He sensed the usual desperation rising in her until the side of his face felt scorched by her eyes.

"I'm not whoring, Wyatt."

Wyatt, keeping his face neutral, turned to her and took in the full measure of her resentment toward the Earps. "I wasn't talking 'bout that neither."

He returned his gaze to the town below and inhaled deeply through his nose. Just beyond the railroad tracks, he could make out great jagged mounds of white he knew to be sun-bleached buffalo bones piled up for the trip back east, where they would be ground up for fertilizer. He thought to point out the mountain of skeletons to Mattie—something to talk about besides themselves. Instead he listened to the distant sounds of men yelling over the railcars banging in the yard.

"Why are you taking this job, Wyatt? Why aren't you going into business like you're always talking about?"

"I got to start somewhere. As a lawman I'll get to know the people that count."

"But you tried that in Wichita. Look where it got you."

Wyatt gripped the reins tighter and watched his knuckles rise under his skin. "Billy Smith's got too many friends there."

"There'll be Billy Smiths in Dodge, too, Wyatt."

He wanted to tell her she didn't know anything about town politics, but instead he snapped the ribbons on the team's rumps. The wagon trundled on, and once again the jingle of the harness, the grind of the axle, and the monotonous turning of the wheels filled the space between man and woman.

Behind them, perhaps a mile back, a train whistle sang out over the land, an unexpected plaintive whine weaving into the layers of the wind. Again Wyatt reined up the horses, and both he and Mattie turned around and watched the dark plume of engine smoke spout upward and arch back over the chine of cars and then spread as a broad black veil that trailed across the prairie and hung there like a stain on the air.

"I like trains," Mattie said. "They make a place feel connected to something."

Wyatt turned to her as though she might explain her thoughts, but Mattie only smiled sadly off into the distance. He popped the ribbons again and didn't stop until they were inside the town.

After securing a room at the Dodge House he unhitched the team at the hotel's livery. When he returned to their room to clean up, he found that Mattie had brushed his hat until its original rich black color emerged from the gray coat of dust he had carried from Wichita. While she laid out their clothes, he cleaned up at the porcelain wash basin and carefully shaved around the broad sweep of his moustaches.

As he dressed, Mattie poured fresh water into the basin and performed her female ablutions. They went about their routines without speaking, and while Wyatt was grateful for the silence, he could see the strain in Mattie's melancholy face. There was no clear answer as to why he had brought her with him, but for the one that had originally thrown them together: he felt sorry for her. He supposed that, by intuition alone, she knew this as surely as if he had spoken the words aloud.

Wearing a clean, starched shirt and his black frock coat, he stood before the mirror and adjusted his hat on his head. Looking at her reflection in the mirror, he watched as she secreted a bottle of laudanum into the drawer of the bedside table. Even before they had left Wichita, she had begun to use the medication on a regular basis. It was taking something from her, he knew, but he could not broach the subject without arousing the brooding anger that had become her defense against such words.

"Thank you for getting my clothes ready," he said into the mirror. She glanced up and smiled, but her smile seemed directed inward at a world she had manufactured inside her head. He watched her for a time as she continued to sort out her belongings on the bed. She began to hum, and her movements took on new energy, like a woman who had fallen into the good fortune of being settled in a life where settling was hard fought and seldom won. As she continued to hum, he left the room, half-sure she did not know that he had gone.

When he announced himself to the clerk at the courthouse, he was given directions to Mayor Hoover's business on the main thoroughfare in town. Wyatt walked Front Street to Hoover's Saloon, stepped out of the wind, and closed the door behind him. Isolated in the main room, three men smoked cigars at a table, two of them leaning forward in quiet conversation. The third man was so heavy that leaning forward might have proved a liability to the table. Wyatt remembered him—the German named Deger. They had played poker together in his buffalo hunting days. When Wyatt approached them, the men quieted and looked expectantly his way.

"Mayor Hoover?" Wyatt stopped at a distance and looked from face to face.

A fleshy man with clear eyes and light-brown moustaches raised a smoking cigar. "I'm Hoover."

"Wyatt Earp."

Hoover's face showed nothing.

"From the Wichita police force," Wyatt added.

"Oh, yes," Hoover replied melodically. He groaned as he stood. After offering a perfunctory handshake, he motioned to the man beside him. "This is our county sheriff, Charlie Basset." Basset stood and equaled Hoover in size, but the skin on his face was weathered from a life in the sun. His eyes pinched in a sly inspection of Wyatt's appearance. His grip was firm.

"And Larry Deger, our town marshal," Hoover said, rounding out introductions. "You'll be working for him." Not attempting to rise from his chair, Deger held out a bloated hand. The German had not impressed him years ago, but Wyatt would have to reassess his opinion of the man if he was to police under him. "Sit down, Earp," Hoover said in the distracted tone of business interrupted.

Deger cocked his head and narrowed his eyes at Wyatt. "Haff we met before?"

"Could be," Wyatt said.

The German's plump facial features tried to squeeze together as he continued to scrutinize Wyatt, but it was Bassett who spoke. "How's the season looking over in Wichita?"

"It's early yet, but I think Dodge is gonna pick up most of the business this year."

Hoover smiled and pointed toward the front windows with

his cigar. "This town's going to double in size inside of two months. Lot of money coming in."

"And a lotta hell to pay," Bassett said. "We've already run through a handful of officers who couldn't handle shit."

Deger grunted his affirmation and shifted in his chair. That the chair held together was a tribute to the woodworker who had crafted the furniture.

Wyatt looked from one to the other. "County and city work together on this?"

"Hell, yes," Bassett said. "Half of my deputies work for the city sometimes. Goes the other way, too. We got to put up a combined front to control these Texas boys." Bassett smiled and took a long pull on his cigar. "Word is," he bobbed the cigar twice toward Wyatt, "you're a hard case."

"I don't back down on the law, if that's what you mean."

Basset's smile widened, his teeth showing around the cigar. "I hear you're pretty quick to bang a man's head for 'im if he steps out of line." The sheriff raised his eyebrows and chuckled from deep in his chest.

"I deal it out fair enough," Wyatt said.

Bassett snorted and waved his cigar like a checkmark in the air. "Hell, I'm all for it. My policy is to crack their heads before they can show me what bad men they are. That way, everybody gets to live a little longer."

Wyatt sat unmoving in his chair. His stillness was made all the more noticeable by the heavy shifts Deger made in trying to hear the conversation over his own breathing.

"Some heads need crackin'," Wyatt replied. "Some don't." He made no effort to match Bassett's smile.

Hoover sat forward. "We want you to be our enforcer, Earp. Let 'em know right up front we keep a tight lid on our town. For all I care, these Texas sons of bitches can eat each other for breakfast on the south side of the tracks." He jabbed a thumb at his silk cravat three times. "Over here, *we* make the rules. *We* enforce them." He changed direction to poke his cigar at Wyatt. "*You* enforce them."

"What's the pay?" Wyatt said.

"You're to be the assistant marshal. We start you at seventy-five a month. You'll get bonuses for arrests and court appearances. One dollar for each."

"What about deputies?"

Hoover stuck his cigar in his mouth and looked at Deger. The rotund marshal turned his lips down in the shape of a hanging horseshoe, the lines of his mouth cutting deeply into his flaccid jowls.

"Right now I haff two," Deger said.

Wyatt looked at Basset. The sheriff held up three fingers.

"We'll need more when the season tops out," Wyatt said. "Do I have power to appoint?"

Again Hoover looked at Deger, who shrugged. The mayor leaned to Wyatt, and the skin on his face reddened and drew tight as a drum.

"Long as it's not from Kelley and Wright's crowd . . . and you keep it to the right number."

"Who're Kelley and Wright?"

Hoover frowned as if he had detected a foul scent wafting through the room. "Dog Kelley and Bob Wright. We just beat out that crowd in the elections. They control a lot of the commerce, and they like the law to look the other way when it comes to their businesses. They'll hamstring our administration if they can." Hoover made a dismissive gesture with his hand and sat back in his chair. Cocking his head to one side, he lifted the cigar but stopped short of inserting it into his mouth. "So . . . you think you're ready for Dodge City, Earp?"

Wyatt tolerated the question without expression. "I'm ready."

Hoover studied his new employee and shot a smile at Bassett before turning back to Wyatt. "I believe you just might be."

After two weeks on the job, Wyatt had met most of the merchants and was careful to avoid all talk on the rival political factions, which were more deeply entrenched in Dodge than they had been in Wichita. Kelley and Wright regularly pressed him for information about Hoover's plans, but Wyatt held a firm grip on the lessons he had learned at Wichita. If the next election brought a new boss, he would need to fit into that possibility.

Like other cattle towns, Dodge had drawn a line to separate respectability from the rowdy arena where the Texas drovers would blow off steam when they flooded the town come June. Unlike Wichita and its wayward sister, Delano, where the river served as such a barrier, here the line was arbitrary. South of Front Street and the rail line, the grid of city blocks was monopolized by saloons, gambling halls, entertainment houses, and brothels—many strategically named with Texans in mind, all of them spruced up in gaudy fashion to draw the rougher element.

Though his future might be better served dealing with the citizens north of the line, Wyatt knew that it was the south side where he would earn his pay. The best he could plan for was to earn a reputation as an enforcer of the law that would carry over to any sector of the social order.

Anticipation of the coming cattle drives was high, and every merchant on both sides of the tracks worked diligently to be ready. This driving ethic suggested the town's visitors held some kind of sway over the town councilmen, which was the very situation that favored a tough enforcer. Dodge needed Wyatt, depended on him to forge the balance that would make the symbiotic relationship work. If he could make a name for himself in the law, in time he should be able to parlay that reputation into a more profitable business.

Just as the cattle season was going full tilt, Wyatt looked up from his faro game at the Long Branch to see a lean, powerfully-built young man standing at the bar. Despite the newcomer's surge into manhood, Wyatt recognized young Masterson from their days in the buffalo killing fields. Bat limped toward a table where a game of monte was in session, levering his every other step over a wooden walking cane with an ivory grip. Wyatt signaled for a dealer switch and excused himself.

Bat's eyes turned by instinct to Wyatt's approach, and when the moment of recognition flashed in his eyes, Bat's face and neck flushed with color. Pivoting on the cane, he smiled and offered his hand.

"Mr. Earp!"

They shook hands, Bat pumping Wyatt's arm with the warmth of an old friend. They moved consensually to an unoccupied corner of the bar, and there the two settled in for conversation.

"It's still 'Wyatt,' " Wyatt said and nodded to the cane. "Heard you took a bullet down at Sweetwater . . . and managed to give one back more effective."

Bat's face steeled at the memory. "Sergeant King," he said through his teeth. "I had to kill the damned sonovabitch."

"Had a run-in with him in Wichita," Wyatt said. "He prob'ly needed killin'."

Bat nodded, and gradually his features softened. "It was over a woman," he said quietly. "She took a bullet for me. Stepped right in the way . . . on purpose, I mean. Can you imagine a woman doin' that?"

Bat's face seemed to fill with heat, and for a brief moment Wyatt saw what the ex-soldier in Sweetwater must have seen in

Masterson's eyes before his life was forfeit. Wyatt gestured with a hand toward the lame leg.

"How bad is it?"

Masterson shrugged off any complaint. "I can ride . . . and I reckon I can walk wherever my horse can't go." He looked down at his hip as if appraising a cut of meat at a butcher shop. "Stoves up sometimes, but a hot bath'll get me goin' again." He looked up with a perverse smile. "I'd say I'm gettin' 'round a lot better'n King is."

"You got work lined up in Dodge?"

Masterson looked around the room and nodded at the table where a winner raked in his chips at a monte game. "Long as there's cards and men who are lookin' to lose some money, I reckon I'll be satisfactorily employed."

"I mean steady wages," Wyatt said. "You interested in that?"

"That depends . . . on what I'd be doin' . . . how much I'd be makin' . . . and who I'd be working for."

Wyatt leaned on the bar and lowered his voice. "You'll be banging Texas heads, making fifty a month, and working for me."

Bat leaned to study the metal scroll pinned to the front of Wyatt's shirt. "You're the marshal?"

"Assistant," Wyatt corrected. "Marshal's job is mostly behind a desk. Like I said, you'll be working for me."

Masterson gazed down at his game leg and pursed his lips. When his head came up, his pale-blue eyes were like steel.

"Hell, yes. And I got a brother in town."

"Ed?" Wyatt asked.

Bat shook his head. "Jim. He's one you ain't met."

Wyatt pursed his lips and studied the room. "Well," he said, "let's go meet him."

They made a good team—Wyatt and Bat and Jim Masterson. Wyatt and Bat groomed the reputations that followed them by way of the town gossips. Wyatt for the stories of his face-offs with Ben Thompson in Ellsworth, and Mannen Clements and Big George Peshaur in Wichita. Bat for killing his man in Sweetwater and for his part as an Indian fighter at Adobe Walls. Such talk, both lawmen learned, was a helpful tool. No one doubted that either man would follow through on his threats to any challenger who tested the law. Reputation, the two friends agreed, was more than half the battle in backing down a troublemaker.

Bat's apprenticeship as a lawman was a short one. Wyatt's method of aggressively keeping the upper hand on the Texans made sense to Masterson. When there was trouble, one officer backed up the point man with a shotgun from an angle visible to the offender but distant enough to allow the arresting officer room to operate in an independent fashion. The appearance of one-on-one confrontation was less likely to agitate the spectating Texans.

When point man, Bat employed vitriolic intimidation, heaping a spate of crude epithets upon his antagonist. Wyatt's way was quieter, letting the unspoken certainty of his unyielding rule make its own statement. Both methods proved effective. Wyatt insisted that, whenever possible, a deputy consider his revolver a club for buffaloing offenders. Among the town merchants there was some criticism about slamming a gun against a man's skull, but Wyatt's response was always the same: "A man would rather have a sore head than a gravestone. And besides, he'll be back to spend his money the next day."

CHAPTER 13

Summer, 1876, through spring, 1877: Dodge City to Deadwood, Dakota Territory, and back

In midsummer Morgan arrived from Wichita and served out the rest of the season as a deputy. He was every inch of Wyatt's six feet, and as soon as he let his moustaches grow, he was often mistaken for his older brother on the streets—a mix-up that never failed to bring a smile to his boyish eyes.

At the end of summer when the drover population dwindled, the two brothers declined the off-season pay cut and struck out for the Black Hills, where the latest gold strike had heated the northern plains country to a grab-what-you-can fever. For Wyatt, prospecting held the potential to put lawing behind him and to lift him up to the successful business status he craved. And the time away from Mattie might do some good for both of them. When she tried to argue the point, it eventually narrowed down to one immutable fact. With her frail constitution, Mattie could not endure a harsh winter in the Black Hills, where the temperature commonly plummeted below zero.

Before he left town, he paid the hotel manager an advance rent to cover four months, and he left Mattie enough money to keep from whoring. Finally, he encouraged her to find work as a seamstress, telling her she needed to see people, to expand the limits of her world. He mentioned nothing about her habit with whiskey and laudanum. There were some things about which he could do nothing, and this was one.

Sitting at the window, she had appeared to listen to every word as she mended one of his shirts. At last she looked up, and, speaking in the breathy, dreamlike voice that had become an anthem of her resigned ways, she offered only four words.

"I'll be here, Wyatt."

With few claims available in Deadwood, the two Earp brothers adapted by reviving Wyatt's old profession of cutting and delivering firewood, this time in several feet of snow. Split wood was "gold" in the camp, and with the inflated economy of the strike, Wyatt could charge three times what he'd made in the Indian Territory. Converting a cheap wagon into a sled, the Earps did more than survive. They turned a handsome profit.

When the spring thaw began a steady drip from the roof of their rented shed, Wyatt returned from feeding the horses and found Morgan still lazing under a pile of blankets on the pallet he had dragged close to the wood stove. Wyatt nudged his brother with the toe of his boot.

"How'd you come out last night?"

Morgan stretched and smiled. "Lost forty at the Number Ten, then went down to the Red Bird and won back forty-two." He laughed. "I think that's what a dog calls 'chasin' your tail.' What about you?"

"Picked up a hundred supplyin' wood for a private game."

Morgan sat up, his eyes alert beneath a veil of disheveled hair. "A hundred!"

"Those boys were serious about their game. Winners didn't want the losers leavin' on account o' the cold. After that I hunted up a game at the Shingle. At the end of the night I sold our sled to a butcher."

Morgan's gaze remained glued to his brother as Wyatt shed his heavy coat, scarf, and mittens. "So how'n hell're we gonna haul firewood without the sled?"

Wyatt opened the firebox and added split sticks of spruce. The resinous aroma of the evergreen sap had permeated everything they owned over the last months.

"How'd you like to head back to Dodge and make good wages just for the travelin'?"

Morg snorted. "I can't leave this ice box soon enough." Then he frowned. "Who's payin' us to leave?"

"Cheyenne and Black Hills Stage Company. They're runnin' bullion to Cheyenne and want you and me to guard it."

Morgan rousted himself from the blankets and began pulling on his trousers. "This is about those holdups we been hearin' about, ain't it?"

Wyatt nodded. "Company can't afford to have this shipment waylaid." He picked up his brother's boots from under the stove. "Still wet," he said and propped them on the bench to better receive the heat.

Morg rubbed at the sleep in his eyes, pulled a blanket from his bedding, and wrapped it around his shoulders as he huddled near the stove. "Shit, it's cold as hell!" He gathered the dank wool tighter to his throat. "So when are we leavin'?"

Wyatt stepped outside and scooped snow into the kettle. When he returned, Morgan was still waiting for an answer.

"Three days," Wyatt said and set the kettle on the stove, where for a moment it sizzled like a hot branding iron pressed into a cow's hairy hide. "We need to start sellin' off the rest of our gear . . . axes, ropes, pulleys, and extra blankets . . . anything we don't wanna carry with us. We'll tether our horses to the stage."

Morgan stretched his arms and arched his spine. "Well, then . . . I'll see can I sell this damned ache in my back from sleepin' on this goddamned cold floor." He stopped the motion and looked at Wyatt with the same twinkle in his eye he had used as a boy when he was up to no good. "You interested?" he quipped and patted his own back. "Bein' family and all, I'll give you a good price."

Wyatt cracked half a smile. "Already got one."

On the second day out from Deadwood, Wyatt caught sight of five men paralleling the stage route off from the main road in the trees. When the horsemen remained steadily just behind and on their right side for a full hour, Wyatt instructed the driver to stop in the next clearing that afforded a view in every direction. Then he leaned off the side, taking a grip on the luggage rail, and spoke into the coach to Morgan.

"We got five riders been doggin' us for as many miles. Keep your eyes open to the north, 'bout sixty yards out. We're gonna stop up ahead and see what happens."

On the rise of a barren knoll the stage rolled to a stop. Wyatt watched as the distant party emerged from a boulder field, stopped, and then backed their horses into a coulee.

"See that, Morg?" Wyatt called just loud enough to be heard inside the coach.

"I saw it," Morgan replied.

The stage stayed put for a full minute. Finally, the nervous driver turned an anxious face to Wyatt.

"Can we get the hell outta here now?"

Wyatt held up a finger for the man to wait. After a few seconds one of the riders showed himself but then circled back to disappear behind the rocks.

"Take 'er forward a little and stop the coach where your team is standing now."

The driver's face tightened with confusion, but he did as he was told. After easing the horses on, he pulled up again on the reins.

As soon as the stage came to its second halt, all five horsemen came into view and immediately reined to a halt themselves.

Wyatt leveled his Winchester and shot into the boulder nearest the group. Pieces of rock shattered and sprayed into the air as the bullet whined off into the distance carrying the sharp whistle of a ricochet. Pumping the lever of his rifle, he sent five more rounds into the same boulder, the air seeming to fill with a sustained explosion. Dust and shards flew off the rock like fireworks. The riders milled about in a small chaos for a time, until they got their mounts under control and sought the refuge of the rocks again.

When the quiet gathered back around the stage, Morgan yelled from the coach, "How the hell'd you miss like that?"

"Didn't," Wyatt replied. "Hold quiet a minute. Maybe that's the end of it."

They waited another two minutes but never saw horse nor rider appear again.

"Can I go now?" begged the driver.

"Go!" Wyatt said.

Picking up momentum again the stage rumbled down the trail. Morgan crawled out of the coach and climbed onto the luggage rack.

"Why in hell didn't you shoot one o' them jaspers?" Morg said as he lay low on the bucking top.

"Didn't need to," Wyatt replied. "I reckon they're sufficiently persuaded to wait on the next coach." He turned to look at his brother. "Wouldn't you be?"

Morg craned around to inspect their back-trail. There was not a soul in sight as far as the eye could see. When he turned back to Wyatt, Morg's eyes crinkled with good humor.

"You reckon they're back there buryin' that damn boulder? 'Cause you sure as hell killed that damn rock."

Because the trip went without further incident, the Earp brothers found themselves in good standing with both the stage line and Wells, Fargo Securities Company. They received handsome wages and a standing offer at employment, which, because Wyatt turned it down, Morg also declined.

Returned to their saddle horses, and with their pack mounts trailing behind, they were four days out of Denver just coming into the Smoky Hill country of west Kansas when Morg turned the conversation toward his disdain for cold weather. He slipped a boot from his stirrup, studied it, and cursed the Black Hills.

"I reckon my toes can stand to never see another drift of snow in this lifetime. I don't know how people live up there in winter."

"People will tolerate a lot to get rich," Wyatt said.

Morg laughed. "Then there's us, a day late and a dollar short, sloshin' 'round in the cold to keep the stove pipes smokin'. These toes o' mine have tolerated a hell of a lot without the gettin' rich part."

"We came out better'n most," Wyatt said. "We packed in there too late, that's all."

Morg nodded, but Wyatt could see in his brother's face that there was more to it. "Wyatt, you gonna stick with lawin'? We ain't exactly getting rich in Dodge."

"Lawin' can lead to other things. You get to know the right people."

"So, why'd you walk away from the Wells, Fargo's offer? They got 'the right people,' too, ain't they?"

"I don't care to be a target settin' up on a coach box every day. The odds are bad for a shotgun messenger."

Bouncing in his saddle like a greenhorn, Morg led the way across the Smoky Hill River, making a point to raise his boots up high. He was smiling on the other side, while Wyatt let his horses drink in the middle of the stream. When they were back into their rhythm on the trail, Morgan grew pensive again.

"So, you're figurin' on stayin' in Dodge?"

Wyatt combed a wayward strand of the chestnut's mane to fall on its natural side. "I still got some things I need to work out there."

Morgan's face was dead earnest now. "Business dealings?"

Wyatt nodded, but it was Mattie he was thinking about.

CHAPTER 14

Spring, summer 1877: Dodge City, Kansas

When they rode into Dodge at mid-morning, Wyatt and Morgan stopped at the Long Branch saloon and found the room almost empty. Chalkley Beeson, the owner, was pulling down spider webs from a corner of the ceiling with a long-handled broom in one hand and a billiards cue in the other.

"Chalk," Morgan greeted, "break out the band. I'm back!"

They shook hands all around. Morgan stepped behind the bar and began checking the kegs on tap. Beeson leaned on his billiards stick and shook his head at the younger Earp.

"I haven't forgot what you like, Morg." He prodded Morgan with the stick. "Coffee, Wyatt?" When Wyatt nodded, the saloon man crossed to the stove and returned with a pot. "Let me catch you boys up on what's happened." He poured two coffees and a beer, and they sat at a table near the bar.

The only other customer sat in a back corner slumped over a table, the flattened crown of his hat serving as a pillow as he snored through his open mouth. An empty bottle stood at his elbow, an empty shot glass still cupped loosely in one hand.

"Well," Chalk began, his smile like that of a man trying to hold back the punch line of a joke, "Kelley beat out Hoover for the mayor's office, but he kept Deger as marshal." Beeson looked from one Earp brother to the other, smiling, waiting for a reaction.

"Kelley is thinkin' about the next election," Wyatt said.

"Tryin' to lock up the German vote."

Beeson pointed at Wyatt and winked. "That's the way I read it, too." The saloon keeper spewed a stream of air through pursed lips. "Why else would he keep the big elephant? Deger can't hardly get out of his bed in the morning.as I hear it."

Morgan wiped his upper lip with the sleeve of his blouse. "Aw, don't be too hard on the old German," Morg said straight-faced. "Not many men could hold down that office as well as he does." When Beeson took on a bewildered look, Morg laughed. "Three hundred fifty pounds worth o' holdin' down!"

Chalk gave Morgan a sidewise glance but couldn't keep from smiling. He turned his focus on Wyatt.

"Ed Masterson, Bat's older brother, has got your old job as assistant marshal. Bat is undersheriff working for the county." Beeson shifted in his chair and leaned forward excitedly. "And get this . . . a month ago Deger arrested Bat for interfering with an arrest. Then, when Deger arrested one of the top cattlemen, Kelley butted in and fired him." Chalk laughed. "Fired him without a town council meeting, mind you." Chalk waited for Wyatt to smile but gave up on that. "But you know Deger. He ignored the dismissal and arrested Kelley, his boss. The court is still trying to untangle the mess."

Wyatt sipped his coffee and watched Beeson's smile broaden.

"Now here's the best part," Chalk said. "Sheriff Bassett took on Deger as a deputy—Deger probably figuring on a short career on the *city's* payroll." The bartender was about to burst to get out the best part of the story. "Then Bat, as undersheriff, up and fires Deger . . . pisses off Bassett, and now everybody's mad at everybody."

Morgan stood and carried his mug behind the bar to the keg tap. "Chalk, I want you to run through all that again, and I'm gonna see if another beer will help me follow it this time."

After finishing his coffee Wyatt left the conversation on

politics and walked his mare and the gelding down the alleyway to the hotel livery. After tipping the stable boy to brush down both animals, Wyatt entered the Dodge House through the back entrance, climbed the stairs, and found his former room occupied by a lumber salesman from Kansas City. Carrying his saddlebags and bedroll downstairs to the lobby, he rang the desk bell. The manager hurried from the backroom but slowed when he saw Wyatt.

"You've got a man in my room."

The manager's flushed face lowered to the register book, and when he looked back at Wyatt, his eyes sagged with apology. "The room was vacated, Marshal."

"I left money for that room."

"Well, yes, you did . . . but your . . . the lady terminated the lease and took a refund." Wyatt's face showed nothing. The man forced a contrite smile. "I'm sorry, Marshal."

Wyatt nodded. "Can I get a room?"

Now the man seemed to shrink. He pulled in his lips and took on a pained expression.

"I'm sorry, we're all full at the moment, Marshal."

Wyatt nodded, looked down at his boots, and then brought his eyes up to the clerk again. "I'm not the marshal."

"Well . . . all right . . . but a room should free up within the week," the man said.

"Can I board my horses in your livery until then?"

"Of course. And I'll promise you our first available room."

The next day Morgan breezed into the hotel livery, where Wyatt was shirtless, grooming the chestnut mare and Rilla's gelding. Without a word of greeting, Morgan—seemingly pleased with himself—leaned against a stall divider and unfolded a newspaper. Without interrupting the rhythm of the brush on the horse's legs, Wyatt turned his head to his brother.

"What're you smiling at?"

Morgan held his grin and struck a pose as if he were reciting a poem at the Women's Literary Club. He cleared his throat, lowered his eyebrows, and spoke in a deep, resonant tone that made Wyatt think of his father.

" *'Wyatt Earp is in town again. We hope he will accept a position on the police force once more. He had a quiet way of taking the most desperate characters into custody which invariably gave one the impression that the city was able to enforce her mandates and preserve her dignity. It wasn't considered policy to draw a gun on Wyatt unless you got the drop and meant to burn powder without any preliminary talk.'* "

Wyatt placed a hand on the mare's rump, hinged around her hindquarters, and picked up a bucket of water. Morgan laughed and swatted the paper against his leg. At the sound, the mare sidestepped and nickered, and Wyatt spoke softly to calm her as he poured water down her flanks.

"Damn, brother, you're startin' to sound like Wild Bill hisself." Morgan raised the paper and shook it as if it were the conclusive evidence in a court trial. "With this . . . and Wells, Fargo wantin' to hire you . . . a fellow might believe you're gettin' to be famous."

Morg held an expectant smile, but Wyatt did not look at him.

"So . . . you gonna take it?" Morg prodded.

"Take what?"

Morg slapped the newspaper against his leg again. "The marshalin' job! What do you think I mean?"

Wyatt lifted the bucket over the mare's withers and poured a steady trickle of water along the spine. "Can't take something that ain't offered," he replied. He looked at his brother and nodded toward the newspaper in Morgan's hand. "That's the *Times* talking. Probably trying to shame Deger and Kelley for all their shenanigans."

Morg laughed with a hint of exasperation. "Well, maybe you should run for governor or somethin'."

Wyatt poised with the bucket as if considering laundering Morgan's dress shirt. "Maybe I should run you out o' here."

Laughing wholeheartedly now, Morgan backed up, using the newspaper as a shield. Wyatt poured water down the mare's corded rear legs and then scraped away the trail muck with the brush. He looked back at his younger brother and straightened at the change in Morgan's face.

"I saw Mattie," Morgan said quietly and squinted one eye in a wince. "She's working for Frankie Bell."

The two brothers stared at one another, until Wyatt began stroking the horse's flanks with short, brisk strokes. Morgan stepped to the mare and let his hand glide down the neck. When he spoke again, there was an uncommon gentleness in his voice.

"Finish up and let's go down to the Delmonico. I'll buy you some dinner." Then, as if hearing the heaviness in his words, Morg tried to lighten the mood. "We'll see if anybody recognizes the celebrity in town."

Wyatt stroked the same place a dozen times, then stopped, staring at the horse's smooth coat, seeing nothing but Mattie's pitiful face the way he remembered it when he had first met her at James's brothel. "Workin' for Frankie Bell ain't no damned good for her," he said.

"Well . . . if it weren't for whores . . ." Morgan said and shrugged.

"I ain't saying nothin' 'bout whores. I'm saying Mattie ain't suited for it."

Morgan narrowed his eyes. "I kind o' thought you were wishin' her on her way."

"I was. Just not *that* way."

He poured what was left of the water over the horse's heels and hung the bucket on a peg. The chestnut snorted and shifted her weight from one leg to the other, trying to see behind her.

Wyatt looked into the mare's dark eye when he spoke. "I'll go clean up. Then we'll eat."

Front Street was dominated by a slow-moving train of covered wagons—eleven of them—stretching from the train depot down to Bob Wright's store. The migrants had come to a stop, and, because most westering bands passed through town on the south side along the old Santa Fe Trail, these travelers were drawing a crowd. One wagon had its sheets down, and there exposed to all the world was the sum total of the family's possessions covered in a patina of gray dust: a cast iron Dutch oven and fry pan, a porcelain wash basin, canvas trunks strapped with thick leather belts and brass buckles, bolts of cloth, a chest of drawers. All of it was neatly packed and bound by tie-ropes.

Wyatt stayed on the boardwalk as Morgan walked out into the street to get a look at the lead driver. Picking up speed Morgan turned to Wyatt with a smile and waved him to follow. From the lead wagon Wyatt heard a gritty voice that opened a floodgate of memories. Nicholas Earp barked a laugh and climbed down by way of the wheel hub to meet Morgan. Wyatt stepped down from the walkway into the hard light and took his time walking toward this unexpected revival of his past.

The three Earp men stood together in the middle of the street, and it was clear even as they shook hands that the father believed he had repossessed his dominion over his scattered family. He spoke of menial events that had passed since last they had been together and complained of the government's ineptitude at controlling the last of the wild Indians. As Nicholas went on about his new journey to California, Wyatt walked to the lead wagon, where his mother watched his approach from the wagon box.

"Going at it again, are you?" he said and took off his hat.

She had aged in ways that made her seem more sedate, even

fragile. Once she had been a woman constantly in motion, her chores never done. Now she appeared to sit back and take what came. It made the time that had passed seem more than a decade. She reached toward him, and Wyatt stepped up on the wheel hub to squeeze her hand.

"You're a sight to see, Ma."

She sighed through a feeble laugh. "For someone who once called himself a farmer, your father seems to have no notion of what roots are."

Her smile was unchanged by the years and took him back to Iowa. In some way that he could not define, he felt sullied standing before her.

"You need to meet Bill Edwards, son," she continued. "Your new brother-in-law."

In the street joining Morgan and Nicholas were Virgil, Warren, Adelia, two dogs, and a slim man, who nodded each time Nicholas made some point during his oration. Morgan held out a palm to hush his father and began reading the article about Wyatt from the *Times*.

"Come on down, Ma," Wyatt said. "Looks like the party's over yonder."

She waved him away. "Oh, I'd just have to climb back up again. You go on. Tell Morgan to come over here and see me."

He started away but turned when she spoke his name. She busied her hands on the tie-cord of her bonnet and waited for him to take the few steps back. The reunion in the street grew louder, and she watched her family as she spoke.

"Lord, but I've made some handsome sons. You all look so grown up in your moustaches." Her eyes shone like smooth creek stones lifted up from clear water. "Morgan seems . . . well . . . he's Morgan." Her eyes lowered to Wyatt, and her mouth turned down at the corners. "But tell me how *you* are, son."

Wyatt rested a hand on the metal rim of the wheel. The

warmth of it was like a symbol for movement . . . for progress. His father had always stayed on the move, looking for that next try at a successful life. Wyatt was surprised how this idea made his presence in Dodge feel like stagnation.

"I'm good as the next fellow, I reckon," he finally answered.

Her expression did not alter. She was, perhaps, the one person who could outwait him, stand him before a looking glass, if only for a moment. She seemed not to breathe as she studied his face.

"You look carved out of stone, Wyatt. Is it Aurilla?"

Wyatt turned his head to the draft horses and watched the flies worry their eyes. The sounds of the town around him congealed into a common blur that now seemed to have little meaning for him.

"Your father lost a wife, too, Wyatt. Newton's mother. Then he moved on, started new." Her voice picked up a trace of hope. "That's how you come to be, you know."

Wyatt nodded but kept looking down the street. It wasn't much of a town, built first on the skins of dull-witted buffalo and then on cattle, but he was making a go of it, especially in the gambling rooms. One thing was for certain: Aurilla would not have liked it here.

"I was stuck on it for a time," he said. "Took me a few places I might not ought to 'a gone. I reckon I got past it." He looked straight into her eyes. "I'm all right, Ma."

Virginia nodded, but her face held a question. "Are you settling here in Dodge?"

"Reckon I'll just wait and see." He began inventorying the signs hanging on the stores, cataloguing the gamut of vocations represented. He considered pointing out the marshal's office but then thought better of it.

"Don't settle like that, son. Figure out the best life and then go to *work* on it. Do you understand what I mean?" Her voice trailed off. "It goes so fast, Wyatt. Before one day . . . you *have* to settle."

The pale sickle moon hung above the day, a washed-out blue against the deeper blue of the sky. It had been a long time—maybe a year—since the haunting face of Valenzuela Cos had risen before his eyes. As a person, she was almost a nonentity to him now. Her dark features had blurred with time. She would be grown now, different in ways he could not imagine, but even now the moon could take on the guise of her personal dispatch.

"Find yourself somebody to share it with, Wyatt."

These words, like a brick hurled through glass, shattered his thoughts and brought him back to the hard light pressing down on the dusty street. Then Virgil was there, slapping him on the back and pulling him down the line of wagons.

"Somebody I want you to meet, Wyatt," Virgil said beaming, turning his younger brother to where Morgan was standing at the tailgate of a loaded-down Studebaker. Morg was pouring on the charm. When they rounded the back of the wagon, Wyatt faced a tiny grasshopper of a woman sitting on a stack of blankets, giggling, and repairing a torn basket with baling twine.

"This here is Allie," Virge introduced. "Al, *this* is the last of the brothers."

Her nose wrinkled with mischief. "Now which one are you?" she teased, pointing one bare foot at Wyatt.

Wyatt looked at the dirt-stained foot for a moment and then back at Virgil, who was smiling as if he'd just won the grand prize at a shooting match. Morgan pinched the girl's toe, and she laughed—a cachinnating cascade that made Virgil's smile spread across his face.

"This here's the one gettin' famous in the newspaper," Morgan said. "But I'm the good-looking one. Hell, anybody can see that."

"This is Wyatt, Allie," Virgil explained and slung an arm

around Wyatt's shoulders.

"Where'd you find this little alley cat, Virge?" teased Morgan.

"Plucked her right out o' Council Bluffs," Virgil said, then wheezed up his familiar laugh. "She's a handful of Irish, I can tell you." He looked from one brother to the other. "You boys got you a woman yet?"

"I got about two dozen," Morgan said straight faced. "I'm thinkin' on goin' Mormon." Allie giggled at him. Morgan had his audience.

"What about you, Wyatt?" Virgil said, his face intent with the question.

"I ain't married."

Warren joined the gathering, listening to the banter of his older brothers. Keeping his eyes on Wyatt, Warren tried to stand as tall as the others.

"You three boys are like peas in a pod," Allie declared, sweeping her index finger to include the three older brothers. "All that pretty yeller hair and moustaches." She made a face at Warren and let her eyes rove over his dark hair. "I swan, Warren! You must'a been dropped on the doorstep by some gypsy woman."

"Least I weren't dropped on my head," Warren shot back. Trying unsuccessfully to hide his hurt pride, he turned his back to her. "Are you the marshal here, Wyatt?" Warren asked.

Morgan rattled the newspaper. "Don't need to be a marshal when you're this famous."

Virgil leaned on the wagon, his arm resting on Allie's knee. "I reckon we'll have to find you a woman, Wyatt." Virge winked at Morgan. "Can't you free up one of yours, Morg? For your brother's sake?"

Morgan squinted and rubbed his chin. "Well, there's one or two gettin' to be a little old for me. I might could spare 'em." They all looked to Wyatt for a rejoinder.

"I expect there's plenty we could talk about b'sides you planning my future for me," Wyatt said and pushed his hat down on his head. "Let me go see Adelia and meet her husband. See if *they* want to run my life for me, too."

As Wyatt moved toward his sister and her husband in the middle of the street, Warren followed anxiously. "You were marshal here in Dodge, weren't you, Wyatt? Did you have to kill anybody yet?"

Wyatt looked down at his youngest brother as the two walked abreast of one another. "I was assistant marshal," he said and slackened his stride to match Warren's shorter stature. "Pretty much the same as bein' marshal, except for the pay. I ain't had to kill anybody." Wyatt could see the disappointment in the youngest Earp's face. He clapped a hand on Warren's shoulder and kept it there. "The whole point of a lawman's job is tryin' to prevent people from killin'. These pistoleers you hear about notchin' their guns . . . that's just a lot of dime novel nonsense."

Warren frowned, but the novelty of a notched gun handle brightened his dark eyes. "I ain't killed nobody . . . not yet anyway."

Wyatt smiled. "Well, why don't you try and hold onto that record."

Warren's eyes filled with a new energy, and Wyatt realized how little he knew the boy. "Hell, I've known a few who needed killin'," Warren crowed, "and if I weren't with Ma and Pa, I might'a done it, too."

Wyatt squeezed his brother's shoulder and shook him once like a gentle wake-up. "Well, don't be killing anybody in Dodge, all right? We got laws against it."

Warren's earnestness for the conversation had colored his face as if he were running a fever. "You ever need help with anybody, I'll be ready to back you," Warren said, his voice as hard and blustery as his father's.

"I'll keep that in mind," Wyatt said. "Now how 'bout you introducing me to our brother-in-law."

CHAPTER 15

Summer, 1877: Dodge City, Kansas

When the cattle season ended, Wyatt lost any chance at finding a place on the police force. He wired Wells, Fargo in San Francisco, and they, in turn, referred him to the Santa Fe Railroad, which had been robbed twice in Kansas in the last year and was looking for a detective to follow the outlaws' trail south to Texas. He signed on, but—before he left—he felt an obligation to confront Mattie.

Frankie Bell ran a string of whores, drifting from one establishment to the other, depending on a particular saloon's popularity and prosperity in a given season. Wyatt found Mattie at the Lady Gay, the reigning watering hole south of the tracks and the current favorite congregating site for all Texans.

The room was noisy, and the smell of whiskey and cigar smoke hung in the air like a thick fog. Jaunty music from a two-man band on piano and banjo could barely be heard over the storm of male voices. The last of the Texas drovers stood two deep at the bar, each man jawing away at some story that he told or retold for whoever would listen. Every man was dressed in the bright colors of new purchases at the local stores, giving the saloon a festive appearance. Wyatt's black coat and white shirt set him apart from everyone else in the front room.

Weaving through the tables to the back room, where the gamblers and the soiled doves plied their respective professions, Wyatt was acutely aware of his lack of a gun and a badge. There were men in the room whose skulls he had cracked just a season past. He walked toward Mattie in the back of the room, where she sat motionless on a bench, her back against the wall. Looking straight ahead, she seemed to be in a trance as a broad-chested man with freckles groped her breasts. Then the man's black, curly hair lowered beneath her chin and remained there—like a dog eating his meal. Mattie closed her eyes, and the skin around her temples tightened to a fan of creases.

Wyatt stood near the faro table, listening to the dealer take bets. The subtle sounds of the game provided a satisfying rhythm to his ear: the click of chips, the flip of cards from the box, the announcement of a winner by the dealer, and the groans of the losers. The game was routine, the house winning most of the time, but the patrons continued to lay down chips on the pasteboard, banking on the change of luck that every man felt was his due after a steady run of losses.

Wyatt quickened his pace when the dark-haired Texan jerked Mattie from the bench and led her through the crowd toward the cribs in back. It was bad timing, he knew, but his momentum was set. He moved to the back curtain ahead of them and waited for her. The man with her was laughing and paid Wyatt no heed, but Mattie's dulled eyes found him, her brow squeezing down like cracked porcelain and her shoulders slumping as though she were surrendering her last hold on a shred of dignity. When she stopped walking, the drunken Texan lost his grip and stumbled through the curtain alone.

"I'd like to talk to you, Mattie," Wyatt said quietly.

The Texan emerged from the curtain with an impish grin aimed at Mattie. When she would not look at him, he spun to see what had her attention. A big smile spread across his face.

"She's all paid for, preacher! Services to be rendered soon as I can unbutton my britches."

Wyatt would not look the man in the face, but in his

peripheral vision he could see the freckles on the Texan's cheeks coalesce darkly against the white flash of his teeth.

"You ain't gotta do this, Mattie," Wyatt said, his voice a low hum in the din of the room.

Her eyelids drooped, hooding her eyes. "Maybe I do," she said. Her voice lacked any melody or timing, as though she were reading words off the floor.

"You're damned right she do. Come on, Sally." The man grabbed her arm and jerked but came to a halt when Wyatt gripped his wrist. The Texan's eyes brightened with a sudden fury, and he stuck his face into Wyatt's. "Get your fuckin' hand off me, you sonovabitch!" Along with the whiskey breath came warm specks of saliva that sprinkled Wyatt's face like cinders. With a violent recoil the drunken cowboy jerked free, lost his balance for a step, and recovered.

"We need to talk, Mattie," Wyatt said. "Give his money back and come outside with me."

The Texan stepped forward until his chest swelled against Wyatt's side. "Listen, pimp! I ain't payin' another goddamn cent, and she ain't backin' out. Look at me, goddamn you!"

For the first time, Wyatt turned his attention to the Texan. The man's eyes were livid, and his breathing came in ragged hisses through his teeth.

"She's done whorin'," Wyatt said, keeping his voice low but clear. "Find another woman." He turned back to Mattie. "I inquired about a job for you at the millinery on the north side. Legitimate. You'd be working as a seamstress."

"The hell you say, *Mar-shal* Earp!" The woman's voice came from behind him, putting Wyatt in an awkward position between two adversaries. The curly-haired man glared at Wyatt and reached blindly to grab Mattie's dress by the low-cut front, tugging her forward. In the same moment fingernails raked down the back of Wyatt's neck, and his shirt collar snapped against his throat.

Spinning, Wyatt swiped at the offending arm and found himself facing Frankie Bell. Big and muscular and reeking of a cloying perfume, she glared at him, her teeth bared and her eyes—the most feminine part of her—white hot with indignation. Nearby patrons turned to watch the confrontation, and the back of the room went quiet, becoming an unexpected and impromptu stage.

"Keep your self-righteous prick away from my girls, 'less you goddamned pay for it like ever'body else."

Wyatt's face flushed. The music continued from the front of the room, but the whoring area in back remained painfully quiet.

"Mattie," Wyatt ordered quietly, "throw down the man's money and walk outside with me."

Frankie Bell propped her fists on her ample hips and burst out laughing. "Mattie!" she roared. "Who the hell is 'Mattie'?"

As Wyatt waited for her answer, Mattie crumpled to the floor, weeping soundlessly. The freckled drover pulled at her to get her on her feet, but she remained crumpled and helpless. Frankie Bell clawed at Wyatt's shoulder to spin him.

"Don't you turn away from me when I'm talking to you! If you can't handle things at home, you can—"

Wyatt slapped Frankie across the face, and the heavy-set madam stumbled backward, almost falling. He let the motion spin him around to face the Texan, who stiffened in a wary crouch. Now the music stopped, and the patrons in the front of the saloon shuffled closer to see the conflict.

"Hold on!"

The big booming voice filled the saloon with the desired effect to freeze every man present. Bat Masterson shouldered through the crowd and stepped between Wyatt and Frankie

Bell. With his right hand resting on the butt of his holstered Colt's, Bat faced the freckled Texan and extended his left arm to point at him.

"Step back, Curly Bill!" Bat ordered, the blue of his eyes gone ice cold.

Masterson's expression and the badge on his shirt provided a palpable weight that eased the tension in the room. The man named "Curly Bill" straightened from his fighting stance, but Frankie Bell tried to shoulder around Bat to get at Wyatt.

"Back off, Frankie," Bat warned over his shoulder. "You're all right. Just got a little pat on the cheek, so just you settle down." Bat turned to Wyatt, and in a lower voice he said, "Easy now, Wyatt."

"I want this sonovabitch arrested," Frankie Bell snarled. She bulled her way around Masterson to thrust a painted fingertip at Wyatt's face. "Everybody here saw this sonovabitch hit me."

When Bat continued to block her way, Frankie swung her fist against the undersheriff's arm to get his attention. Bat slowly turned to fully face her, and his eyes went as flat as two dull coins.

"Unless you want to get slapped a bit more, you'd best keep your hands to yourself."

She heaved all her weight against him, but Bat didn't give an inch. In the same motion he drew his pistol and wrapped her up in a bear hug, his walking cane still gripped in his hand.

"Wyatt," Bat said, "you and me and Frankie are going over to the jail." Bat looked pointedly at the man named Curly Bill. "The rest of you, settle down, and go about your business. Drink the place dry, and use up the women. Let's just don't all kill each other, all right?"

Some of the customers chuckled, and conversations began to pile up one upon the other. Bat raised his chin to the musicians, and the festivities recommenced with a lively melody.

Wyatt knelt to Mattie and started to whisper to her, but she surprised him with a hoarse scream that tore from her throat. It was like the baying of a wounded animal.

"You can't just leave for eight months and expect to come back to a wife!" The music stopped again, and every voice quieted, rendering a silence more fragile than before. In this damning quiet, Mattie glared at Wyatt through a thick lens of tears.

Slowly, Wyatt stood. He didn't need to look at anyone in the room to know that everyone was watching him. Curly Bill smiled, cocked his head, and let his head bounce once with a private laugh.

"Well, hell, preacher," he said and froze midway through an expansive shrug. "I didn't know she was your wife." He turned at the waist to grin at the men behind him, as though he had finally found some measure of humor in the situation. When he turned back to Wyatt, he squinted with a pretense of curiosity. "Say, preacher . . . if she is your wife . . . then what in hell is she doin' in—"

The ice in Wyatt's eyes cut off the man's words. "This ain't between you and me," he said in a low raspy voice that only the ones up front could hear. "But you could get it there real quick."

This time when Curly Bill laughed, there was a hollow ring to it. Wyatt turned and made his way for the front door, the crowd parting for him as he crossed the saloon floor. When the music started up again, he felt it play to his back, mocking him like a chorus of crows badgering a hawk.

He spent a night in the city jail and paid a one-dollar fine to Frankie Bell's twenty. The next morning he started for Texas with no grander goal in mind than to be moving . . . anywhere. If he didn't see Kansas again . . . or Mattie . . . it was reason enough to call it a fresh start at something.

CHAPTER 16

Fall and winter 1877–1878: Ft. Griffin, Texas

The land lay flat as a skillet, the distance from horizon to horizon giving Texas a sense of unending space. The blue canvas of the winter sky dominated the colorless monotony of the southern plains, but even the sky was forfeit to the harshness of the unyielding sun. It had swung toward its southerly winter arc, and Wyatt rode into its glare in a grueling face-off. After sweating through the day, he wrapped up against the unforgiving cold of the prairie night and then the next morning repeated the cycle again.

On a cold afternoon after the New Year he rode into Fort Griffin. The civilian encampment that had spread from the adobe-built military post was now expanding into rows of wooden buildings, laid out in the formal grid of a proper town. Every other construction was a saloon, and, judging by its lighted interior and swell of music, the moneymaker was The Cattle Exchange.

Wyatt stabled his horse, secured a room, and ate a steak dinner before wandering into the Exchange. The main room, lavishly furnished, rivaled any of the plush watering holes of Dodge. A long cherrywood bar stood before matching cupboards of shelves filled with gleaming glassware. The smells and sounds of the establishment were reminiscent of the peak of the cattle season in Kansas, the difference being that here the ranch hands looked more at home in their everyday work clothes rather than

157

the fanciful array of gaudy colors purchased at the end of a cattle drive.

Working his way through the crowd, Wyatt heard a heartfelt tenor laugh that jostled his memory. Behind the bar stood John Shanssey, the Irish boxer who had trained Wyatt in the art of fisticuffs in the Wyoming rail camps. Capping a bottle Shanssey held court with a trio of smiling customers, who drank up his story along with his liquor.

Hat in hand, Wyatt approached the bar, where he waited for the Irishman to serve him. Shanssey broke from his conversation and, with a few words of perfunctory introduction, set down a clean shot glass before Wyatt. Then when his eyes fixed on Wyatt, Shanssey's big square face lit up like a lantern.

"Saints above," he purred in what remained of his native brogue. "Wyatt Earp." Shanssey thrust a big open hand across the bar. The retired boxer's grip recalled the intense workouts the two had shared in their days with the railroad. Whatever Shanssey might have lost in fighting skills, he was still every bit the friendly gentleman he had been a decade past. He appeared genuinely delighted to see his former protégé.

"John," Wyatt said. "Good to see you." Wyatt glanced at the inventory of bottles lined up on the shelves. Never had he seen such an array of brands. "You the owner here?"

Shanssey leaned forward and stacked his meaty forearms on the bar. "That I am, Wyatt," he said, pushing a grin to one side of his face, his eyes sparkling with pride. Sliding the glass aside, Shanssey laced his thick fingers together.

Wyatt nodded toward the crowded room. "How is it, running a saloon business?"

Shanssey dipped his head to one side. "Profitable. It keeps me a bit busier than I might want to be, keeping up the inventory, and keeping a lid on these Texas boys. But hell's bells, Wyatt, drinking and gambling are as constant as the prairie wind. Always will be, I suppose." He pushed his wide chin toward Wyatt. "I've heard your name a time or two." He lifted both eyebrows and inhaled deeply. "Can't say it was flattering to you, boyo, not coming from these Texas cow hands. Working with the law up in Kansas now, are you?"

Wyatt shook his head and leaned in closer. "Workin' for the A.T. and S.F. Railroad. I'm looking for some men who held up one of their express cars a few months back. Who might I talk to about that?"

Shanssey pursed his lips and surveyed the room. "Well . . . I don't know how much talk you'll get out of them, but there's some boys from over at the Clear Fork of the Brazos. They drink here most every Saturday night." He pointed across the room. "Set up a game right there. If there's anybody up to no good in north Texas, they'll likely know about it."

Wyatt eyed the back tables. "Poker or faro?"

Shanssey waggled his head. "Poker for the most part. Faro is popular with some, but to most of these Texans, it's a Yankee conspiracy."

Wyatt turned back to the bar. "Might be a good idea to forget my name for a while, John."

Shanssey gave Wyatt a hard look. "Done." Then he fixed his attention over Wyatt's left shoulder at the back corner of the room. "Now that one there . . . the thin dandy with the washed-out face . . . he seems to get along with those Clear Fork boys. Plays with them pretty regularly, I'd say."

Wyatt looked into the long mirror above the cupboard. At a table of four, the sallow man was easy to pick out—lean and dapper in a gray suit with black trim, his back to the wall as he considered his hand of cards. When the man's head came up, Wyatt saw a mix of desperation and spite in his eyes, the same conflict of emotions he had discerned in whores he had known who were worn out from their profession.

"He's an odd one," Shanssey mumbled, "a Southerner . . . name of 'Holliday.' " The Irishman poured water from a carafe into the shot glass and slid it toward Wyatt. "He'll treat you like a brother one minute and then threaten to cut your tongue out in the next. And he probably knows how to do it. They say he's a doctor."

Shanssey pivoted his head to acknowledge two customers at the other end of the bar. When he turned back to Wyatt, the barman straightened and lightly slapped the polished counter-top with his big hands.

"Anything else, sir?"

When Wyatt shook his head, Shanssey winked and pushed away to walk the length of the bar and take new orders. Wyatt sipped from the glass and observed Holliday for a time in the mirror's reflection.

The pallid gambler's delicate appearance seemed a veneer, Wyatt thought. Like a thin rime of ice apt to melt from a fire within. The men sitting in on Holliday's game appeared cautious and uneasy; their quietness seeming to create a palpable tension at the table. Wyatt set down the glass, left a coin on the bar, and walked out of the saloon. He would talk to this Holliday, he knew, but the timing was not right just now.

On the evening of the following day he joined three men in the only game in progress in the Exchange. Shanssey had glanced his way upon his entering but offered no gesture of recognition. For an hour, Wyatt placed unremarkable bets and won enough hands to stay in the game. He offered nothing about himself other than his intent to play poker, and—as was the tacit protocol of the frontier—no one inquired about his name, his past, where he'd come from, or his destination.

At ten o'clock Holliday strolled in, sporting a bone-handled cane in one hand and a small, rouged-up woman on his other arm. On this night, he wore a fawn-brown suit and vest and a crimson cravat neatly folded into his white blouse. The woman flaunted a plum-colored gown worthy of a stage show.

"Fifty dollars," Wyatt said, loud enough to be heard by the new arrivals. Holliday stopped and leaned both hands on the cane to watch the action. Wyatt lighted a cigar and waited as the men seated at his table stared warily at the proffered bet. When Wyatt's gaze came up again to Holliday, he recognized the woman staring a hole through him—the Hungarian whore from James's brothel in Wichita. The hellcat. Kate.

"Too rich for my blood," said the man to Wyatt's left. He tossed his cards into the dead-wood and picked up his hat off the floor. "I'm done." Two others folded their hands but remained in the game, leaving one to meet Wyatt's raise. When Wyatt lost the hand, Holliday tipped his hat and made a small bow to the table at large.

"May I round out your table, gentlemen?" Holliday offered, his voice purring with a courtly Southern lilt. His smile was a decidedly comfortable smirk. When his woman slunk off to the bar, he tapped his way to the vacated seat and settled in. By appearance alone, his presence added a sense of formality to the game. His movements seemed fluid and practiced, like an actor on a stage. His hands appeared as soft as a woman's. Only his eyes told the truth, and those eyes seemed to say: *Tread lightly; nothing is what it seems.*

Holliday proved to be a man of contradictions—displaying in equal measures a calculated aloofness and a personable charm that often overstepped the boundaries of familiarity when it snapped to vicious insult. Then, just as quickly, he might voice a self-deprecating assessment of his own foibles with the cards. His drawl was educated, but he took every opportunity to curse. Passing this man on the street, Wyatt might have thought him a refined traveler who had stepped off a train at the wrong destination, but, to hear him speak so carelessly with strangers, Holliday was, by Wyatt's estimation, trouble in the making.

With the cards the Southerner was driven, sometimes reckless, hell-bent on fleecing a man out of his money or going broke in the process. Though not much older than Bat Masterson, Holliday seemed already used up in some fragile way that Wyatt could not identify. The man's faded-blond hair and gray pallor marked him as someone who seldom ventured into daylight. A feminine quality sometimes emerged in his face, but his cool eyes could be predatory, taking in everything, even when he laughed . . . even as the lids fell partway to shield his thoughts. He drank enough whiskey at one sitting for three men, yet he never appeared drunk.

With Holliday on a streak, Wyatt folded early on three hands, and then, after winning once, he folded again three times. Holliday's foxy eyes seemed to bore into him as though digging into his thoughts.

"You appear to know your way around the cards, suh," he said, smiling at Wyatt as though they were old acquaintances.

Wyatt sat with his wrists crossed on the table. The cigar loosely clamped in his fingers sent up a thin string of gray smoke that snaked before his face.

"I have my moments."

"Indeed," Holliday said and began dealing. "Let us see who will have this one."

The play came down to Wyatt, Holliday, and a heavy-set Texan, whose scarred cheeks were pitted with tiny craters. "Are we to believe that you have suddenly come into good fortune after so many staggering losses?" Holliday said pleasantly to the Texan.

The thick-necked man stared at Holliday long enough to stretch the moment into an awkward standoff, but Holliday merely smiled, laid his cards face-down, and threaded his fingers together on the tabletop as though expecting an answer to his rhetorical question.

"We gonna play poker?" the Texan drawled. "Or yap?"

Amused, Holliday glared at the man and then picked up his cards again, laughing like a rebellious adolescent. After another glance at his hand, he stared at the Texan with a look of cool disdain. Without breaking his gaze he dropped a card on the table.

"I'll take one," he said, his eyes shining with mischief inside their pale-blue irises.

When Wyatt folded, Holliday looked at him with feigned disappointment and then raised the pot again. It went back and forth three times before the play was called. Holliday showed two pairs—sixes and nines. Laying down three queens and two sevens, the Texan broke into a wide, gap-toothed grin.

Holliday chuckled as the money was swept away. "And here I thought *I* was someone to be reckoned with." He turned to Wyatt. "But you apparently knew to be less foolish than I."

"Guess that was one of my moments," Wyatt said evenly.

The Texas winner leaned on his forearms and smiled. "I'd say that was one o' *my* goddamned moments!"

Holliday was still chuckling when the general laughter tapered off. "And so it was, suh. Yet the night is young. Many *moments* yet to unfold." Then the humor dropped from his expression as if a mask had been ripped away from his face. His voice turned acid. "Now deal the cards!"

Every man at the table stared at Holliday, but he only ignored them and drew on the slender, silver flask he kept inside his coat. Each time he drained the flask he called for Shanssey to refill it, which the Irishman did six times throughout the night.

When the game closed at dawn, Holliday's pockets were heaviest. Wyatt had come out thirty dollars ahead, and the others seemed satisfied with the play. When Wyatt stopped at the bar to leave a tip for the management, a silver eagle rolled in a spiral next to his elbow and came to rest on the polished-wood counter.

"Buy you a drink, suh?" Holliday's voice was now warm, almost confiding. He stood nearly as tall as Wyatt, but, beneath his finely tailored suit, he appeared to be little more than skin and bones. He hooked his cane over the edge of the bar and, plucking at the lapels, adjusted the hang of his suit.

" 'Preciate the offer," Wyatt said. "I don't drink."

"God in heaven," Holliday drawled sourly. He leaned in and squinted at Wyatt. "Is that true?"

Shanssey approached, smiling and wiping his hands on a towel. "Fill your flask for you, Doc?"

Holliday surrendered the flask from his inner coat pocket. This time when his lapels parted, Wyatt caught the gleam of a nickel-plated revolver tucked under one arm in a compact holster.

"So, you're a doctor," Wyatt said.

"*I* am a *dentist*," he announced with an obvious undertone of irony.

When Shanssey returned, Holliday pocketed the flask and patted the coin lying on the bar. "I'll have a glass now, too."

Shanssey poured, and Holliday picked up the glass to assess the color of the liquid. The barman watched as his customer threw back the amber fluid and wiped his mouth with the back of his scrawny hand.

"Now I'll have one to savor, suh. Pour me one more."

As Shanssey accommodated with another tilt of the bottle, his smile stretched across his face. "Nectar of the gods," he declared and capped the bottle.

"And for the rest of us," Holliday amended.

"Anything for you, sir?" Shanssey asked Wyatt. Wyatt shook his head, and the Irishman moved away.

Holliday sipped the whiskey and closed his eyes when he swallowed. A faint smile played at the corners of his mouth, but only for a moment. When he opened his eyes he looked at Wyatt with a sense of genuine curiosity.

"And what do you do to empty men's pockets, if I may ask, suh?"

Wyatt nodded back toward the table. "I reckon you just saw me at work."

Holliday frowned. "It *is* a profession, of course, but I'll warrant there's more to you than that." He raised the glass to his lips and paused. "You strike me as a man who has more on his mind than the random fall of the cards."

Wyatt averted his eyes and studied the room. "No more'n any other man, I reckon."

Holliday waved away the unanswered question, drank the remains of his refreshment, and slapped the shot glass down on the bar. "John Holliday," he said and held out his pale, slender hand that looked like it might be nimble enough for a dentist to maneuver inside a man's mouth.

Wyatt took the offered hand, and they shook. The strength in Holliday's grip was unexpected.

"My friends call me 'Doc,' " the dentist said, intoning the remark as both a disparagement and an invitation.

The Hungarian whore approached and attached herself to Holliday's arm. She gave Wyatt a self-satisfied glare just short of scathing. Holliday turned to her and raised his eyebrows.

"Kate, have you been cavorting around and distracting men from their better judgments at the tables?"

"No," she said, "I haff been on da prowl t'inkin' maybe I find someone prettier d'an you." She laughed and leaned in close enough to bite Holliday's ear. When she propped her arm on the bar and stared at Wyatt, her eyes were as cold as beads of glass.

Any plan for Wyatt to use an assumed identity in tracking the train robbers was dashed by the woman's hostile eyes. Like Mattie, she had resented James and, by extension, any of the Earps.

"Name's Earp," Wyatt said, completing introductions with the Southern dentist. "Wyatt Earp."

Wyatt was surprised when the whore thrust a stiff hand toward him and waited to shake his hand. "Kate Elder," she announced, the message on her face insistent and clear: *The two of them would declare no common past.*

When Wyatt took her hand, it was as cold and limp as a cut of raw meat.

" 'Wyatt Earp,' " Holliday repeated quietly, delivering the name in a singsong melody. He made a small bow from the waist toward Kate. "I've got a little story Mr. Earp might want to hear. Will you excuse us, dahlin'?"

Kate smiled and bent at her knees to perform a shallow curtsey. Then her face darkened like the sudden approach of a cloud casting its shadow over a hillside. Flashing a private warning to Wyatt with her eyes she sulked away. Holliday laughed at her performance.

"I'm afraid we're just too much alike to stand each other for much longer," Doc quipped, still watching her sashay across the room. He swung back to Wyatt and shrugged. "What about you? Are you tied up in the hopeless plight of all men, Mr. Earp?"

"What would that be, Dr. Holliday?"

Holliday pocketed the flask. "Please, just call me 'Doc.' " He spread his hands with the obvious. "Why . . . the fairer sex, of course!" When Wyatt did not answer, Holliday looked around the saloon and pointed to a table. "Let's have a seat over there, shall we?"

They laid their hats side by side on the table and settled in like two men striking up a business deal. Across the room Kate Elder sat with two soldiers, drinking and chatting as if she were the guest of honor at a private party. Holliday acknowledged her by raising his flask as a toast, but he did not drink. Laughing quietly, he set the flask aside and leaned toward Wyatt.

"Wyatt Earp," he breathed, as though wanting to hear the sound of the name again. "I sat in with a crowd of ruffians a few weeks ago," he began in a muffled monotone. "They were talking about a man coming down from Kansas . . . a *de-tec-tive* for the railroad." The dentist smiled as if he had said something clever. "They got your last name wrong . . . 'Arp' . . . but the first one is dead on."

Holliday beamed with a wicked smile and leaned in with a conspiratorial gleam in his eye. "Have we been using an alias, Mr. Earp? I tried it once myself for a time. Never did grow accustomed to it. It always made me feel I was cheating my past." He straightened and raised both eyebrows with regret. "When a man gives up his beginnings, he can feel a little lost."

Wyatt looked around at the patrons closest to them. All were preoccupied with cards, whiskey, or women. Turning back to Holliday, Wyatt decided to take a chance with the Southerner.

"Didn' change my name," Wyatt said. "The newspapers were always getting it wrong. I was a marshal in Dodge City. Now I'm workin' for the Santa Fe Railroad. I'm after some men who waylaid a couple o' their runs and busted into the mail cars." Wyatt lifted a hand off the table and tottered it back and forth like a seesaw. "Never used any other name but my own . . . not yet anyway."

Holliday pursed his lips and shook his head. "You shouldn't."

Wyatt held dead eyes on the smug dentist. "Why's that?"

Holliday shrugged and turned his gaze to the room at large. "Oh, I don't know. Pretending to be someone you're not just doesn't suit some people. I think maybe you're one of those."

Wyatt let that go. Most of what Holliday said seemed to be for his own entertainment, and this he considered to be more of the same.

The dentist's eyes narrowed. "So you were the marshal in Dodge City?"

"Assistant," Wyatt said.

"But now you're a railroad detective."

Wyatt leaned and adjusted the hang of his coat over his revolver. "I go wherever the money takes me."

Doc sat back in his chair and studied Wyatt's face with interest. "Well, I'd say you came to the right place if you're looking for thieves and scoundrels, but you're a little late." He laughed. "The reprobates you are after were in here last month with the Clear Fork crew. I had a good run of the cards against those boys. I guess maybe I'm living off some of that railroad money as we speak."

"They actually talk about stopping a train?" Wyatt asked.

Doc shrugged. "They talked *around* it." He turned suddenly and coughed repeatedly into his fist. Then he pulled out a white handkerchief and waited as if expecting more of the spasm. When it did not continue, he dabbed the cloth at his watery eyes and put it away.

"That crowd has not been back," he resumed hoarsely. "They were flush with money, yet seemed unaccustomed to such fortunes. If their conversation can be believed, the party you seek struck out for Missouri." He spread his hands. "Thus, you—as a detective—may be wasting your time here, suh."

"Any names to go with these boys?"

Holliday smiled as if both he and Wyatt were the brunt of a joke. "All Smiths and Joneses." Then his face turned hard and his eyes distant. He cleared his throat with a rough cough that caused him to wince. "I don't tell stories like this often," he snapped.

Wyatt looked into Holliday's pale, ice-blue eyes, seeing nothing there that would explain the enigma that seemed to exist at the core of the Southerner. "Any reason you're tellin' me this one?"

The skin on Holliday's face tightened, and he flicked the backs of his fingers at the air. "I don't need a goddamned reason for everything I do," he barked. Now his expression was as sour as his tone. He looked around the room, as if searching for something better to occupy his attention.

Wyatt assumed the conversation had come to its natural end. He expected Holliday to leave, but a series of hacking coughs overcame the dentist. Doubling up in his chair, he whipped out the linen handkerchief again and clapped it to his mouth. When the seizure finally abated, he wiped his mouth with the linen and angled his teary eyes away. For a time he held the cloth in place as if another spell might be forthcoming. Wyatt waited.

"I'm sorry," Holliday said, his voice now as soft as a mother's lullaby to her child. "I am often rude for reasons that would not seem evident to my acquaintances." He drank the flask dry, folded the handkerchief, and stared at Wyatt with unabashed interest, as though he were only now seeing him well enough to make an appraisal.

"Can I buy you another?" Wyatt said, nodding to the flask.

Holliday cleared his throat loudly and shook his head. "It's not that I like the stuff so much, but it eases the pain, you know." He laughed quietly to himself. "Sometimes I convince myself it's a medicine."

When Wyatt made no response, Holliday discreetly opened the handkerchief and privately inspected it. He made a thin smile and stuffed the linen back into his pocket.

"You're not going to ask?" he said.

Wyatt shook his head. "None o' my business."

Holliday laughed. "Well, *that's* refreshing. Most of the people

I've met in Texas think *everything* is their business." Now his face turned earnest, and he looked pointedly into Wyatt's eyes. "Anyone ever tell you . . . your eyes are like ice?"

Wyatt felt a memory cut free of its moorings and float from a deep place inside him to the front of his mind. He'd been sixteen in a peach orchard in San Bernardino when Valenzuela Cos had guided him through the initiations of manhood. She had told him about his eyes . . . about how they sometimes turned to ice.

"People say that about me, too," Holliday continued and made his ironic smile. "But I'll wager that's where our similarities end." He sat back gloating with a grin that suggested he knew the whole of Wyatt's story.

Wyatt tolerated the inspection and said nothing.

"They say that opposites attract, you know," Holliday went on. "I'm inclined to believe that. I, for instance, could play any part on a stage, whereas you, Mr. Earp . . . you are, suh, what you are. I like your direct manner. And you play the gentleman's game like a seasoned gentleman. But, of course, you will never do as the undercover sort." He chuckled, which led into another racking cough. He retrieved the handkerchief and pressed it to his mouth again until the fit subsided.

As soon as he was able to regulate his breathing Doc turned, held up the flask, and signaled to Shanssey for more whiskey. The two men sat without speaking, letting the ambient noise of the saloon fill the gap in their conversation. When Shanssey arrived with a bottle, he filled Holliday's flask. Wyatt laid money on the table.

"This one's on me, Doc. Maybe I can return the favor someday."

Shanssey scooped up the money with a deft movement of his thick hand. "Thank you, sir," he mumbled and returned to the bar.

"There *is* a favor you could afford me, suh," Holliday suggested. "You could tell me about this Dodge City of yours. How're the pickings up there in Kansas for a professional of the green cloth?"

Wyatt pushed his lower lip forward. "During the cattle season, pretty good." He nodded toward the noisy room. " 'Course your clientele will be the same as what you've got here—mostly Texans—the difference bein', in Kansas every one of 'em will have three-months' pay in his pocket."

Holliday nodded thoughtfully. "I might want to visit your fair city."

Wyatt took in a long breath and let it slowly seep from his nose. "It ain't my city. I reckon you can go where you please." He stood, donned his hat, and plucked down on the brim. "Take care of yourself, Doc. Tell your lady friend it was a pleasure to meet her."

"Where're you headed?"

"North," Wyatt said. "I might want to see Missouri again."

Holliday cleared the phlegm from his throat and wiped his mouth with the handkerchief. "Hang on to your good name, Mr. Earp. It might be all we ever really have."

"It's 'Wyatt,' " Wyatt corrected.

When Holliday put away the cloth and offered his hand again, Wyatt took it and watched the man's face fill with color as though he were in the prime of his health.

Wyatt wired the A.T. & S.F. Topeka office and awaited instructions. The message that came back was brief: *Forget Missouri. Wire Dodge City mayor immediately.*

He did just that.

While waiting for a reply, Wyatt read a dated issue of a Kansas newspaper with Dodge's last election returns: Bat Masterson had been elected sheriff. His brother Ed was assistant marshal under Charlie Bassett. But there was more crime in Dodge reported in this paper than during the whole of Wyatt's last season on the force.

When the agent brought out the folded message, he made a little bow of his head and took a step backward, giving Wyatt some privacy. Wyatt opened the paper and turned to the light from the window.

Ed Masterson killed. Wire immediately if return as assistant marshal to Bassett.—J. Kelley, mayor.

Wyatt carried the telegram closer to the window that looked out over the prairie. Clouds were piling up in the west. In the muted light, a few drab-colored birds flitted through the chaparral and nested beneath the eave of the roof.

He had been thinking of moving on from Dodge. Mattie would be there, and he could see nothing good coming from being in the same town with her. But the telegram had been a personal vindication of sorts. There were people in Dodge who saw what he was and recognized in him something of value.

"Mr. Earp?" the agent said, his fingers laced before him. "Will you be sending a reply, sir?"

Wyatt crumpled the telegram and turned again to look north out the window. He allowed the other side of the argument to surface. He had wasted his time in Texas. Being in pursuit of law breakers would always contain a certain amount of futility. Not to mention liability. Being a lawman might never help to better his position in the world. It hadn't worked for Ed Masterson.

The massive cloud moved north, looking angry and ominous above the bleak landscape. If it cut to the east, he thought, some of the dry springs he had encountered on the trip down would benefit, and, in thinking this, he knew that he was considering the trail back to Dodge. By going back, he would be in motion, heading toward something to sink his teeth into.

But if he was going to do it, he would need more from the job. Something to nest away for the future.

He turned and walked to the telegraph desk where the clerk waited. Wyatt wrote three words: *Arrive three weeks.* Then he signed his name. The clerk read his penciled note and nodded gravely, as though grasping the full import of Wyatt's decision.

"Good luck, Mr. Earp," he said and sat to tap out the message.

Wyatt thought of correcting the obsequious man. Luck played its part, just like in gambling, but it was what a man did—or didn't do—that played the more decisive role in his life.

"Wait a minute," Wyatt said. "Add this." He scratched more words on a square of paper.

The clerk lifted his hand off the key and read the note aloud. " 'Must increase monthly salary by twenty-five.' " He checked Wyatt's face. "Yes, sir."

Wyatt walked outside to his horses and studied the volatile sky for a time. It was a long trip back through the Indian Territory to Dodge . . . and longer still through a driving rain on the open prairie. But he felt a momentum building inside him. And he sensed a purpose with definable borders. He unlashed his slicker from the bedroll on his pack horse and suited up just before the rain began to spatter down on the dry caliche and brittle scrub surrounding the telegraph office.

By the time he was mounted, the sky opened up and hammered the ground with big heavy drops of rain that snaked over the ground in rivulets that coalesced and ran with purpose into the pockets of low ground and over the edges of shallow ravines. Facing into the storm, he kicked his heels into the mare's flank and began the long push back to Kansas.

CHAPTER 17

Summer, 1878: Dodge City, Kansas

The spring of '78 was a record season for longhorns in Ford County, Kansas. Dodge was the center of the market in the plains, and the herds that spread out and cropped the grasses for miles around fed an all-consuming fire of commerce. At night the off-duty drovers gave birth to a new city south of the tracks. It was loud, festive, and unpredictable—as though a great slumbering creature had been roused from a day of fitful sleep, and the officers waited to see what name to put to the beast on any given night. Even with the firearm-carrying ban in effect, the south end of Dodge was real estate leased from hell . . . with alcohol fanning the flames.

The team of Sheriff Bat Masterson and Assistant Marshal Wyatt Earp descended upon the urban chaos like a new book of the Bible. Swift, authoritative, and unrelenting. A flash of gunmetal and the dull thud of steel collapsing the crown of a man's hat. Earp and Masterson. Their names were often joined as one, a bicephalous force that suffered no exceptions to the law in Dodge City.

On a summer night in June Wyatt stood at the bar in the Long Branch drinking coffee and reading with interest a card in the *Times,* informing the public that Dr. John H. Holliday was now providing dental services at the Dodge House with a money-back guarantee. The pallid man's sly face surfaced in Wyatt's mind like the recollection of an old friend. This surprised Wyatt, having not thought of the Southerner since leaving Texas.

He had just paused to consider stopping by the dentist's office the next day, when two gunshots rang out south of the tracks. Wyatt stepped outside in time to hear two more pistol reports that pinpointed the disturbance as a block deep into the saloon district south of the deadline.

Coming up Locust Street he saw Bob Rachals brandishing a nickel-plated revolver with fancy pearl grips. The popular trail driver took a wavering bead on something in the alley next to the Comique Theater and fired. A water barrel spumed a spray of water over a terrified fiddle player trying to cover his instrument with his coat.

"If you're gonna play the damn thing," Rachals yelled in a drunken slur, "the least you can do is learn 'The Yellow Rose.'" He cursed and cocked the gun again. Without prelude Wyatt crashed the barrel of his Colt's into the back of Rachals's head.

As they reached the city offices, businessman Bob Wright ran toward them, yelling from half a block away. "Hold on, Earp!" Wright, wearing a knee-length coat over a white nightshirt, burst into the office. "Earp! What are you doing with Rachals? What's the problem?"

Wyatt's eyes traveled down and up Wright's hastily donned attire. "There's no problem. He *was* shooting on the street. Now he's not."

Wright approached Rachals solicitously, stood on his toes, and sorted through the cattleman's hair, trying to assess the damage to his bleeding head. Still groggy, Rachals opened Wright's lapels, trying to make sense of who this was combing through his scalp.

"He's running the biggest cattle drive we've seen this season," Wright said to Wyatt, pressing the information on him as though it were a mandate from the city council.

Wyatt moved Wright aside and ushered Rachals into a cell. "I know who he is."

Wright lunged after Rachals and jerked him back by his sleeve, causing the drowsy trail driver to bobble like a puppet. "Look here! You can't arrest him, Earp. I've made promises to this man."

Wyatt broke Wright's grip on the prisoner and eased him out of the way. After a startled silence, Wright cursed into Wyatt's face, spraying flecks of saliva that touched his skin like sparks from a fire. Wyatt heaved Wright into the cell with the Texan and locked it. Wide-eyed, Wright gripped the bars and rattled the door.

"What in the *hell* are you doing! I'm on the town council . . . an alderman . . . one of your employers! I order you to open this door."

Keeping his anger in check, Wyatt stared as the merchant finished ranting. "You're interfering with an officer during an arrest."

Wright's skin color deepened, and his eyes bulged. When Wyatt closed the dividing door between office and jail, the cell-block filled with the echoes of the councilman's strident threats.

Wyatt locked the office and started his last patrol of the streets before dawn.

He found Marshal Bassett dealing faro at the Lady Gay and apprised him of the new prisoners. Bassett looked up from the layout long enough to show a sly grin. When he returned his concentration to the game, Bassett laughed quietly and shook his head.

"You don't bend for nobody, do you, Wyatt?" Bassett said and cut his eyes back to his head enforcer. He raised his eyebrows. "This'n might come back to bite you in the ass."

"Law's the same for Wright as it is for anybody else," Wyatt said.

"Well," Bassett laughed, "we'll see."

After his night in jail, Bob Wright would not look Wyatt in the eye whenever they chanced to meet on the streets. Nor would he speak to Wyatt, unless out of necessity during a meeting of the town council. A month passed with Wyatt indifferent to the wasted energy of Wright's resentment. If the alderman wanted to spit and fume behind closed doors, that was his privilege. For Wyatt, the book was closed on the affair.

On a warm night in late July, Wyatt and Charlie Bassett sat in the back of the Long Branch, Wyatt sipping coffee while Bassett thumbed through a deck of cards over a game of solitaire.

"All I'm sayin' is," Bassett repeated, "you gotta play the politics if you wanna keep the job."

Wyatt watched the marshal's tired eyes hide his disappointment at the card he drew. "I reckon things are set straight enough," Wyatt said. "I doubt that any councilmen will want to butt in on my arrests again."

Bassett tilted his head to one side. "As long as you're assistant marshal, you mean."

"Wright tried to boot me out," Wyatt confided. "Couldn't make it stick with the others on the council."

"Look, Wyatt, I know the rest of the council respects you, but Bob Wright has got a wagonload of money. For the right price, a feller can go at a problem from a lot o' different angles."

Wyatt timed his drinking, balancing the hot coffee against the warmth of the evening. "What do you reckon Wright woulda paid Bob Rachals to stop his shootin' on the street?"

With the queen of diamonds hovering over the king of clubs, Bassett looked up from his game and went as still as a tintype portrait. "Did you just make a joke?"

Wyatt raised his cup and drank, keeping his face expressionless. When the marshal's attention shifted to the door, Wyatt turned to see Jim Masterson cross the room in his quick, cat-like pace.

"Hey, Jim," Bassett announced, "Wyatt just made a joke." The marshal frowned. "Least I'm pretty sure he did."

Jim stepped to the table and stared at Wyatt as if he had not heard Bassett. "There was some ruckus down at the Comique . . . but I hear it quieted down."

Wyatt finished his coffee, stood, and strapped on the gun belt he had hooked over the back of the chair. "How 'bout you and me make the rounds together. We'll swing by the Comique first."

When the officers stepped inside the Comique Theater, the room was as subdued as a church service, as Lillie Beck's sweet, springwater-clear voice held the audience captive from the stage. The pure delivery of her melancholy song had brought a sheen into the eyes of Doc Holliday, who sat with Bat Masterson at a poker table, where business was suspended for the moment. Holliday was turned around watching the singer, one hand holding his cards, the other on the back of his chair. Standing behind him, Kate Elder rested a hand on the dentist's frail shoulder.

When the song ended, the audience broke into wild applause, with whoops and cheers that asked for more. Lillie—the "darling of Dodge"—smiled graciously and threw kisses toward her admirers. Wyatt and Jim waited until she disappeared into the wings, and then they moved outside into the pleasant night air.

"*That* is one damned beautiful woman," Jim said, his voice as earnest as the oath he had sworn to wear a badge. "Whatever the trouble here was . . . I reckon it was Lillie smoothed it out."

Wyatt said nothing as he watched three horsemen approach from the east at a walk. Each man wore a loose bandana tied under his chin and a hat pulled low over his eyes. After taking their horses at a walk down the street, the horsemen turned at the end of the block and started back. When they passed through the light streaming out of the Varieties Theater, each man began pulling his bandana up over the lower half of his face. Wyatt caught a flash of metal in one man's hand. He touched Jim's arm, and the deputy followed Wyatt's gaze. The three masked riders kept their eyes straight ahead as they paraded east.

"What the hell is this?" Masterson whispered.

Wyatt said nothing. His right hand settled on the butt of his revolver at his hip, then he was as still as the awning post.

Inside the theater Eddie Foy was taking charge of the festivities, singing a farcical song in his high, comic voice. One horseman whipped his mount with a quirt, and the others spurred their horses until all three came on at a sudden gallop.

"Jim!" Wyatt called, pulling his gun and extending it forward. "They're throwin' down on us."

The two lawmen instinctively retreated from the lighted doorway and held their guns at the ready. When the riders were almost abreast of them, the rumble of hooves fell away beneath the explosions of multiple guns firing. Bullets slapped into the theater's clapboard front like the banging of hammers from a team of industrious carpenters. The music inside stopped, and throughout the room there was a collective scraping of feet and furniture. Wyatt jumped down to the street and grabbed at the last horse's tail but missed. He dropped to one knee and took aim against the faint backlighting of the sky.

"Crouch down," Wyatt ordered quietly. "Keep your shots above the buildings."

They let go with several volleys as the riders made a dash down the street. When two rifle shots barked from an upstairs window in the theater, Wyatt spun but refrained from shooting when he recognized the Comique's bouncer levering another round and aiming east where the riders had turned down Second Avenue toward the river.

"Lay off on that shootin'!" Wyatt ordered, his voice filling the street. "And get out o' that damned window!"

The two lawmen ran toward Second Avenue, rounding the corner in time to hear the three horses rumble like thunder on the wooden bridge. When the horses appeared across the river, Wyatt could make out only two riders.

"Must've hit one," Jim said between breaths.

At the near end of the bridge they found a body sprawled across the planks. The felled man moaned and rolled off his side onto his back. Wyatt spread the man's shirtfront to inspect the wound. By the dim cast of light from town, he could see a shoulder wound and splinters of bone slick with blood. The Texan tried to lift his head, digging his chin into his collarbone to inspect the damage.

"My shoulder . . . it's shot all to hell!" he wailed. "Goddamn . . . it hurts like a sonovabitch!"

"You think about that when you and your friends were pouring lead into the theater?" Wyatt said.

"We weren't shooting at the damned theater!" he snapped. Then his head dropped back onto the hard planking, and he bared his teeth. "God-*damn*! It hurts like a fuckin' sonovabitch!"

Wyatt took hold of the man's greasy hair and jerked his head to better see his face. "Then what the hell *were* you shootin' at?" he demanded, tightening his grip on the man's dirty hank of hair.

The wounded man's eyes flared with contempt. "I'd like to a' hit you, you damned sonovabitch."

Letting go of the hair, Wyatt gathered up the man's collar in a fist and raised him several inches off the ground. "Who talked you into this?" he demanded, but the drover's head fell back limp when he passed out.

When Doc McCarty arrived, Wyatt walked down the riverbank and washed the blood from his hands at the edge of the muddy Arkansas. Jim Masterson followed, and together they stood watching the currents swirl around the bridge pilings and slide away into the night.

"Bad wound for a cowhand," Jim said. "He's lost a lot of blood. If he even makes it, he'll sure as hell need to find himself another line of work."

Wyatt rolled down his sleeves and buttoned the cuffs. "No need to start feelin' sorry for 'im 'cause he's hurt," he said and turned to Jim to drive home his point. "Could be you or me bleeding out on the sidewalk up at the Comique right now," he explained. "Just like your brother." Wyatt shifted his attention back toward the business district, taking a fierce hold on something among the flickering lights of the town. "Somebody made a goddamned bad choice tonight."

Jim hissed and spat. "Yeah, guess he'll just have to live with a busted shoulder."

Wyatt's voice was clear over the shearing of the water. "It ain't him I'm talking about, Jim."

When the wounded Texan died, Wyatt felt the gazes of the citizens hold a little longer on him whenever they passed him on the street. The Texans lost no opportunity to show their disdain, most of them simply giving Wyatt a cold stare, but the bolder ones condemning him with an arc of tobacco spat from a safe distance.

In truth, there was no way to know whose bullet had killed the young drover. But Wyatt knew. He had known it was a hit when he squeezed off the shot. What surprised him was how little it meant now that it was done. The Texan—Hoy, his name was—had played a high-stakes game and lost. He had to have known the risk. Wyatt supposed money had been the incentive that made the cowhand lose sight of the possibilities, and he was half sure where that money had come from.

As for Wyatt's part in the cowhand's death, he knew that he had prepared himself for it ever since he had witnessed the

street fight back in Omaha City when he had been little more
than a boy. What mattered now was that the Texans understood
the rule of the law in Dodge City. It was uncompromising. You
broke the law, you paid a price. Wyatt had no control over who
did or did not decide to cross that line. His job, as he saw
it, was simply to supply the consequences.

He let three days pass before walking to Bob Wright's store.
There under the awning he leaned on a post until the store's
few customers had left. Upon entering he walked to the counter
and watched the alderman enter figures in a ledger, the scratching of his pen the only sound in the room.

"Be with you in a moment," Wright mumbled absently. When
he lifted the pen to examine his work, the complete stillness of
the room seemed to speak to him. He brought up his head
quickly. "Oh, it's you," he said, trying to cover the dry catch in
his throat with a forced cough.

"You heard about Hoy?"

Wright's face flashed through a gamut of twitches and frowns
as he licked his lips. "Who?"

Wyatt's expression was wooden. "The young Texan who died
out on the street. You knew him?"

Wright's face darkened suddenly with the hostility of a sulk-
ing child. "I don't know what you are talking about." He
snapped down the front of his vest with both hands, and a daub
of ink from the pen bled into a small dark sunburst on his
trousers. Seeing the stain, he slapped the pen on the counter
and fussed with the stain using a rag. "What is it that you want,
Earp?"

Wyatt looked over the shelves of new clothing behind the
counter and raised his chin to a stack of new denim trousers
neatly folded on one of the shelves. "Bob, do you reckon if I
wanted to own a new pair of those work trousers, I could send
down one o' the deputies to try them on for me?"

Wright frowned. "What are you talking about?" He wet his lips again and looked around the room, his head jerking in small increments as if he were desperately trying to locate something. "Why would you do something like that?"

Wyatt waited until the man's gaze met his own. "I wouldn't," he said and walked out leaving the door open.

The next time a disturbance brought Wyatt and Jim Masterson to the Comique Theater, they employed a standard tactical maneuver: Wyatt entered first, walking into the crowd alone; half a minute later, Jim came in quietly and sidled along the wall to back him up from a strategic angle and unobtrusive distance.

The only part of the room functioning normally was the back section where the gaming tables were busy. Holliday, the dentist, was there concentrating on his cards. Kate Elder stood behind him. On stage the performers stood motionless in their costumes watching the standoff in the main room. The new bartender lay on the floor with his head bleeding. Standing over him with his legs spread, a tall, gangling Texan wearing a fresh-off-the-shelf striped shirt and a bright red scarf emptied a whiskey bottle onto the supine man's chest.

"Which one of you Kansas bastards wants to water down my drink now?" The Texan's laughter rattled through the quiet of the room until he saw Wyatt. His face suddenly lost its celebratory glow and shut down with a hostile glare that hardened the line of his jaw.

"You're done here," Wyatt said and hitched his head at the door. "Let's go. You're heading down to the jail."

Though the Texan's bravado had dissipated palpably, he would not back down. He wore no gun, but he widened his stance and stood his ground as if his boots had been nailed to the floor.

"Hard or easy," Wyatt offered, "it's your choice."

Ten heartbeats passed, but the man would not submit. Wyatt slowly pulled his Colt's from its holster and let it hang by his leg.

"Looks like you go hard."

From Wyatt's side a new voice broke in. "Not this time, tin star. You just stepped into a nest of Texas rattlesnakes."

This one was broad-shouldered, an inch taller than Wyatt. When he swaggered forward and took his position, his closed fists hung down his legs almost to his knees. Three more men in fancy cattleman garb wove through the crowd to stand beside him.

Jim Masterson stepped up behind the first challenger and swung his revolver into the man's skull. As the man fell, the Texans closest to him instinctively shuffled away. But one patron reconsidered and closed on Jim, trying to get his gun away from him. Wyatt had his hands full with three others who came on in a surge. The two lawmen swung their guns wildly, slashing at whoever came near. When Masterson's gun went off, Wyatt capitalized on the momentary lull to knock a man senseless. The crowd backed up, and Wyatt pivoted his gun in a slow arc to cover them all.

"Next man who moves," Wyatt growled, "I'll put in a grave." He looked at Masterson, who lay on the floor, his lip bleeding, and his shirt torn down one side of his body. The Texans who had not fallen under the sting of a gun barrel straightened up, relaxing from their fighting stances.

"Back away from my deputy," Wyatt ordered.

Masterson stood up and began turning in half circles, searching the floor around him. "Lost my damned gun, Wyatt."

Behind Jim a Texan raised the lost pistol, cocked it, and brought it to bear on Wyatt. The gunshot that went off was like the jolt of a giant buckboard, making everyone in the room jump. The man holding Jim's gun bent double and appeared to tie his body into a knot as he reached across himself to clap his left hand over his right ear. He silently worked his mouth as if testing the hinge of his jaws.

Behind the deafened man, Doc Holliday cocked a smoking nickel-plated pistol and pressed it into the Texan's neck. The dazed man let the still-cocked gun pivot upside down by the trigger guard and surrendered it to Masterson.

The brawl had come and gone like an unexpected gust of wind on the prairie. Now the room went silent. A red string of blood ran down Wyatt's forehead and mixed with the sweat beading on his face. Extending his arm forward, he swept his gun in a half circle to include every Texan standing before him.

"Pick up your friends lying here and clear out! I want you all across the river in five minutes or I'm going to arrest every god-damned one of you, even if I have to lock you up in the stockyards. You can pick up your guns tomorrow. Now git!"

Without comment the surly patrons began shuffling out the door, some using their friends as crutches, others oblivious as they were hauled out by their boots and armpits. Standing on the boardwalk with their weapons drawn, Wyatt, Doc Holliday, and Jim Masterson watched the sullen parade—Wyatt fully expecting carbines to burn powder in a rousing Texas farewell as soon as the cowhands were mounted. Instead, the unorganized mob moved out with their horses at a walk and crossed the bridge without a disturbance.

Wyatt holstered his gun and turned to look at Holliday. In the dark outside the building, the dentist's complexion was paler than Wyatt remembered, his cadaverous face even more emaciated. The hollows in his cheeks made dark shadows that contrasted starkly against the washed-out slate-blue of his eyes. Holliday looked as out of place in Dodge City as he had in north Texas.

"I'm obliged, Doc."

Kate Elder attached to Holliday's arm and tightened her mouth into a vindictive smile. The venom in her penetrating eyes still seemed to be her natural reaction to anyone whose name was Earp.

"Well," Holliday said, "I suppose I took umbrage at the interruption. I was winning my game." The dentist tucked his plated pistol into a scabbard hanging against the ribs of his gaunt body.

"We got a law about totin' guns in town, you know," Wyatt said.

Kate bristled. "You two *of-fi-cers* can t'ank Godt Doc was dar to break da law, Mar-shal. Maybe it be you d'ey haff to carry out uff dis saloon."

Jim blew a stream of air from his lips. "You sure as hell saved our hides . . . that's for damned certain."

"Still got the law," Wyatt said. "Nobody carries in town, Doc."

Holliday coughed up a laugh, unscrewed the cap of his flask, and downed two gulps. "I'm not quite the physical specimen that you two gentlemen are," he said, handing the flask to Kate. "My bite will have to be my bullet." He smiled, patted the gun's bulge under his coat, and produced a stained white handkerchief. Turning away, he bent forward from the waist and started coughing just as the cloth covered his mouth. Kate leaned with Doc and wrapped her arms around him as the racking continued.

Wyatt bent at the knees to get his face level with Masterson's. "Your lip's busted open, Jim," he said. "Better go and let Doc McCarty see to it."

Jim touched his mouth gingerly and then checked his fingertips for blood. He nodded and headed up Second Avenue. At Doc's request, Kate went inside to refill his flask, leaving Wyatt and Holliday standing in the light from the Comique and listening to the bartenders cleaning up inside.

"What made you do what you did in there, Doc?"

Holliday cleared his throat roughly and gazed down the street at the abundance of saloons and entertainment houses. Two doors down a lively out-of-tune piano poured an upbeat melody from the Lone Star out into the thoroughfare. After a brief pause a deep-throated woman's voice attached itself to the tune, and the roar of the crowd welcomed her.

"Hell, I don't know," Doc said. "What makes *you* walk into a room of Texas trash and risk your life over a beat-up barman?" Holliday coughed up phlegm and spat into the street. "I read in the newspaper you're one of the Republican delegates headed for the convention in Topeka. Maybe I figured you were getting too important to get shot."

Wyatt looked down Front Street and considered the idea of dying in such a place as Dodge City. It made him realize that— except for Morgan—there was nobody in this town who really knew him. Not even Mattie. *Especially* Mattie.

"Whatever it was made you do it," Wyatt said, "I ain't likely to forget it."

Holliday snorted quietly through his nose, his mood turning quickly to sarcasm. "Does that mean I can keep my shooter next to my skinny ribs?"

Wyatt watched the dentist's body curl up as if a drawstring had been pulled tight along the length of his frail body. Holliday's face reddened, and he exhaled a long wheeze that led to another spate of wrenching coughs. The handkerchief pressed to Holliday's mouth muted the sound, but the man's eyes teared up as though he were trying to contain the last shreds of his life. When he pulled away the handkerchief to inspect it, flecks of blood glistened brightly on the soiled linen.

Wyatt kept his eyes on the saloons and stores across the railroad tracks, giving Holliday a modicum of privacy in which to compose himself. Between the Alamo and the Alhambra, he could see the shop light shining from Zimmerman's. He imagined the gunsmith busy with repair work at his workbench. The German had a secure job with a good income. And a future. A gun was always going to be one of the primary tools a man counted on. In some cases it was the difference between a man's life and an early grave. Zimmerman also sold lumber. Here was a man with vision. Compared to the merchant's life, Wyatt knew his own occupation could not claim the security of a crapshoot.

"Keep the gun hidden, Doc," Wyatt said. "Far as I'm concerned, you can wear it to church."

"Hell, Wyatt," Holliday laughed weakly, "I doubt there's a chance of that happening any time soon."

CHAPTER 18

Late summer, 1878: Dodge City, Kansas

Sitting at a table in the Delmonico, Wyatt was reading the newest issue of the *Times* when Jim Masterson hurried inside, his face at once both solemn and agitated. Wyatt lowered the paper and spoke to the waitress as she set down two breakfast plates. Masterson frowned at the double order.

"My brother, James, is in town," Wyatt explained.

Masterson removed his hat, sat, and leaned close to Wyatt. "There's some talk Clay Allison is coming into town to put it over on us," he said in a low monotone.

"Us?" Wyatt said.

Masterson nodded. "The law." Jim made a concerned face and lowered his voice to a whisper. "Well . . . people are sayin' it's mostly 'bout you."

Wyatt folded the paper and set it aside. "People like to talk."

"I'm talking about Clay Allison—the shootist. You know who I mean?"

Wyatt positioned one of the plates before him and broke open a steaming biscuit with his fingertips. "I've heard of him," he said and inserted a slice of butter that quickly melted and spread out to the crusty sides of the bread.

"He's a mean sonovabitch," Jim said. "Said to 'a killed two marshals down in New Mexico."

Wyatt sawed at a slice of ham. "Far as I know, we've got no warrants that have come in on him."

189

When James Earp walked into the dining room, Masterson picked up his hat and stood.

"James," Wyatt said. "This is Bat's brother, Jim."

The two men shook hands, and James sat down before the second plate. Wyatt wiped his moustaches with the cloth napkin and turned to Masterson.

"Anything else, Jim?"

The deputy held his hat before him, his arms extended down with both hands clutching the brim, tapping it against his knees. He frowned at Wyatt.

"You ain't worried 'bout Clay Allison?"

Wyatt bit into his biscuit, chewed, and sipped coffee. "Just circulate and keep me posted."

Masterson hesitated, took a step closer, and licked his lips. "Word is . . . he's comin' into Dodge on a paid-up job, Wyatt."

Wyatt smoothed the napkin in his lap, rested his elbows on the table, and looked out the window. He sat like that in deep thought for several seconds. Finally he turned back to Masterson.

"Would Allison hire out like that?"

Jim nodded. "They say he's a little crazy in the head. Probably love to kill us *all* and get paid for it, to boot." He waited for a response, but Wyatt began sawing at another slice of ham. "Who do you reckon would put up the money for that kind o' thing," Jim said, " 'round here in Dodge, I mean?"

Wyatt forked the ham into his mouth and, chewing, looked out at a crew of men rolling the fire hose into a coil just beyond the railroad tracks. The saloons lined up south of the deadline appeared to laze in an off-duty slumber. The only other activity to be seen was an occasional tenant going into or coming out of the Great Western Hotel.

"Bob Wright can be a mighty tiresome fellow," Wyatt said simply.

When Masterson left, James watched Wyatt continue to work on his breakfast. "Is this Clay Allison of the Washita we're talking about?"

"The same."

"And he's looking for you?"

"If he is, he can find me. Prob'ly just a lot o' talk."

The waitress appeared and poured fresh coffee for both brothers. Wyatt nodded his thanks, but James barely gave her any notice. Still watching Wyatt, James set down his silverware and sat back deeper in his chair. The furniture made a little ticking sound and then quieted.

"That ain't what I heard about Clay Allison," James said. His voice was as flat as a preacher's last words at a funeral.

Within an hour Jim Masterson came marching into the city office and stood before the desk where Wyatt was reading through a stack of new circulars. Jim spread his boots and propped his hands on the sides of his cartridge belt, waiting for Wyatt to meet his eye.

"He's here," Jim said.

Wyatt looked up.

"Allison," Jim said. "He's in Dodge. He was down at Springer's saloon asking about you."

Wyatt returned to the papers and sorted out the ones he knew to be outdated. "He can ask," Wyatt allowed.

Masterson kept his attention fixed on Wyatt's face. "Is your younger brother still in town?"

"Morgan? No. Gone back to Montana to seek his fortune . . . again."

Masterson walked to the window and leaned on the sill to survey the goings-on in the plaza. On the side track a big Santa Fe engine built up steam west of the depot as a man with a mail sack ran toward the express car.

"I can't tell if Allison is alone with an audience . . . or if he's got men with him backing him up."

Wyatt dropped the obsolete papers into the trash barrel and slipped the active ones into a drawer in the desk. "Go to the sheriff's office. Tell Bat we need some backup." Jim started to leave, but Wyatt stopped him. "Jim . . . we don't go looking for Allison like he's got our attention, understand?"

Jim stood very still, frowning as though memorizing every feature of Wyatt's face. "He ain't got your attention?"

"He's got my attention. No need to give him that kind of satisfaction."

Wyatt waited until Masterson nodded. Outside they heard the train building up its powerful rhythm as it moved west along the rails. The whistle blew two short blasts and then a long strident wail that filled the plaza with its urgency. The sound was like a periodic, celebratory scream keeping inventory on the town's thriving commerce. The wheels *clack-clacked* over the coupling onto the main track, and the long line of cars rolled out of town bound across the prairie.

"Jim, I want everyone to stay clear of Allison till I tell you how this will go. Is that understood?"

The deputy nodded again. "Can I go tell Bat now?"

"Go," Wyatt said.

Twenty minutes later Wyatt was writing up an invoice for delousing powder for the cell mattresses when Jim returned and stopped in the doorway. "Allison is over at the Alamo Saloon, Wyatt. Ab Webster wants 'im out o' there."

"You get that from Webster?"

Jim shook his head. "That German boot-maker's the one that told me. But I dug into it a little. You wanna guess who told him?" Jim screwed a tight smile onto his face and arched an eyebrow. "Bob Wright."

Wyatt stood, put on his coat, and nodded at the gun rack.

"Get a rifle and put plenty o' shells in your pocket. I want you down at the Opera House, taking an angle from the east. Hang back in the doorway and keep your eyes open." Wyatt walked to the door and opened it. "Go tell Bat to take the other angle from the drugstore. I'll go over to Webster's and see what this third-hand complaint is all about."

Jim frowned. "You're not carrying a gun?"

Wyatt patted the bulge in his coat pocket. "Less invitation this way."

Wyatt crossed the plaza diagonally toward Ab Webster's Alamo Saloon. There was no outward sign of unusual activity. The door was closed to the dust, but lighted lamps could be seen inside. The silhouettes of men standing at the bar showed clearly through the window—no more than three or four men.

Stepping up on the boardwalk Wyatt paused and listened. He heard nothing more than the clink of glasses and the normal murmur of conversations coming from inside the saloon. Looking one building west, he saw Bob Wright staring back at him through the front window of his clothing store. When Wyatt walked toward him, Wright widened his eyes, turned, and moved deeper into the store.

As Wyatt stepped through Wright's door, he saw the councilman busily smoothing the buckled creases in a long spool of muslin. Even when Wyatt crossed the room—his boots tapping a blatant cadence on the bare boards—Wright did not look up. Stopping at the cutting table Wyatt tossed down his hat, and Wright jumped as if he'd been surprised by a sharp cattle prod.

"Buy you a drink, Bob?" Wyatt said quietly.

Wright quickly wadded the unwrapped muslin to the spool and shoved it beneath the table. Without looking at Wyatt he walked to his cash register, where he busied himself with a stack of receipts.

"Didn't know you drank," he said, his voice dry and cracking.

"I might on special occasions."

This brought up Wright's guarded face. "And this is one?"

Wyatt stood as still as a store mannequin. "Could be."

The two men stared at one another without a word between them. Wright was first to lower his gaze.

"Thought you might want to step over to the Alamo with me," Wyatt said. "See what we might find over there . . . to quench our thirsts."

Wright swallowed audibly and began shuffling through the papers again. "I can't get away now," he said irritably. "Some other time."

Wyatt watched the man's discomfort turn to anger as the merchant kept sorting uselessly through the same papers. Wyatt looked slowly around the store at the shelves filled with various items of clothing.

"Prob'ly make a good livin' at this, don't you, Bob?"

Wright lost his count again, hastily gathered up the papers, and shut them in a cigar box. "I do all right," he snapped. "Why?"

Wyatt pursed his lips. "Ever hire on anyone special . . . to help out with special problems?"

Wright straightened a ledger and pencil on his counter. "I don't know what you mean. Look . . . I can't have a drink now. I have some work I have to do." He opened the box again, snatched out the stack of papers, and flattened them on the counter. Licking a finger he began flipping through the pages with a practiced dexterity that did not match the disconcerted expression on his face.

When Wyatt walked to the door and stood looking out at the street, he heard the papers stop rustling behind him. Pushing Bob Wright from his thoughts, he took in the scene on the plaza. The traffic on Front Street was typical for a late morning: an empty wagon from Zimmerman's lumberyard returning to its livery; laborers from the stockyards walking in pairs toward the diners; a skinny boy loading boxes into a wagon in front of the grocery; two women carrying covered trays of food toward Doc McCarty's infirmary.

Across Second Avenue Wyatt spotted Bat Masterson hurrying into the district attorney's office. Inside a minute Bat reappeared holding a shotgun. Moving more cautiously now, he eased into the shadowed doorway of the post office and nodded to two men who walked past him under the awning.

Wyatt stepped from Wright's store out onto the boardwalk, leaving the door open behind him. Turning immediately left into the Alamo, he saw Ab Webster behind his bar conversing with a customer. Webster looked up, his eyes open wide and bright as candle flames.

"Everything all right here, Ab?"

Webster motioned Wyatt closer and leaned over the bar. When Wyatt approached, the barman lowered his voice to a whisper.

"Clay Allison, the gunman . . . he was in here. He was heeled and talking about running the law officers into their holes."

"Where is he now?"

"Don't know." Webster pointed east. "Paid for his drink, then breezed out o' here like a ghost. Might've walked down to the Long Branch."

Wyatt stared at the saloon owner for several heartbeats. "Did you send word for me to come see about Allison?"

Ab Webster's face twisted into a mass of creases. "What? I never sent for nobody . . . not today anyway."

Wyatt nodded once. The other men in the room watched him with their drinks held suspended in their hands. In the complete stillness of the saloon Wyatt heard laughter coming from next door at the Long Branch. He walked to Webster's front entrance and paused with a hand on the swinging door. Marshal Bassett now stood in the alleyway on the east side of the post office, shotgun in hand. Duffy, a sheriff's deputy, was on the west. Bat had relocated to the corner of Wright's store.

Wyatt pushed out the door, turned left toward the Long Branch, and came face to face with a lean man dressed in a dark blue blouse and gray trousers. His slate eyes were as empty as spent shell casings. A sparse beard spread across his scarred cheeks. A bone-handled Colt's jutted from a holster strapped high on his waist.

Neither man spoke. Watching Wyatt carefully, Allison sidestepped toward the building, his movements uneven as he favored one leg. The boot of that leg turned inward a few degrees, like a badger's. Letting indifference dominate his face, Allison slouched against the wall and began rolling a cigarette. He appeared at once relaxed and defiant. After licking the paper and sealing the tobacco, he smiled.

"You the law around this pig's sty?" He continued to look down at his cigarette, his thick southern drawl like the lazy slither of a fat snake.

Wyatt stood relaxed, his weight evenly distributed over both legs. He eased a hand into his coat pocket.

"I am."

"Well, well," Allison purred and looked up. He allowed an amused smile to tighten his lips into a shallow vee. "Which one are you?"

"The one you need to see," Wyatt said.

Allison nodded as if he had expected such a reply. When he pinched the rolled smoke in his lips and smiled around it, the cigarette rose like an erection. Wyatt stepped beside Allison, so close that they stood shoulder touching shoulder, each with his back to the wall.

"On your way out of town?" Wyatt asked.

Allison smiled again, this time showing his teeth. They were small and surprisingly white in orderly rows.

"What makes you say that?" he said, with feigned curiosity.

Wyatt stared into the formless gray void of the man's eyes. It was like looking into an abandoned well of tainted water.

"You're wearing a gun. That's against the law unless you're comin' or leavin'. I figure you're leavin'."

Allison breathed a whispery laugh that hissed through his teeth. "You ain't even heeled, so I can't see what you'd have to say about it."

Wyatt's expression remained unchanged. "I got everything to say about it. You're leaving."

Allison smiled and eased his right hand toward the butt of his pistol. Feeling the movement, Wyatt, with his right hand gripped on the Colt's in his pocket, pivoted toward Allison and pressed the muzzle of his revolver through the pocket into the gunman's gut. The gun barrel pressed against Allison like a railroad spike about to be sledged into his spine.

The surly man had taken hold of his weapon but stayed his move. Now his face went slack, losing all its defiance for the moment. Realizing his error, Allison parted his lips, causing the cigarette to dangle. His nostrils flared rhythmically like the slow wing beat of a dying moth. He tried to affect a smirk, but his embarrassment was as obvious as the salty scent lifting off his skin.

In the silence as they stared at one another, the crisp *click, click* of the hammer of Wyatt's Colt's delivered its own message. The hard muzzle of the gun drove deeper into Allison's belly, and all traces of humor left the gunman's face as his hands slowly rose to the height of his shoulders.

"Put your right hand inside your shirtfront," Wyatt ordered.

Allison plucked the unlighted cigarette from his mouth and flipped it into the street. Then, sliding his fingers between two buttons at his chest, he stood like a man posing for a photographic portrait. His eyes narrowed as he spotted the lawmen across the street and at the east end of the block.

"That hand comes out of your shirt," Wyatt said quietly, "and I'll open up your gut." With his left hand he lifted the gunman's revolver and stuffed it in the other coat pocket. Then he backed away two steps.

Something new registered in Allison's face, and Wyatt realized the gunman was weighing the odds. If Allison carried a backup gun, Wyatt could not see it. The mercenary's cool gaze turned to amusement, and he cracked a crooked grin. Wyatt had heard the rumors that Clay Allison was crazy. Or maybe he was one of those rogue saddlers who simply didn't care whether he lived or died.

The moment hung like a stone just before it's dropped into the dark eye of a well. Then, just as quickly as the wild look in the killer's eyes had flared, it snuffed out. His face turned guarded. He filled his chest with air, and then he let it seep out slowly, the sound like a hopeless sigh.

"Guess I *am* leaving town," Allison said, chuckling. With his thumb he pointed over his shoulder in the direction where Jim Masterson approached along the boardwalk. Allison cleared his throat and swallowed. "My horse is just around the corner."

"Keep your hand in your shirt until you reach your horse," Wyatt instructed. "You turn around . . . I'll kill you."

Allison touched the tip of his tongue to his upper lip and raised his chin to point toward Wyatt. "What about my gun?"

"Just walk," Wyatt said.

Allison's eyebrows lifted as he pushed away from the wall. He pursed his lips and blew a stream of air like a man who had forgotten how to whistle.

"I'm going now."

"Go ahead," Wyatt said and removed from his pocket his

right hand with the Colt's. His motion was smooth, slow, and efficient as he leveled the barrel at Allison's chest. The hammer was still fully cocked.

When Allison turned and walked, Jim stepped off the walkway into the street and stood like a sentry with the shotgun held diagonally across his torso. He looked briefly at Wyatt, as though instructions might be forthcoming, but Wyatt's attention on the visiting gunman was complete.

Clay Allison turned the corner at Beatty and Kelley's restaurant, his arm still awkwardly bent and his hand remaining inside his blouse. Wyatt stepped into the street and stood with his body turned sideways to the empty corner where the gunman had disappeared. The Colt's hung down beside Wyatt's leg.

In half a minute the sound of a horse's hooves clopped on the side street and Allison reappeared on a dappled gray stud. Pulling up the reins with his left hand, he stopped and looked at Wyatt. Half smiling, he glanced at Jim Masterson in the street and then at the three officers who had moved closer from their assigned posts. Then, squinting at the sky, he smiled openly, like a man who had just remembered a good story from his past.

"I don't ordinarily come out on the short end of these things," he said easily. He leveled the smile on Wyatt and made a little two-fingered salute that he thrust forward from the brim of his hat.

"I'd say you came out pretty good," Wyatt said, "considering the alternative."

Allison's body bounced once with a silent laugh. "Yeah, well . . ."

"You make any money off this deal?" Wyatt asked.

Allison shrugged and allowed a passing glance at Wright's store. "Man's got to earn a living somehow," he drawled, his tone almost friendly.

Wyatt slipped his revolver back into his pocket, walked to the gray, and opened one of Allison's saddlebags. Into this he stuffed the confiscated pistol and lashed the leather flap back in place.

"Go earn it somewhere else. You ever come back to Dodge City . . . I'll shoot you on sight."

Allison gave Wyatt a long, hard look. When he got no rise out of Wyatt, he smiled at the other officers who had gathered. There were faces crowded in the doorway and windows of the Long Branch, but he paid them no mind. Leaning, he made a *chick, chick* sound in the side of his mouth. The horse wheeled around and started at a slow walk paralleling the railroad tracks along Front Street.

"Cocky sonovabitch, ain't he?" Bat said as the backup lawmen assembled around Wyatt.

" 'Loco' is more like it," said Bassett. "He'd kill his mother if there was good money in it."

Wyatt gave a nod to the men gathered in the street. Walking past them, he stepped up on the boardwalk in front of Wright's store, where he stopped before the window. On the other side of the glass, Bob Wright stood staring back, pale as a sheet. The councilman opened his mouth as if to speak but then thought better of it. Briskly he turned and straightened the drape of a veil covering the blank face of a female mannequin.

Wyatt turned on his heel and began crossing the plaza, making his way steadily toward the city offices.

CHAPTER 19

Late summer, 1878: Dodge City

Wyatt walked his rounds in the heat of the September night, first checking the shops and saloons on the north side of the deadline. Walking up the side street by the Dodge House, he passed the hotel livery and paused to consider the private homes lined up along Walnut Street. Here was a class of people who seemed to have set their course by a star that made their lives more stable, more secure than that of a policeman on the frontier. They had families. And their children would probably follow along on the same path and bypass the suffering that seemed to wait in ambush for those men without a good course of action defined for them.

At thirty years old, Wyatt stared at these upper-class homes, lighted from within, and wondered about their interior lives, considering them to be as foreign to him as sovereign nations on another side of the world. He realized his aspirations for higher office had transformed from an unspecified plan waiting somewhere in the future to a nagging sense of urgency. Charlie Bassett, he figured, would make a bid for county sheriff again, now that he was eligible after a term as city marshal. The county tax collecting carried out by that office made the sheriff's badge pure gold. Wyatt could probably slip right into the marshal's job. No one was better positioned for it.

As chief enforcer, Wyatt had shown that he could control the rowdy Texans, often with only words and only as a last resort by the blow of a pistol barrel to the head of a troublemaker. The people of Dodge had seen him perform his duties, but that witnessing was a double-edged sword, he knew. Ordinary town folk wanted to be protected, but they did not want to be an audience to the ruthless cracking of a man's skull. That was the irony of it all. A foot soldier like a deputy or an assistant marshal was forced to advertise his violent reputation. A reputation served him well in this regard, but it set him apart from the higher class of citizens.

Meanwhile a marshal or a sheriff was seen mostly at his desk or attending community affairs. He even sent his underlings to collect the taxes, which gave him some distance from the unpopularity of that stigma. When elections came around, people were probably more inclined to vote for the administrative version of a lawman over a head basher. They seemed to forget that it was all the head bashing that put a lid on the city. If an administrator was polished enough, Wyatt had learned, he could take credit for the law and order in a community without connecting himself to the brutal nature of enforcing it on the street.

As he did with most issues that grated together in his mind, Wyatt decided people would have to come around to his way of thinking. He was not going to be a hypocrite. He also knew he was not a politician. He didn't have the pretention for it, just as he had no intention of loosening his grip on his duties for the sake of votes.

But he would be the marshal. The citizens of Dodge would have to understand that he would pour just as much proficiency into his administrating as he had into his enforcing. Once he wore the marshal's badge, he would leverage that position into something more profitable outside of the police business. He had convinced himself of this plan for years, but now he was determined to prove it.

Heading back to the business district, he crossed the railroad tracks in the plaza and strolled past the open saloons on the south side of the line. Walking the boardwalk, he moved in and out of the lights spilling from these establishments, their interiors flashing with scenes that seemed to be part of a never-ending story that looped around on itself without promise of a proper ending.

Through his experience here in Dodge, he could assess a room through a window and just that quickly check for any trouble. This late in the season there was little to be found. But he stopped in front of the Lady Gay, leaned against the window frame, and observed for several minutes. Doc was there, a drawer of poker chips sitting before him at the faro table, his quizzical smile giving away none of his internal thoughts.

The Lady Gay Saloon had been the unofficial headquarters for most of the cattle outfits for the season . . . and, therefore, the most frequently visited point on the rounds of the law officers of Dodge City. Only a few hangers-on of the Texas crews remained in town, but Wyatt had instructed the deputies to maintain their vigilance . . . especially here. The season's crime record had been a good one, and Wyatt intended to keep it that way.

Stepping into the main room he moved to the bar, leaned an elbow on the polished countertop, and observed the clientele. Three soldiers drank whiskey with Kate Elder at the far end of the bar. Behind the bar at a small table sat the manager dipping a pen into a tiny inkwell and scratching figures into a ledger. Never looking up from his work he asked questions of the bartender, who stood beside him and counted whiskey bottles by poking his finger at the air as he inventoried the shelves.

At the west wall, five drovers played poker at a table, each man dressed in a natty new outfit and well on his way to intoxication. A sixth Texan sat off to one side on a bench, his hatless head angled back to the wall as he snored loudly through a mouth hanging open like the bore of a cannon barrel. Two of these Texans had felt the sting of Wyatt's gun barrel late one night outside the Varieties, but on this night every customer seemed as docile as a gray-whiskered dog.

Zimmerman from the hardware store was talking business with two men at a front table. In the middle of the room a few merchants laughed together over a round of beers. In the back of the saloon where Doc ran his game, a blue-gray cloud of cigar smoke had spread and flattened against the ceiling.

Holliday smiled for his customers and spoke with his soft Southern charm as he loaded the card box. Wyatt could not hear the words, but judging by the faces of the players at the lay-out, it was evident the dentist took his side profession seriously. For a time Wyatt kept his eyes on the thin gambler with an unpredictable demeanor, trying to discern the man's shoulder holster and nickel-plated shooter. Wyatt couldn't see it, but he knew it was there. Holliday had called it right, Wyatt knew: without that gun, the skin-and-bones dentist would be easy pickings for any man who ran up against him.

Kate Elder disengaged from the knot of soldiers at the bar and walked to the back of the room. Standing behind Doc she put her hands lightly on his thin shoulders and leaned to whisper in his ear. Holliday laughed and looked up as he patted Kate's behind. When he saw Wyatt, his perfunctory smile snapped off and was replaced by one more earnest. When Kate glimpsed Wyatt, her pouty face hardened like porcelain.

"Wyatt!" Holliday called and waved him over.

Wyatt nodded and signaled for the bartender. The big-bellied pourer waddled along the creaking floorboards for the length of the bar and stood before him with both eyebrows raised like a question.

"Any trouble tonight, Cyrus?"

The barman narrowed his eyes and pursed his lips as though he had to think about his answer. "No, sir. No trouble." He waited, arching his eyebrows again. "How 'bout some hot coffee, Marshal?"

Wyatt nodded once. "That'd be good." He pointed to the faro game. "I'll be back at Holliday's table."

As he approached the gamblers, Wyatt noted Kate's glare of growing hostility, but he only nodded her way and then ignored her. He watched Holliday pull the winning card from the box, and a groan made its way around the players gathered there.

"Well . . . no winners this time. Sorry, friends." Doc allowed a wicked smile. "All the more reason to stick it to the house next time . . . right, gentlemen?"

He gathered the chips from the lay-out and dropped them into the dealer's till. Then he pushed back his chair.

"Take over for me a moment, will you, dahlin'," Doc said as he stood. Pulling Kate down into his seat, he made a partial bow from the waist toward the players. "If you gentlemen would excuse me for a few minutes?"

Kate glared at Doc's back, but her hands began to take over the dealer's job as if by instinct. Then, like an actress changing roles, she smiled at her customers and offered the kinds of bawdy pleasantries that make men smile and temporarily forget their gambling troubles.

Coming around the table Doc clapped a hand to Wyatt's shoulder and turned him toward a back corner where an empty table sat in the dark of an unlighted lamp. Wyatt took off his coat and laid it on the bench at the wall. As soon as they had settled into chairs, the bartender arrived with Wyatt's coffee and set it down.

" 'Preciate it, Cyrus," Wyatt said.

"Anything for you, Holliday?"

Doc looked up at the portly barman and delivered a thin

smile. "Did you mean to say 'Doctor Holliday'?"

Cyrus looked from Doc to Wyatt and then whipped a towel from his apron strap and began to clean the fingers of one hand a finger at a time. He took in a deep breath and began again.

"You care for a drink, Doctor Holliday?"

From his inside coat pocket Doc produced his flask and smiled as if he were greeting an old friend. "If you'll just fill that with bourbon for me, please. You can put it on my tab." Holliday smiled as he dug into a vest pocket. "And here's a little token of my appreciation for your part in the dissipation of my body." He held up a dollar, pinching the coin between two outstretched fingers like a forceps.

Cyrus cupped his hand under the gratuity, and Doc let it fall. With a meek smile that seemed equal parts apology and gratitude, Cyrus made an awkward bow and started away in his wobbling gait.

Wyatt sipped coffee and then set the cup aside, pushing it to arm's length across the table. The brew tasted like it had been boiled in a rusty can.

"How's your dentist work goin', Doc?"

Doc laughed quietly, but his expression was one of contempt. "Well, it's not quite what I had in Atlanta."

Wyatt nodded toward the gaming tables, where Kate kept the players in good spirits. "So is this your supplementary income?"

Doc laughed again, and still there was no trace of humor. "Oh, I'd say it's the other way around." He pointed toward Kate, who managed Doc's lay-out with deft and fluid movements of her slender hands. "And there sits my lovely partner in crime."

"Looks like she knows what she's doin'," Wyatt said.

Doc widened his eyes at the understatement. "She's half wildcat and all business," he said, watching her with an amused smile. Coughing wetly, he hunched forward and produced his ever-present linen handkerchief to wipe his mouth. As always he waited to see if a spate of coughing would follow. When it seemed his chest had settled, Doc folded the handkerchief and put it away.

Cyrus returned the flask to the table, and, apparently expecting nothing more from Holliday, he looked at Wyatt. "Coffee all right?"

"I've had better," Wyatt said.

Cyrus's face seemed to compress with confusion. "Bring you anything else then, Marshal?"

Wyatt shook his head and then pointed at the abandoned cup. "You can take that with you."

The barman lifted the cup, frowned into the dark liquid, and then sipped off the top. "Tastes all right to me."

Wyatt stared at him for several seconds. "Maybe we just have different standards, Cyrus."

As the bartender walked back to the bar, Doc began to chuckle in earnest. "You know, Wyatt, everybody doesn't expect you to tell the truth all the time." When he got no response, he laughed again, leaned forward, clapped his hand to Wyatt's forearm, and delivered a friendly jostle. "But that's one of the things I like about you, you know. A man will always know exactly where he stands with Wyatt Earp."

"The truth always seems easiest, Doc."

"Maybe so," Doc said and cocked his head as if he had heard a good joke. "But it'll bring you just as many enemies as it will friends." Right away, Doc's face sobered. "On the other hand, I'll warrant those friends might be willing to walk through hell for you."

Wyatt pursed his lips. "Wouldn' know. Never had to ask anybody to do that."

Doc nodded and chuckled at Wyatt's answer. "I doubt you'd even need to ask 'em, Wyatt."

Cyrus appeared again, carefully balancing a new cup on a saucer, which he lowered to the table. His movements reminded Wyatt of the explosives setters he had known on the railroad crew in Wyoming. This new porcelain set was adorned with a fancy, floral pattern in browns and blues.

"My wife had some fresh-made upstairs," Cyrus offered. "See if this'n here is any better."

Wyatt picked up the cup by its tiny ear-shaped handle and sampled the replacement coffee. Setting it down, he began to nod.

"Good," he said.

Cyrus looked like a man who had bucked the tiger for all the money on the table. When he left, there was a little less waddle in his walk.

Holliday beamed. "I rest my case, suh."

Wyatt studied the dentist's self-satisfied expression and drank more of the coffee.

"I hear you had a run-in with Clay Allison," Doc probed and gave Wyatt one of his wry, enigmatic smiles.

Wyatt hinged a hand partway from the table and then returned it palm down again. "Didn' amount to much."

Doc curled his lip and shook his head. "Allison is a vile abomination . . . a degenerate who has no regard for human life . . . not even his own. I would think any encounter with him would be a little more noteworthy than that."

"How'd you hear about it? There wasn't any mention of it in the newspapers."

Keeping his elbows on the table, Doc spread his hands to the room. "I gamble with the Texas boys. A man can hear a lot of news that way. Most of it not good." Doc twisted his smile into a conspiratorial smirk. "So what happened?"

"I run 'im out o' town," Wyatt said plainly.

"Did he misbehave?"

Wyatt turned the fine chinaware cup in its matching saucer. "I reckon I run 'im out before he had a chance to misbehave."

Doc's eyebrows shot up. "And he just left . . . just like that?"

"He left."

Doc waited for more, but Wyatt relaxed in his chair and offered nothing. He picked up the cup with both hands and worked on his coffee.

"No gun play?" Doc probed.

Wyatt shook his head.

Now Doc sat forward to better stare into Wyatt's ice-blue eyes. "You convinced Allison to leave without resorting to Mr. Colt's almighty equalizer?"

Wyatt set down the cup and tilted his head to one side, just enough gesture to show he had not revealed the whole story. "Allison was lookin' into the muzzle of my Colt's when he made the decision to leave."

Doc smiled and drank from his flask. "Ah . . . yes," he sighed, "a most poignant persuasion." Then his brow furrowed. "Well, something as exciting as that should have found its way into print. I thought the newspaper editors in Dodge ate up stories like that and served them out with a manure shovel."

Now Wyatt's attention turned to Doc to let his friend see the disgust in his expression. "It appears some things don't make it to the papers if they got to go through Bob Wright first."

"Wright?" Doc repeated. "The storekeeper?"

"And town councilman," Wyatt added.

Doc frowned. "What's his stake in all this?"

Wyatt turned his attention to the faro game, but he was seeing the image of Bob Wright standing wide eyed behind the glass of his store window. "I reckon he's one of those enemies you were talkin' about."

Doc frowned again and followed Wyatt's eyes to Kate at the lay-out. When she shot him an impatient glare, he flattened his pale hands on the table and pushed himself up.

"Duty calls," Doc announced with the droll insouciance of a jaded soldier.

"Take care, Doc," Wyatt said and leaned to his coat to check the pockets for a cigar. Finding none he finished the coffee, stood, and was surprised to see Doc still standing next to him.

"I don't care how goddamned important a man thinks he is," Doc said quietly, his voice as personable as Wyatt had ever heard it. "If he's the enemy of my friend . . . then he's my enemy, as well."

"Forget it, Doc," Wyatt said and patted Doc on the upper arm. Under Wyatt's hand the frail dentist's shoulder felt like a sack of sticks. "You already saved my skin once. I figure I'm the one in debt to you."

"Friends don't keep score, Wyatt. You ever need my help, all you've got to do is just ask."

Moving back to his faro table, Doc changed places with Kate and quickly assumed his professional deportment, talking to the players as if he had never left the game. Wyatt stopped at the bar and pointed at the shelf to the cigar brand he favored. Cyrus brought down two, and Wyatt laid down his money.

"Tell your wife she makes good coffee."

"Yes, sir. I'll do just—" Cyrus's mouth stopped moving, and he froze in a frown as he stared over Wyatt's shoulder.

Wyatt half turned to see Kate Elder approaching him, her eyes fixed on him and glowing with an internal heat. Pivoting on his heel he straightened to face whatever was coming.

"Kate," he said by way of a tentative greeting.

She stopped so close to him that he could see individual specks of powder she had applied to her face. Her breathing came more quickly than it should have.

"I vant to talk vit' you . . . alone."

"All right," Wyatt said.

Kate turned her hot-coal eyes on Cyrus, and the barman closed his mouth and moved away. She pivoted to the bar where Wyatt would shield her from the back of the room where Doc gambled.

"When I leaf da Earp *empire,* I leaf it for goodt! I vant it to stay dat vay! Do you understandt?"

"Can't say as I do," Wyatt replied.

"I vant you to stay da hell away from Doc. We don't need anyt'ing you or any uff da Earps have godt."

Wyatt looked into the mirror behind the bar, and in the reflection he watched Doc dole out two bills to a winner. By the look on Holliday's face, it was clear to Wyatt that Kate's tirade was a private one Doc knew nothing about. When Wyatt turned back to Kate, she appeared ready to spit.

"I got nothin' to do with my brother's whorin' business," he said quietly. "Never did. Anything that ever happened between the two o' you . . . or Bessie . . . it's got nothin' to do with me."

Kate smirked. "You men haff godt no idea vhat it's like to whore all da night with a bunch of stinking strangers. But you make all da rules and tell us when we godt to do dis and godt to do dat! Don't you?"

Wyatt looked down at his boots briefly and tried to muster up the patience he had once needed with Mattie. Then he looked Kate squarely in the face.

"I don't reckon James forced you to whore for 'im. I reckon you made up your own mind 'bout that."

"Vhat else vas I to do?" she hissed. "You tell me!" Leaning to her right she looked past Wyatt to the table where Doc plied his trade. When she focused again on Wyatt, her face tightened, and her voice lowered to a raspy whisper. "You godt-damn men . . . you Earps . . . and everyone like you . . . you don't know vhat it is like for us girls in dese rail-roadt towns. Da men make all da godt-damn rules."

"Men gotta follow rules, too, Kate," Wyatt said and with his forefinger tapped the badge pinned to his blouse. "And they hire someone to make sure they do."

She glanced at the metal shield, spewed air through her lips, and coughed up a cynical laugh. "And you t'ink dat badge make you somet'ing better dhan da rest uff us?"

Wyatt stood quietly before the spiteful woman, taking her insults like a boxer with his hands tied behind his back. Conflict with a female was nothing like the confrontations he was accustomed to facing as an officer of the law. He didn't know how to fight what he could not understand.

"Kate, there ain't—"

"Just stay avay from Doc!" she said in a rush. "He don't need to be mixed up vit' you Earps!" She rose up on her tiptoes, leaned toward Wyatt, and stabbed her finger to his chest. "You don't control Doc." She turned the finger on herself and tapped her breastbone where it showed above the lacy border of her dress. "Doc and I . . . vee are toget'er . . . vee decide vhat vee do."

Wyatt felt a strange chill pass through him, as if a window had opened up somewhere behind him. He turned his head and caught Cyrus and the manager staring at him from the far end of the bar. The bookkeeper returned to his work, but the bartender stood stock-still holding a whiskey bottle by the neck in each hand. Now Cyrus seemed to awake from a trance, and he set the bottles on the counter before him and began clinking glass as he rearranged other bottles on the shelves.

Turning back to Kate, Wyatt began shaking his head. "I got no control over Doc, Kate. He's the one citizen in Dodge I gave some leeway on the gun ordinance. Seems to me I—"

"Dat's right . . . he safe your life dat night at da Comique. So now vhy don't you repay da favor and leaf him be?"

When she brushed by him to march toward the back of the

room, Wyatt felt the space around him open up as if he had been loosed from a trap. He watched her angry stride smooth out to approach Doc's table. As for Doc, he was completely absorbed in his game.

Cyrus made his way slowly along the bar and stopped behind Wyatt. He leaned both forearms on the countertop and quietly observed the faro game until Wyatt made a motion to leave.

"You ask me," Cyrus mumbled in a deep monotone, "that lady is a little tetched in the head." When Wyatt turned to face the bartender, Cyrus was staring at Kate and shaking his head in tiny increments. "I wouldn' worry about what she told you, Marshal." He pushed his lower lip forward, shook his head more deliberately, and then turned his gaze on Wyatt. "You ask me, she ain't to be trusted."

"Why do you say that?" Wyatt asked.

Cyrus frowned and shrugged. "She'll say whatever comes into her head if it'll git 'er what she wants."

Wyatt rested an elbow on the bar and watched Kate laugh with Doc's customers. "I got no idea what she wants."

Cyrus laughed quietly and nodded toward the faro game. "Wants *him*," he whispered, "all to herself."

"Who . . . Doc? She's got 'im, don't she?"

Cyrus gave Wyatt a skewed smile. "Doc thinks a lot o' you. Talks about you. She don' never seem to like it when he does."

Wyatt turned to grip both hands on the bar. He stared at Cyrus and lowered his voice to a bare whisper.

"What're you sayin'?"

Cyrus shrugged again but held a confident gleam in his eyes. "I know it don't make sense, but you can't always make sense out o' some women." He allowed a conservative smile. "She's jealous."

Wyatt frowned. "Of me?"

Cyrus's expression turned sly. He lifted an eyebrow and nodded once. After watching Wyatt's face for a time, he began to shake his head.

"There ain't no logic to it, so don't even try."

A collective groan arose from Doc's customers. Doc, himself, was smiling as he picked up the chips from his lay-out.

"I won't," Wyatt said and walked out of the Lady Gay.

CHAPTER 20

Fall, 1878: Dodge City to Cimarron River

In the predawn of a cool October night, Wyatt lay in bed staring at the water stains on the ceiling of Lillie Beck's hotel room. He wondered how long a man could hold a job like his in Dodge City and still fool himself into thinking it might lead to something more profitable. Or, for that matter, how long could he expect to live? There were only so many moments of grace in his profession—like the night Doc Holliday had saved him from a fate like Ed Masterson's.

He rolled his head to one side and looked at Lillie, deep in slumber. She was young, not yet prey to such thoughts about mortality. He wondered why he didn't want her more than he did. She could have any man within earshot of her angelic voice . . . or close enough to appreciate the allure of her finely sculpted face. If an admirer got as close as Wyatt was now, there was no question. She was the kind of woman who caused practical men to dream beyond their means.

Lillie had no ambitions, Wyatt decided. Even Mattie had carried inside her a hunger to get to a better place. Wyatt remembered the day she had fled James's brothel and set out across the frozen prairie. He could not imagine Lillie doing something like that. Lillie Beck had already arrived at some complacent, self-deluded destination with which he could never be satisfied. Wyatt wanted more, he realized, than Dodge City could give.

Unable to sleep, he sat up on the edge of her bed and set his feet to the cold floor. His clothes were folded neatly on her chair. The symmetrical drape of shirt and coat on the chairback was like a stranger in the room, mocking him for his failures. He had watched Lillie arrange his clothes as she had described to him the new Celtic song she was learning for her performances. He had not understood most of what she had said, but he doubted she would grasp the meaning of much of his police work, if ever he tried to explain it to her.

Behind him, she stirred in the sheets, stretching and purring like a cat. "Are you leaving, Wyatt?"

He reached to the chair for his trousers and began pulling them on. "I'm still on duty, remember?"

"This is your duty, too, Wyatt." She poked him with a long-nailed finger and giggled, and then her hand dropped to the sheets and was still. Within seconds the rhythm of her breathing told him she was asleep.

He had just tucked the tails of his blouse into the waistband of his trousers when a gunshot broke the quiet of the night, close enough to be in the next block east. Then three more shots followed, the reports almost blurring into one sound. Wyatt finished dressing and took his revolver from the top of Lillie's bureau. Just before he closed the door to her room, he heard a light airy snore from the bed. For Lillie, those gunshots may as well have been in Topeka.

As soon as Wyatt stepped into the street behind the hotel, he saw Jim Masterson running around the corner of the Varieties. Jim slowed when he saw Wyatt, and his hand took a grip on the revolver at his hip.

"Wyatt?"

"Where'd it come from?" Wyatt called out.

Masterson visibly relaxed, released his hold on his weapon, and approached. "I was on the other side of the tracks." He pointed east. "Sounded like this block."

Together they left Bridge Street and walked into the alley behind the Great Western Hotel. Several lamps were lighted in the rooms at the back of the building. When they reached the corner of the hotel, Wyatt slipped his gun from his waistband and outstretched his free hand to clamp down on Jim's arm. Masterson stopped and turned a taut face to Wyatt.

"What?" Masterson whispered.

Wyatt pointed with his gun toward the back of the lot where Mayor Kelley's squat cottage hunkered in the dark. As they got closer, they heard a high-pitched wailing. In the open back door of the little wood-frame building a woman stood in her nightgown, fingering the tie cord knotted at her collar.

"Who's there?" Wyatt called.

"Dora's dead," the woman cried out. "Someone shot through the wall and killed her." She tried to say more, but her words trailed off into a pitiful sobbing.

"Fannie?" Jim said. "Is that you?"

Shivering, she collapsed by degrees in the doorway, her cheek pressed into the jamb, forcing her open mouth into a skewed oval. Her eyes were clamped shut so tightly that three deep lines etched across her brow. Tears streaked down her face as she moaned into the emptiness of the night.

Jim crouched to check her for a wound. Wyatt moved past them into the cottage, his gun extended before him.

"Mayor Kelley?" Wyatt called. The dark house was quiet. It smelled of perfume and candle smoke.

"Fannie says he's at the army hospital," Jim called from the door. "Says Dora and her were staying here while he's gone."

A match flared in a front room, and Wyatt made out the figure of a man standing over a candle. He was naked from the waist up, staring back wide-eyed and licking his lips. He approached, carrying the candle before him, the flickering flame illuminating his face.

"Weren't me done the shootin', Marshal. You know me. Name's Wilden. I's with Dora. The shots come from out front. Four of 'em." He pointed back toward the room from which he had emerged. "Dora's in there. Somebody kilt her, sure 'nough."

"How do I know you didn't shoot her?" Wyatt said, putting some iron in his voice.

Wilden was shaking his head even before Wyatt had finished the accusation. "I ain't even got a gun here, Marshal." He gestured toward the back stoop. "You can ask Fannie. She seen me come in."

Wyatt took the candle from the man and walked into the front bedroom, where he found an unmoving mound beneath a bedsheet. A tangle of long hair spread across the pillow, and a dark stain on the sheet glistened black in the candlelight. In the south wall four rough holes were ringed by splinters in the wood. Wyatt combed the hair back from Dora Hand's relaxed face. He felt for breathing with the backs of his fingers, but there was none. He returned to the back doorstep, where Wilden stood barefooted, watching Jim Masterson comfort Fannie. Across the alleyway, two women stood on the rear stoop of the hotel.

"Who did the shootin'?" Wyatt called out, but the women did not reply.

Fannie looked at Wyatt through her tears. "I heard a horse," she sobbed.

Wilden began nodding enthusiastically. "Yeah, I heard it, too . . . and after that first shot, I might'a heard somebody work the lever on a rifle. The rest of the shots were so fast . . . I couldn' be sure."

"Why would anyone want to hurt Dora?" Fannie whimpered to no one in particular. "She was so good."

Wyatt called across the alleyway to the hotel. "I need one o'

218

you to get a doctor! The other come over here and see about Fannie. She'll be needin' you."

Fannie pointed east. "I heard the horse run that way . . . and then I think it went up toward Front Street."

Wyatt stuffed his gun into his waistband and carried the candle around to the front of the house. The bullet holes were erratically grouped. From the position of Dora's bed in the room, he estimated the assassin had shot from horseback—a horse that had probably spooked at the first shot. Returning to the back of the cottage, he dripped wax on the doorstep and perched the candle to light the entranceway.

"Take care of things here, Jim. Keep Wilden with you. Have the girls take Fannie to the hotel. I'm going to have a look around."

He ran out to Front Street and sent two men from the train depot to find Sheriff Masterson and Marshal Bassett. Then just beyond the rails of the side track he stopped. Tethered to an awning post in front of the Long Branch was a familiar stallion, powerfully built with every fine equestrian point that marked a prime racer. On its back was perched a silver-studded saddle with a fancy fringed saddlebag.

Wyatt walked to the saloon window and saw only two customers, who shared a bottle at one of the back tables. Up front, Chalkley Beeson put away whiskey bottles on the shelves behind the bar. Looking back at the drinkers, Wyatt recognized the puckish face of Spike Kenedy. The young Texan sat with his back to the wall. He was a troublesome brat who had spent many a night in the city jail. As the son of a wealthy cattleman, his habit was to throw his father's money at the court fine and pout for a day before finding some way to get himself arrested again. Wyatt had seen Kenedy's recent scrap with Mayor Kelley right here in front of this saloon just a few days before.

Kenedy was dressed in a scarlet shirt adorned with fancy

white embroidery along the bib, a yellow scarf, and tall, studded boots. He downed drinks with a balding man who talked as fast as he poured. The young Texan laughed, stretched his legs before him, and crossed his showy boots at the ankles.

Keeping his eyes on Kenedy, Wyatt entered the saloon and walked to the bar, where Beeson turned at the sound of his boots. Kenedy never once looked his way.

"Wyatt," Beeson said and leaned on the bar. "What's the ruckus out there tonight?"

Wyatt turned his back to Kenedy and lowered his voice. "How long have these boys been here, Chalk?"

Beeson's eyes cut to Kenedy, and his face drew cautious. "Come with me," he whispered.

Wyatt followed the saloonkeeper into the backroom, where Beeson lighted an oil lamp and hunched so close for privacy that Wyatt had to step back from the flowery scent of the man's pomade. Beeson was not a nervous man by nature, but now he leaned in close to Wyatt again and began to whisper in a rush.

"That Kenedy boy was waving his gun and making threats I couldn't understand. He's not as drunk as he wants you to think he is."

"Is he heeled now?"

Beeson's eyes jumped away in thought. "I can't say for certain. He came in a couple of hours ago, started juicing up. He had a Schofield on him then. He left just about a half hour ago and came strolling back in about . . . what . . . maybe ten minutes ahead of you?"

"I don't know, Chalk. I'm asking you."

Beeson shook his head quickly, impatient with his flustered state. "All I know is he's not shown a gun since he came back in. What were those shots about out there?"

"Was Kenedy here when you heard them?"

Chalk frowned, looked away, and rubbed the whiskers on the

side of his face—the sound like fingernails on parchment. "No. Just the other one. The little bald guy and me. That was it. I remember when we heard the sound he and I looked at each other but didn't speak. Kenedy wasn't with him. I'm sure of it."

Wyatt turned his head to the closed door. "Put out the light, Chalk."

Wyatt's gun was in his hand when he stepped out. Kenedy's chair was empty. The other man sat slouched forward with his fleshy cheek pressed flat against the polished wood tabletop. One hand still gripped the empty bottle.

Wyatt tapped the drunk's shoulder with his revolver. The bald man's eyes half opened, and when they tried to focus on Wyatt, his head rose up from the table an inch, and he licked his lips.

"Where is Kenedy?" Wyatt said.

The man lowered his brow over wandering, blurry eyes. "Who?"

Wyatt jerked the man to his feet and slammed him into the wall. A glass-framed picture of the Dodge City Silver Cornet Band rattled on its hook, but Chalk Beeson caught it before it could fall.

"Where's Kenedy!" Wyatt growled. "The man you were drinking with!"

The man winced at the force of Wyatt's words. The fist twisting his shirt collar into a knot threatened to cut off his air.

"He's gone," he squeaked. "I don't know where."

Wyatt pushed the drunk toward Beeson. "Hold him here, Chalk, until I send somebody down for him."

Wyatt hurried out the door to find the stallion gone. One door down at the Alamo Saloon the nightshift bartender swept dust over the threshold onto the boardwalk. When he saw Wyatt, he stopped the motion of his arms and raised his eyebrows with a question.

"Marshal?" he said. "What was all the shooting about?"

"You see a man ride off on a high-strung stallion that was tied here?" Wyatt nodded toward the vacant awning post.

The man set aside his broom on the doorjamb and wiped his hands on his apron as he stepped forward. At the edge of the boardwalk he stopped, looked west, and pointed far down the rail tracks.

"That Kenedy kid with the rich Texas daddy. The one that got into it with the mayor here a while back. He rode out o' here and on down past the lumberyard . . . looked like a swarm o' hornets was on his tail."

Across Front Street beyond the tracks, Wyatt spotted Bat running for the city police building. When Wyatt whistled, the shrill, high-pitched note carried across the plaza, stopping Bat. They met in the street, and Wyatt quickly apprised him of all he had learned.

"Dora is dead?" Bat said, his face stricken.

Wyatt nodded. "Shot through the heart, looks like." He shook his head. "Killed while she was sleeping."

Bat's jaws hardened like rocks. "And you think it was that damned, snot-nosed kid, Kenedy?"

"Last time Kenedy was in town," Wyatt reminded him, "Kelley kicked him out of his saloon, humiliated him on the street. The boy made a poor showing of it."

Bat cursed and turned steely eyes down the street. "That's a damned fast horse he's on. The sonovabitch will be out of our jurisdiction before the sun is up. Let's go see Judge Cook about getting a federal appointment."

Rufus Cook was quick with a warrant but uncertain as to his authority in appointing a federal marshal. Standing in his library in his nightgown, he combed through law books and muttered to himself as he thumbed over pages. The long wait stiffened Wyatt's back and rankled Bat into pacing the floor.

"Goddammit, Rufus!" Bat finally erupted. "We're losin' too much time!"

Cook, his patience clearly waning in this too-early hour, pinned his finger on a page and looked up at the lawmen. "Look, dammit, I've got no choice in this other than to go through the proper channels. You can't jump from county to federal authority at the drop of a hat. Just give me a—"

"If you can't find a law, then make one up!" Bat spat and spun partway around to fling his arm to point south. "Rufus, right now I'm thinking Ford County extends all the goddamn way to Mexico!"

Exasperated, Judge Cook leaned both arms on his desk and glared at Bat. "I've issued the warrant," he scolded. "That's the best I can do!" He frowned at the window as if he could see out into the night where the killer of Dora Hand was galloping hard across the prairie. "Both of you go do whatever it is you think you've got to do. We'll try to sort out all the legalities on this later."

Wyatt picked up the warrant, folded it, and sidled between the judge and the young sheriff. Facing Bat, he spoke in a calming voice.

"Let's round up who we can and gear up for light traveling."

Bat marched for the door but turned before opening it. "Fix this, Rufus! If you have any trouble figuring it out, I want you to consider what Dora Hand would think about jurisdiction restrictions!" Bat pinned the judge with a fierce gaze. Cook tried to hold Bat's stare, but he was sorely outmatched.

Sheriff Masterson, Assistant Marshal Earp, Marshal Bassett, and deputy sheriffs Billy Tilghman and Will Duffy rode out of town just as the first light spread across the prairie. The tracks led west, but Wyatt placed bets on the fugitive swinging south to ford the Cimarron at Wagon Bed Springs. From there Kenedy could cross into Indian Territory and cut the Texas Trail.

The posse struck out cross-country, riding all day and into the night, when a vicious hailstorm unloaded on them out of the dark sky. Crowding their horses beneath an undercut creek bank, the posse men huddled together with their animals and unrolled their slickers. As they waited out the storm, Wyatt had time to describe in more detail the scene of carnage at Kelley's cottage. By the time he had finished painting the picture of the murder, Bat was so mad he ordered everyone to mount up.

"Our horses need rest," Wyatt reminded. "We keep our heads . . . we might catch Kenedy."

Bat rose up and stood stiff as a board, glaring out at the relentless barrage of ice hammering the dried-up creek bed. Some of the pieces were the size of a hen's egg. Cursing, he kicked at a dirt clod and sent a spray of dust and pebbles out over the ice that had accumulated. Finally, he sat down again, wrapped his arms around knees, and seethed.

"That goddamned, mollycoddled sonovabitch! He thinks he can just take his go-as-you-please rich-daddy's rules with him anywhere he goes. We'd *better* catch him. The whole town's gonna want to watch him swing for killin' Dora."

When the hail slacked off to rain, they buttoned down their slickers and rode through a driving downpour all that second day. Taking periodic rests to spare their horses, they pushed on into pitch dark, finding their way by their knowledge of the country from their days as buffalo hunters. At dawn they silently rejoiced at the sight of the Cimarron River and a cloudless sky ushering in the light. Bassett and the sheriff's deputies stayed at the ford, while Wyatt and Bat checked the riverbanks for a quarter mile in each direction. No horse tracks had been laid down since the rain. It was Tilghman who voiced what no one else would.

"If you figure in what that racehorse of Kenedy's can do, he might 'a got here before the rain stopped."

Wyatt squinted south into the Nations. "If he's out there, we'll keep after 'im until we get 'im. But I don't think he'd 'a lasted that hail storm. Prob'ly holed up like we did and waited out the rain, too. Might still be behind us. Either way, we've got to rest our horses. We're no good on played-out mounts."

They unsaddled and let their horses graze in the steam that lifted off the prairie like a floating gauze. After spreading their wet clothes on rocks at the riverbank, they stretched out in their union suits behind a low mound of earth—all but Masterson, who needed to work his game hip. Within minutes, Basset and Duffy were snoring, and Tilghman began to drowse in and out of sleep. Bat was too angry to rest, but he finally perched next to Wyatt and began recounting all the good deeds Dora Hand had bestowed upon the less fortunate souls of Dodge City over the last year. Wyatt said nothing as he kept watch over the mound.

Less than an hour had passed when Bat saw a change in Wyatt's face. Bat scrambled to his hands and knees, parted a swath of yellowing grass, and peered north over the low berm of earth.

"There he is," Wyatt said.

"Son of a bitch," Bat breathed.

The solitary rider appeared as an apparition on the horizon. He must have been six hundred yards distant. The heat rising off the prairie gave his silhouette a watery shimmer that made positive identification close to impossible. Wyatt crouched behind the mound and shook the others awake.

"If that ain't a goddamned racehorse," Bat whispered, "I'm the fuckin' Queen of Canada."

Wyatt leveled field glasses on the interloper. "Red blouse, yellow scarf, calf-high boots. And the horse has the right markings. That's him." Wyatt turned and considered their loose remuda of horses. "Too late to round up the horses." He bent low and peered over the mound. "He'll need to come to us."

Masterson checked the breech of his Sharps rifle and turned to Bassett. "Charlie, if he gets close enough that I can take a bead on him, stand up and call him down off his horse. If he don't dismount, I'll shoot the murderin' bastard."

Duffy appeared anxious. "What if you miss?"

Wyatt kept his eyes on Kenedy and said, "I'll drop his horse."

Duffy winced as though he had bitten into a sour apple. "I'd rather shoot that damned woman killer through both eyes than touch a hair on that horse."

"Sometimes you do what you can," Wyatt snapped, "not what you want."

Hatless, Wyatt stretched out on his belly and eased his Winchester through the grass until he could sight on Kenedy. Behind him the Cimarron murmured. A flock of cranes cried somewhere high in the vast blue of the sky. The steady wind bristled the desiccated grasses and set up a faint tapping sound. Now three hundred yards off, Kenedy came on, his head nodding with the relaxed rhythm of the horse's walk.

"Keep comin', you sonovabitch," Bat whispered.

Less than a hundred yards out the Texan slowed, and Bat clicked back the hammer of the Sharps. "Get ready, Charlie." Bassett got his feet underneath him. Kenedy prodded his mount on, but now his approach seemed staggered and wary. At sixty yards Wyatt sighted high on the seam of soft muscle bisecting the horse's chest.

At fifty yards, Kenedy reined up and stood in the stirrups as he stared at the five horses grazing by the river. One of the posse horses nickered and lifted its head, acknowledging the distant rider and mount. But for the flow of the river, the world seemed to stop.

"Better do it, Charlie," Wyatt said.

As soon as Bassett stood and yelled, Kenedy's horse reared and pirouetted a quarter turn. Bat had not shot, and Wyatt knew he would never have a better chance than he had now as the horse flailed its forelegs and offered its flank. Aiming high behind the foreleg he squeezed off a shot, the Winchester bucking into his shoulder and shattering the silence all around them. In the next instant Bat's "big-fifty" boomed. Kenedy and the horse crashed to the earth, and the five lawmen were up and running in their long-johns and boots, covering the open ground in long, awkward strides.

Above the swish of their boots in the prairie grass, they heard Kenedy's scream pour out into the prairie. Slowing their pace, they leveled their rifles at their quarry. The Texan's bright red shirt was stained dark and wet at his shoulder. The horse lay on top of him, its finely tuned body now nothing more than a mountain of dead weight.

"Get me out from under here!" Kenedy pleaded, his voice like a panicked child's. "I think my leg is broke!"

For a full minute they struggled to get the enormous corpse of the racer off the Texan's leg, but the weight was too much. Finally they resorted to dragging Kenedy out. When Bat and Tilghman pulled him by his arms, the kid's soul poured out of his mouth in a piercing scream that eventually trailed off in a strangely feminine wail. A fresh spate of blood seeped through his shirt.

"You goddamned sonzabitches!" he shrieked. "Are you tryin' to tear my fuckin' arm off?"

Bat leaned down into Kenedy's face. "I wouldn' care if we pulled you apart right here, you murderin' little piss-ant brat!"

Kenedy's face distorted like a wrung-out rag. "You go to hell! I hope I *killed* that fuckin' Kelley!"

Bat clamped Kenedy's jaw with the heel of his hand and pushed his head back into the grass. He leaned roughly into the boy, putting his face just inches from the killer's.

"You kilt Dora Hand, you bastard! That's who you kilt!"

Kenedy's wild eyes held on Bat, then darted to each man. "Well, damn all of you assholes standin' around in your underwear! Why didn't you kill me!"

Bat spat in the grass. "Well, I tried to, goddammit, and prob'ly would have if your damn horse hadn't reared."

Wyatt stood over the racehorse, assessing its mass of finely proportioned muscle. Within a few days, he knew, the animal's sleek coat would bloat and burst open to the will of coyotes and vultures. It was a senseless waste, just like the killing of Dora Hand had been senseless. Blood painted the grass beneath the fallen steed—a glistening wellspring of bright crimson color. Turning from the carnage, Wyatt walked toward the river to fetch his clothes and round up the horses . . . but mostly to give himself more space to think.

As he neared the river, his mind painted the picture of Dora Hand's lifeless body in the mayor's bed. Like the racehorse, she had been brought down in her prime. Then the mental image seemed to shift through a will of its own, and Dora's face became someone else's. It was his dead wife, Rilla, and the stillborn baby who lay beside her on the bloodied sheets. Here was the memory he had not allowed to take form for years, and now it had found him out at the edge of the Indian Nations where it seemed the world was too vast for a man to be found by even his worst demons.

Stopping at the water's edge he looked up at the great dome of Kansas sky and understood, perhaps for the first time, that the life intended for him had been permanently taken from him in Missouri. And, just as surely, he knew life owed him nothing for that. There was nothing owed to anybody. There was only what life threw at a man and what he did in return to survive it.

If he was going to have any future at all, it was up to him to piece it together. And the sooner the better. There were no guarantees about what time a man had left. He doubted that Ed Masterson or Dora Hand had ever entertained such thoughts. Rilla herself had never spoken of the fragility of life. And his baby son . . . well, of course, he never had the chance to speak any words at all.

Wyatt pulled on his trousers, and as he did he thought of Mattie. She probably knew something about time running out, but he couldn't imagine her finding a way out of the self-imposed misery that had become as much a part of her as her timid voice. He had done little for her, he knew—in spite of the pity she had evoked from him. It was time to cut her loose to the past . . . along with the lingering guilt. At thirty years old, Wyatt knew it was time to find a life that would see him through the rest of his days. He had pressed his luck with a badge long enough.

He dipped his hand into the Cimarron, but, instead of drinking, he watched the water dribble through his fingers and fall back into the murmur of the current. The cobbled surface of the water flashed with mosaics of broken light, all of it unchanged and indifferent to any grandiose gesture he might conceive. He looked back at Bat and the other lawmen, still in their drawers, each preoccupied with some aspect of preparing the prisoner for travel.

This one last job, he thought. *One last duty.* Wyatt gathered up his clothes, untied his lariat from his saddle, and started off to round up the horses. Already he felt that he was in motion toward something better. He just didn't know what.

CHAPTER 21

Late fall, 1878: Dodge City, Kansas

Wyatt, Doc Holliday, and a mercantile broker from Kansas City sat before a spectacled dealer in the Lone Star. The game was five card draw, and Doc was having a good run of the cards, which had propelled him through a gamut of moods—from delight to impertinence and then finally to the indifference that was his most notable reaction to the quirks of fate.

It was a cool night, just an hour before daylight, and the dance area had dwindled to one couple until, in the middle of an Irish ballad, they too quit the floor and shuffled upstairs. The three musicians remained loyal to their performance and continued to play their instruments to a proper ending.

"Wyatt, I have a profound question for you," Doc said in his sly, singsong way of initiating a conversation.

The salesman looked with interest from Doc to Wyatt, but both gamblers kept their eyes on the dealer's hands.

"What's that?" Wyatt mumbled.

Doc lifted a hand and swept it toward the front of the room. "What the hell are we doing in this Godforsaken town?"

Wyatt made a deep humming sound in his chest as he kept watch on the dealer. "Playin' poker, Doc."

Holliday sat back and smirked. "Yes, I'm playing against a city policeman and a corset salesman, both of whom probably make half the wages of the bootblack down at Mueller's. And the three of us are playing against a dealer who's so nervous he's probably forgotten how to palm a card out of his trousers."

The dealer's hands froze and he looked tentatively from Holliday to Wyatt. His face turned as red as a man who had spent a summer lost on the prairie. His mouth opened as though he might reply to defend himself, but he only removed his spectacles and began wiping the lenses with a soft scrap of cloth he kept for that purpose.

"Meanwhile," Doc continued, "all you optimistic gentlemen are trying to squeeze funds from a dentist who has no clientele to speak of." He looked around the room and made a grim smile. "And the four of us are playing the gentlemen's game in a place boasting the charisma of an outhouse."

Doc leaned forward, stacking his bony forearms on the table. He hitched his head toward the lone drover sleeping off his drunken spree on the bench beside the wall.

"The few cowhands still in Dodge are the hard luck down-and-outers with little left in their pockets. And if it's not a stinking cowman it's an out of luck traveling salesman in a cheap suit."

The corset man offered a nervous laugh and smiled at the joke in which he assumed he had played some part. The four men picked up their cards and studied them for a time. After the discards and hits, Doc took the hand and raked the meager winnings toward his stack.

"Shall we call it a night, gentlemen?" Doc said.

Wyatt nodded, and the salesman sat back as though relieved.

Doc leaned on his elbows again. Keeping his attention on Wyatt, he raised both hands a few inches and turned them palms up for an instant before letting them fall back to the table.

"We can't very well make our livings gambling against one another, can we?"

The dealer packed up his accoutrements and shook his head

at Doc's pile of chips. "You're gonna put me out of a job, Holliday."

"Well," Doc said, feigning a stroke of heartfelt empathy. "Maybe you should take up dentistry. There's an office set up at the Dodge House. You could move right in."

When the dealer frowned, Doc quietly shook with a self-amused laugh and then coughed into his fist until his eyes were teary. Bringing out his linen handkerchief, he waited to see if more was to come. He got his breath and cleared his throat with a wretched scraping sound that made the bartender look his way.

"Study what and where the demand is . . . then supply it," Holliday offered curtly. He spat into the handkerchief and shot a look of disdain at the dealer. "That's all the free advice I'm giving you."

When the salesman excused himself and stood, the dealer filled his cheeks with air and exhaled with a quiet flutter of lips. Then he, too, stood and nodded a good night to the table. Picking up his diminished tray of chips he made his way to the bar.

"What else is in demand, Doc?" Wyatt said. "I'd sure as hell like to know."

Doc began counting his chips. "Why? Are you considering a change of vocation? Are you finally tired of hammering your gun barrel over the heads of miscreants and desperados and Texans in general?"

Wyatt pulled a cigar from his shirt and watched the fiddle player nod to the guitarist as they began a new piece of music. With the room so nearly emptied, the musicians had turned their chairs toward one another. And so began a waltz that poured through the saloon like a redemptive prayer.

"I'm burned out on the law," Wyatt said. The tone in his voice brought a soft light into Doc's eyes.

"You surprise me, Wyatt," Doc said. "I thought that you'd be basking in the light of heroic repute after bringing that Kenedy boy back to stand trial."

Doc patted Wyatt's shoulder, but he said no more when he saw the look on his friend's face. They listened for a time as the artistry of the musicians seemed to elevate the room into something more than a dusty saloon in a Kansas cow town.

"Kenedy's father was in town today," Wyatt finally said as he put away his pocket watch that had lain next to his chips before him. He pulled out a cigar and fingered a match from the box on the table. Before striking the match, he looked Doc in the eye. "The trial was held behind closed doors, and the boy walked out of court free as you please."

As he sorted through his chips, Doc pursed his lips into a contemptuous smile. "Ah, yes, my friend . . . the age-old story of mankind's inviable system of jurisprudence . . . and the quiet jangle of heavy coins on the scales of justice."

Wyatt turned the match between his thumb and index as though inspecting its straightness. "It appears that some people can commit a murder . . . and then just pay for it." He struck the match and lighted the cigar. When he extinguished the match flame with a stream of smoke, he looked at Doc again. "Makes what I do sort of the horse's ass, don't it?"

"Maybe all of us," Doc said. He gave up on counting his chips and swept them into his hat. "Whose life would you say *is* meaningful, Wyatt? The judge? The mayor? Rutherford B. Hayes? Dora Hand?" Doc coughed and laughed at the same time. "We like to think we make a dent, don't we? But it comes to the same for all of us. One short song then the curtain falls." Doc's mouth tightened into a wicked smile. "We all just end up tucked away in a wooden box, don't we? Wyatt, nobody is going to remember you or me after they cover us with dirt. So what's the point?"

When Wyatt said nothing, the two men remained motionless

for a time, listening to the lilt of the waltz as though it were reaching them from some foreign place to which they might never gain access. When the last note was played, Doc watched the musicians pack up their instruments, then he tossed his hat brim-up on the table, the chips rattling inside the crown.

"Most of the poor bastards I've known tell me there's some kind of immortality in simply passing on their seed."

Wyatt pulled the cigar from his mouth and narrowed his eyes. "You figure on doing that, Doc?"

Doc scowled and coughed up one more laugh. "Hell, no." He groaned and turned his head away to hock up sputum from his chest. He pressed his handkerchief to his mouth, folded it, and put it away.

"Where's Kate tonight?" Wyatt asked.

Holliday snorted. "Probably in the stockyards bedding a prize bull. She claims I'm not enough for her these days." He tapped his fingertips to his chest. "Says this stuff is wearing thin on her feminine sensibilities."

Wyatt turned his cigar and studied the orange coal glowing from the tobacco. It was the first time Doc had acknowledged his disease in Wyatt's presence. Wyatt reasoned that because Doc had saved his life, he could broach the question that few men would.

"You're dying, ain't you, Doc?"

Holliday laughed and assumed a philosophical tone. "We're all dying, Wyatt. I'm just doing it faster than most."

They sat without talking, listening to the silence expand inside the room now that the momentum of the music was no longer there to push time forward. Wyatt checked his pocket watch again, snapped the case shut, and let the simple gesture announce his intentions. He nodded to Doc, stood, and carried his chips to the cashier at the bar. With the transaction complete, he walked outside to the boardwalk.

The night air carried a chill, and the change of season felt hopeful to Wyatt, as though the welcome cycling of the plains toward autumn might just as naturally bring transition to his life as well. He drew on the cigar for a dose of reality. The street was quiet but for the tinkle of a piano down the street.

Doc stepped out on the boardwalk and took a pull on his flask. He closed his eyes, exhaled his pleasure, and then pocketed the whiskey.

"That stuff help?" Wyatt asked.

Doc smiled and patted the flask under his coat. "Better than a prayer."

A horseman passed by at a trot and crossed the tracks to the south side. Then a collective laugh erupted two blocks away from the Varieties Theater, and, in the lull that followed, the quiet of the prairie seemed to stake its permanent claim over the town . . . and over all the foolish dreams of the people who lived in it.

"Doc, I reckon you already made a dent."

"Oh, really?" Doc replied, his voice both hoarse and doubtful.

"Weren't for you," Wyatt said staring out into the plaza, "I prob'ly wouldn' be standing here right now."

Doc lowered his gaze to the edge of the walkway and tumbled coins in his trouser pockets. "Wyatt," he said with an uncharacteristically nervous laugh, "did you ever consider that you might be saving *my* life?"

Wyatt paused with the cigar an inch from his mouth. He turned to see Holliday's smile fade to a contemplative frown.

"How many brothers do you have, Wyatt?"

"There's six of us in all."

Holliday drank heavily from his flask and exhaled a burst of whiskey-scented breath. "I've met Morgan and James. What are the others like?"

"We're all different . . . and all the same. You know how it is with brothers, Doc."

Holliday screwed down the cap on the flask and turned his head to the pink glow spreading through the clouds in the east. He took in a deep ragged breath and then let it out so slowly it might have been a sigh.

"Not really," he said.

The sun appeared then like an ember smoldering inside a mass of cotton. The two men watched it rise above the yellowing prairie grass, spreading its scarlet color across the land like blood resurfacing from a mythical battlefield. Neither commented on the display. When the red hue faded and the morning yielded to the prosaic drab tones of dying buffalo grass, Wyatt stepped down into the street.

"I'm going to make the rounds," he said. "Walk with me."

They did not talk as they crossed the plaza and started down Bridge Street on the way to Locust. Turning toward the row of lighted saloons, they moved along the boardwalk and let the footfall of their boots mark time. Their shadows moved ahead of them on the tread boards, two dark, elongated shapes that sometimes fused into a single amorphous wraith floating across the sunlit walkway.

"You know, Wyatt, when I first met you in Fort Griffin, you told me your line of work was on the green cloth. Maybe you should follow the boomtowns while they're still booming. That's where the money is. There is really not much left in this town but cow shit and contentious whores."

Wyatt nodded. "The mining towns show promise. I expect miners, engineers, and investors are easier to live with than these Texas boys, who think it's their sworn duty to raise hell at the end of a trail."

"Ever try to have a civil conversation with one of those cattle pushers, Wyatt?" Doc laughed. "They're about as enlightened as the Godforsaken animals they drive to the slaughter. They even dress funny."

Wyatt kept his face neutral and his eyes on the saloons ahead. "You were just raised different, Doc."

Doc conceded the point with a laugh. "Well, old habits and good clothes might be all I have to remind me I'm not a stinking Texas drover . . . now that I'm not a dentist anymore."

Without altering his pace, Wyatt turned to look at his friend. "So you've given it up for good?"

Doc made a wry laugh. "I think it would be more accurate to say it gave *me* up," he quipped. "The public does not appreciate a consumptive breathing down their throats. It was a star-crossed ambition for me." This time there was no flippant humor in the confession, nor were the words shored up with self-pity.

"You plan to gamble your time out, Doc?"

"It seems as good a way to go out as any. Not here in Dodge though. I might head down to New Mexico. I've heard that the gambling is good there, and the dry climate might suit me better."

"What about Kate? Will you take her with you?"

"Kate?" Doc said, surprised at the question. He snorted quietly through his nose. "Who knows? Our relationship seems to be redefined each week. She's a handful, I admit—a fire-cat out of hell, if truth be told—but there aren't too many women willing to share a bed with someone in my condition. What about you? Will you pull out alone?"

"I reckon so."

"Any time soon?" Doc asked, turning now to see Wyatt's expression.

"Soon as I figure out where the hell I'm goin'," Wyatt replied, his voice edged by the lack of deliberation in his plans.

Doc slowed, put a hand on Wyatt's shoulder, and let it slide off as Wyatt kept walking.

"Well, whenever we do ride out of this piss hole of a town," Doc called out to his back, "here's to the good fortunes waiting for us out there." Wyatt stopped and turned to see Doc raising his silver flask with a flourish. Doc struck a dramatic pose and waxed poetic. "May our wayward paths cross again somewhere, Wyatt." Then Doc's voice smoothed out with a hint of tenderness. "I certainly hope they will."

Wyatt watched him pull at the whiskey like a man condemned to swallow his own poison. "Good luck, Doc," Wyatt said, wondering which would kill Doc first—the disease or the alcohol.

Dawn had fully spilled across the prairie when Wyatt finished his rounds and returned to the Dodge House. He walked the hallway toward his room and, turning the last corner, stopped to let his eyes adjust and assemble the details of a dark figure slumped on the floor.

"Lillie?" he said, loosening his grip on his holstered gun.

He walked the length of the hall and came within inches of the visitor before recognizing Mattie. Slowly, she stood and covered her face with her hands, sobbing quietly, the muffled sound reminiscent of that first night they had stayed together on the prairie after she had run off from James's brothel.

"Can we talk inside, Wyatt?" she mumbled, her voice blurring inside the cup of her hands.

The familiar sound of the key in the latch was strangely disturbing to him. With Mattie drying her eyes behind him, he wasn't sure what he was walking into. The dark room smelled of cigar smoke and gun oil, and the caustic scent reminded him how Mattie had once kept the air sweet with rose petals floating in a bowl of water.

She remained just inside the doorway as he walked to the

table by the bed. There he struck a match and lighted the lamp. He blew out the match, tossed it in the tin can he used as an ash receptacle, and stood looking out the window. When the strain of the quiet drew out, he unbuckled his gun belt, hooked it on the back of the chair, and leaned into the window frame.

"I'm getting out of this line of work, Mattie," he said.

He had not heard his own voice in this room for months, and now his words came back to him off the glass like a third person mocking him for his procrastinations. He turned to look at her, and her face appeared uncommonly resolute. She continued to stand in the doorway with one hand still on the doorknob. When she offered no response, he turned back to the window and looked across the roofs of the saloons and other businesses toward the vastness of the prairie sprawling far to the west.

"I'm leaving Dodge," he continued in a rare soliloquy. "Time to do something with more promise to it . . . something with a future."

The door closed, and he turned to see if she had left or come inside. A wrinkled shirt lay on the bed, and she picked it up, folded it, and smoothed it against her stomach. Wyatt turned back to the window and peered north, taking in the respectable side of Dodge. He did not know the names of the people who owned some of those homes, but he knew they had something he did not.

"Wyatt," Mattie said and stepped quietly to him.

She turned him by his shoulder and flattened her hands on his chest. When he looked down, she began unbuttoning his shirt. He started to speak, but she quickly pressed two light fingertips to his lips.

"It's all right, Wyatt." She smiled wanly. "Just tonight."

He had not seen her act in such a straightforward manner since the night she had stolen James's horse and struck out across the prairie. Watching the calm certainty in her face, he let her lead him to the bed and push him back so she could pull off his boots.

Months passed before he saw her again. He had bided his time in Dodge merely to finish out the cattle season, and during this time of fulfilling his last stint as a lawman, he had heard nothing about her. Then, just like before, Mattie was waiting in the hallway, her arms wrapped around her midsection as she pressed her back into the wall. As he approached her, he reminded himself of her long-suffering dependency on him in Wichita. He began putting together the words for a final good-bye . . . words that would leave no doubt as to the separate paths they would take. There were other things that needed saying, too, he supposed, but he would rather say them here in the hallway than in his room. He wasn't going to repeat the show of weakness and compromise that had marked his last concession to her.

"Got a letter from my brother Virgil," Wyatt said, trying to establish an aloof tenor for the conversation—any topic that did not involve Mattie. "Soon as I finish up the season here, we're plannin' to throw in together and join the silver strike in the Arizona Territory. James, too." He'd almost said *and their wives.*

She blinked at the floor. "Arizona," she whispered, as though trying out the sound of a new word. Then she looked up. "I need to talk to you, Wyatt. Can we go inside?"

He pushed a hand into the pocket of his coat. "That's not a good idea, Mattie."

She was so still, she seemed not to breathe. Wyatt lightly slapped his hat against his leg.

"Wyatt," she whispered, and then her eyes went dead. "I'm pregnant."

Her words leapt out at him, like the flapping of a bird, a sound that seemed to fill his ears. Then the noise buried itself somewhere deep inside him, like a tough piece of food that he had to chew into something manageable enough to swallow. The hallway grew so quiet, Wyatt could hear a jingling harness and the rattle of a wagon as it moved along the rutted thoroughfare of Front Street.

Then before he could ask, she added, "I'm carrying your child, Wyatt."

CHAPTER 22

Fall to winter, 1879: Dodge City to Arizona Territory

It had been a bad season for all the cattle towns. The drought that had dried up the Kansas plains in the summer of '79 cut the beef business by half in Dodge City. With the season over and the majority of Texans returned to their home state, policing the town had grown so mundane that Wyatt decided to stop waiting for proof of Mattie's claim of pregnancy. He might as well go ahead and face what had to be faced and get started on this new life in the hinterlands of Arizona. Having Mattie with him altered nothing about the fortune to be gained. The rewards were there for any man bold enough to stake his future on the new silver mines.

Virgil's latest letter described rich veins of ore waiting for them beneath the sandy floor of the southeastern Arizona deserts. It was all there for the taking. A place called "Tombstone." When Wyatt instructed Mattie to be ready to leave by September, she held a stoic expression on her face, but she could not hide the relief and exhilaration that showed like tiny candle flames flickering deep in her dark, homely eyes.

Wyatt bought a freight wagon with a substantial ash frame that, once he was settled in, he would convert into a stagecoach. It was not as grand an enterprise as he had hoped for, but it was at least a plan that did not involve a badge. That alone seemed to him a promising start.

On the day Mattie brought her belongings to the Dodge

House for packing the new wagon, she seemed touched by a new purpose in her prosaic life. Her mood was hopeful and her hands industrious. As she helped gather up Wyatt's personal belongings scattered around the room, she picked up a Bible off the dresser and opened the cover.

" 'To Wyatt S. Earp,' " she read aloud, " 'as a slight recognition of his many Christian virtues and steady following in the footsteps of the meek and lowly Jesus.' "

She looked up, as if expecting an explanation from Wyatt. When he held his attention on buckling the straps of the clothing trunk he had packed, Mattie looked back at the cursive inscription inside the book.

"Who are Sutton and Colborn?" Mattie asked, frowning.

Wyatt lifted the trunk and carried it just outside the door to leave in the hallway for the porter. When he came back inside, he started consolidating his gun-cleaning kit.

"Couple o' lawyers who work for the city and the county," he finally replied. He shook his head. Then his grim expression barely altered when one side of his mouth curled into a false smile. "Prob'ly their idea of a joke," he said, "after I told the city council I would need something more than what they were willing to pay me if I was to stay on."

"I don't think it's a joke, Wyatt," Mattie said with a rare and convincing tenderness. "You've been an excellent officer here. You held your position with honor, and people respect you for it."

Wyatt thought of the scores of Texans who had fallen under the sting of his revolver barrel. "You don't know what all I had to do as a marshal, Mattie. No need to overplay what I did or did not do here in Dodge."

She frowned and studied the profile of his face as he wrapped a pistol in muslin and stowed it inside a canvas rucksack. "You didn't become a killer, Wyatt . . . like so many other lawmen."

Now he looked at her, and the expression in his eyes caused her to swallow her words. "I've killed, Mattie."

Her frown deepened. "You don't know that, Wyatt. That young Texan who died could have been shot by—"

"It was my bullet," he said.

She pressed her upper teeth into her lower lip and began shaking her head. "Wyatt, you can't know—"

"It was my bullet," he interrupted again, this time in a flat tone of finality. "I know."

She looked down at the Bible again, closed it, flattened her hand on the front cover, and stroked it as if she had learned to calm the soul of a book. "Wyatt, people don't write jokes inside a Bible."

Wyatt allowed a look of distaste and hooked the rucksack over a shoulder. "Mike Sutton might hire a juggler and a fire-eater for his own funeral if he thought he could get one last laugh out of it."

"Well," she said, and began folding the book inside a work shirt he had not yet packed, "we'll want to take good care of this, Wyatt. One day it might mean a lot to you." To cut off his argument, she quickly placed the package in the valise on the bed. "What will you and your brothers do first in Arizona? Will you be mining the silver? Do you have a plan?"

Wyatt set the rucksack outside the door and gave the hotel boy instructions on how to pack the wagon out back. When he returned, he propped his hands on his hips and surveyed the room for any item he might have missed.

"We're gonna open a stage line. That wagon out by the livery is the first step in building a business. I'll convert it into a passenger coach once we get there, and we'll be transporting people to the new boomtown from the railroad and then carting bullion away. That last one . . . that's a service as important as chipping the ore out of the ground and smelting it down to pure grade."

"But it sounds dangerous, Wyatt. Someone will have to guard that silver on the trip, won't they? *You* won't do that, will you?"

"If necessary, I'll ride shotgun, if that's what it takes to get the business off the ground. Later we'll hire guards."

Wyatt shouldered the last of the bags and waited for her.

"I hope you don't have to do that, Wyatt," she said. "We don't know anything about that place . . . or the people down there."

Wyatt picked up the lever-action Winchester by the door. "You ready?"

Mattie hurriedly closed her last garment bag and hoisted it inside a circle she made with her arms. She walked to him, freed up one hand, and lightly touched his upper arm as though feeling for heat through the fabric of his blouse.

"I'm ready," she said and braved a smile for their new beginning. "I'm ready, Wyatt."

Without any more words, they walked out of the hotel for the last time and packed the last pieces of their gear in the wagon bed. By the time Wyatt had checked the harnesses and helped Mattie into the driver's box, James's wagon rolled into view out on Railroad Avenue and stopped. Bessie sat in the box with James, and her daughter Hattie nestled between them with a pale blue bonnet tied to her head. Wyatt snapped the reins and pulled his wagon out onto the street to flank his brother's.

"Damn, son," James laughed, making a show of examining Wyatt's belongings, "is that all you got to call your own?"

Wyatt looked at the furniture, cedar chests, boxes of cookware, and bulging stuff-sacks piled into his brother's spring wagon. James's two draft horses appeared sorely lacking for the journey ahead of them. One was the old sorrel mare Mattie had stolen the time she had run away from Bessie's brothel.

Wyatt patted his shirt pocket, where he kept the modest roll of cash he had saved from his last season as an officer. "Most o' what I got is right here. The rest is what I'm sittin' on." He nodded to the draft horses and poked a thumb over his shoulder at the string of horses tethered to the tail gate. "And the horses."

James eyed the two stout bays standing in the traces of Wyatt's rig. Then he leaned to admire the two saddle ponies, the high-legged racer, and the four braces of coach haulers.

"That the Thoroughbred you won in that poker game with the Pierce crowd?"

Wyatt nodded. "Took him with a full house . . . jacks over nines." He turned to consider his most valuable possession.

James couldn't help but concede Wyatt's primary assets with a smile and a bow of his head. "You keep drawing cards like that, little brother, and you'll be set up like a king in the Arizona Territory. Tombstone will pull in sporting men like a cow patty draws flies. And horse racing is gettin' to be the bull's balls . . . all over the country. Hell, we might open a high-class gambling room with faro tables as the centerpiece. We can grade a track somewhere outside of town and set up horse races on the side."

Wyatt considered the possibilities. He did love gambling. Almost all forms of it. It was in his blood.

"Maybe after we get the stage line off to a good start," he replied.

James made a point of admiring the Thoroughbred. "What'd you name that purse-stealer?"

Wyatt made the little sideways shrug with his head that he rarely used. "Already had a name. I didn' figure on changin' it."

"Yeah? What's that?"

Wyatt almost checked Mattie's face, but instead he re-threaded the reins through his fingers. "Dick Naylor."

"That's right!" James laughed. "One o' the Mastersons told me." He smiled at the regal steed standing behind Wyatt's wagon. "Said that horse is so fast out of the start, looks like the others got their peckers nailed to the gate."

Bessie laughed and held her hands over her daughter's ears. Mattie had not even heard the crude joke. She looked up at the second floor of the Dodge House, as if she were paying a farewell homage to a milepost in her lackluster life.

Wyatt nodded toward the river where the Santa Fe Trail skirted the south end of town. It was the same well-used wagon route his father had taken to California with the family. He wondered how many parties had struck out on this trail in search of their El Dorados. Now it would deliver Wyatt to the Southwest for *his* fresh start. At thirty-one years old he felt as though he were pushing all the chips to the center of the table. He was betting everything on this place called "Tombstone."

They made the long haul to Prescott, where Virgil and Allie ran a saw mill at the edge of town. Virgil still owned the Studebaker with bows and canvas sheeting—the wagon in which he and Allie had traveled with Old Nick when they had passed through Dodge City two years past. For the Tombstone trip, they had packed more housewares than the other families combined. It was Virgil, it seemed, who had sunk his roots deepest into domesticity, but now all the Earps had joined in the common quest for respectability. James even declared his and Bessie's intent to stop pimping whores.

Because Virgil had once served as a spur-of-the-moment deputy and provided the crucial firepower during a shootout in Prescott, US Marshal Crawley Dake stopped by the Earp train and asked him to wear a federal deputy badge in the Tombstone district.

"You'll need more'n one deputy, won't you?" Virgil said.

"I will." Dake sighed. "I figure you're a good start. There's one or two more I'm considering."

Virgil's laugh rumbled quietly from his chest. He beckoned

the marshal with a curl of his finger.

"Come over here and meet my brother," said Virgil, grinning.

As they walked toward the back of their small, three-wagon train, Virgil snapped his fingers, and his little caramel-colored dog trotted on short legs to keep up. Virge turned to smile at Dake. He lowered his voice but his face shone with pride.

"Wyatt was assistant marshal in Dodge City . . . and before that . . . Wichita."

Dake lifted his eyebrows and nodded.

Wyatt crouched by the Studebaker, where he helped Allie tie her sewing machine to the side panel. Smiling openly now, Virge showed off his badge to Allie, who seemed not to know how to react to the commission. Wyatt straightened up and said nothing as he stared first at his brother and then at the federal marshal and his well-manicured beard.

"Crawley Dake," the marshal began affably and offered his hand.

Wyatt met the man's smooth grip and shook, but let his eyes angle away to the half-lashed sewing machine. Dake propped his hands on the sides of his pear-shaped hips, exposing the bright silver federal shield pinned to his vest. He made a crisp nod toward Wyatt.

"Your brother tells me you were a lawman in Kansas."

"Was," Wyatt said.

The marshal nodded encouragingly. "I need some reliable agents in the Tombstone district. Are you interested?"

Wyatt faced Dake and studied the little hammocks of sagging flesh beneath the man's eyes. The bureaucrat must have been desperate to rise so early before the Earp train departed Prescott.

"I already got plans," Wyatt said and let the marshal see the determination in his eyes. "Gonna open up a stage line."

Dake's brow furrowed in a show of regret. "You might be a little late on that, I'm afraid. There are two lines running a price war in Tombstone right now. Might be hard to elbow your way into that business."

Wyatt looked away, and his gaze fell on Mattie, already seated in the driver's box of the wagon. She was fitting a bonnet over her new way of piling her hair on top of her head. The wagon she sat upon was his hope for a future, and now this pasty-faced bureaucrat with a woman's hands was telling him his plans were for naught. He snugged the rope on the sewing machine and fixed it fast with an unforgiving hitch.

Dake smiled. "I admit the pay is not so enticing. You only draw wages when you are on assignment. But I need another good man. You'll be reimbursed for time, mileage, meals, and horse rentals. You would supply your own weapons and ammunition."

"Don't hurt to have a badge, Wyatt," Virge prompted.

Wyatt tightened the last knot and pushed his anger back into its cage. "No," he said in a flat tone. "I reckon I can get my hands into something." He plucked at the lashing with a forefinger, and the rope thrummed with a deep, taut note.

Virgil picked up the dog and laughed quietly as he moved Dake away. "Having Wyatt down there with me will work in your favor, Crawley. He'll help me out when I need it." Looking into the dog's eager face, he tousled the fur at the base of its ears. "Ain't that right, Frank?"

"You'll have the power to appoint deputies," Dake said and nodded back in Wyatt's direction. "I hope he'll be first on your list." The marshal offered his hand to Virgil. "I know Dodge City's reputation. I can use a man who stood up to that."

Virgil shifted the dog in his grip and shook hands. He smiled as he watched Wyatt secure an extra rope to the sewing machine.

"Hell, Crawley," Virge said and grunted as he lowered the dog to the ground. "Wyatt was born to it. He just won't admit it."

When Dake walked away, Wyatt climbed up into the driver's box with Mattie and found that she had cushioned the plank seat with folded blankets. He nodded his appreciation and began untying the reins from the brake handle.

"Reckon you'll be all right bouncing 'round up here?" he asked. "We could set a pallet in back. Might go easier on you."

Mattie smiled at him and then looked out over the stretch of desert and its unfamiliar plant life. The plains of Kansas had been stark with the sameness of its endless grasslands. Now this sandy terrain beyond the mill Virgil and Allie were leaving was no less stark by its own right.

Venturing forward, for Mattie, was as daunting as setting out into a foreign land whose story was known only through rumor. Sitting straight backed on the seat, she shook her head in tiny increments and lifted her chin.

"I want to see where we're going, Wyatt."

She pushed a loose strand of hair from her forehead and tucked it under the bonnet. When she turned to Wyatt, he leaned from the box to check the status of the horses behind them.

"Who was that man you talked to?" Mattie asked quietly.

Wyatt settled back on the seat and took up slack in the reins. He propped his boots on the front of the box and rested his elbows on his thighs.

"US marshal."

She frowned and kept studying the profile of his face. "What did he want?" she probed.

Wyatt pursed his lips and looked down at the reins laced through his fingers. "Appears Virge accepted a federal appointment."

Mattie frowned. "What does that mean? What kind of appointment?"

Wyatt squinted into the distance. "Means he's a deputy US marshal in the district where we're headed."

She was quiet for a long time. He could feel her stare burning into the side of his face. It was like heat radiating from an oven. He rubbed his thumbs against the smooth leather straps in his hands and watched the horses twitch at flies with controlled shivers from isolated muscles along their flanks.

"I thought the Earps were through with lawing and whoring," she said as gently as she could.

Slowly Wyatt began to nod. Then he turned to her and saw the worry that had spread across her simple face.

"Virge is gonna do whatever he wants to. I can't control that."

"But they listen to you, Wyatt."

He huffed a quiet laugh through his nose. "Apparently, not all the time," he said.

"What about *you,* Wyatt?" she whispered.

"What *about* me?"

"Are you a deputy, too?"

He shook his head and looked as far down the trail as the morning light allowed. In the east the red smoldering sun was still broken into shards of burning light behind the low canopy of an orchard. As he watched, the top of the blood-red orb bobbed above the treetops and cast an eerie glow on everything it touched.

Wyatt had hoped to be traveling by first light, but already he was making the necessary adjustments that are part and parcel of joining up with family. The benefits, he knew, would eventually outweigh the inconveniences.

"Mattie, all I want to do is travel down there to this new silver strike and fill this wagon up with money. Enough to set us up for life." He turned back to her and nodded toward her belly, where the promise of a child lay hidden beneath her handmade outfit. "Then we'll find us a more hospitable place to set down roots."

When he gazed back at the horizon, she slid closer and hugged his arm. "Do you think we'll be rich, Wyatt?"

He gently swung one of the reins in a shallow arc and shooed a fly from the off-wheeler's rump. "There's lot o' people gettin' rich in Tombstone, Mattie. No reason we can't be a part o' that."

She squeezed his arm tighter and pressed her cheek into his shoulder. "Why would they want to name a place 'Tombstone'?" she wondered aloud.

Wyatt said nothing. Up in front, the dog made a series of yipping barks until Virge climbed down from the Studebaker to lift the animal into the crowded bed of his wagon. With the addition of the dog, James was teasing Virgil and Allie about the volume of freight in their wagon. Virge knew better than to play into James's bantering, but Allie was holding her own.

Wyatt slipped from Mattie's grip and leaned to check on his brothers. James made a little salute from his receding hairline, and Virgil brusquely waved at the air as a semaphore to get moving. Wyatt jerked the brake handle free and set his boots down on the floor of the box.

"Reckon when we get down there, Mattie, we'll have to ask somebody 'bout that name," he said and lifted the reins to snap them lightly on the backs of his team.

When the wagons began to roll, there seemed to be something more than wheels and horses set into motion. Wyatt and his brothers were on their way to find their fortune. Joined together as they were, it seemed improbable that they could not succeed. Just like the light filling the morning sky, there was promise in the air. The Earps would make their mark in Tombstone. Wyatt was betting it all.

BIBLIOGRAPHY

Wyatt Earp, The Life Behind the Legend by Casey Tefertiller: John Wiley & Sons, Inc., 1997

Doc Holliday, The Life and the Legend by Gary Roberts: John Wiley & Sons, Inc., 2006

Wyatt Earp; The Search for Law and Order on the Last Frontier by Gary Roberts, from *With Badges and Bullets,* edited by R. W. Etulain & G. Riley: Fulcrum Publishing, 1999

Wyatt Earp: A Biography of the Legend by Lee Silva: Graphic Publishers, 2002

Wyatt Earp: Frontier Marshal by Stuart Lake: Houghton Mifflin Co., 1931

Dodge City by Frederic Young: Boot Hill Museum, Inc., 1972

The Illustrated Life and Times of Wyatt Earp by Bob Boze Bell: Tri Star-Boze Publications, 1993

The Illustrated Life and Times of Doc Holliday by Bob Boze Bell: Tri Star-Boze Publications, 1994

The Buffalo Hunters by Charles Robinson III: State House Press, 1995

Great Gunfighters of the Kansas Cowtowns: 1867-1886 by Nyle H. Miller and Joseph W. Snell: University of Nebraska Press, 1963

The Cowboys by William H. Forbis: Time-Life Books, 1973

The Gunfighters by Paul Trachtman: Time-Life Books, 1974

Inventing Wyatt Earp: His Life and Many Legends by Allen Barra: Carroll & Graf Publishers, Inc., 1998

Bat Masterson: The Man and the Legend by Robert DeArment: University of Oklahoma Press, 1979

Famous Gunfighters of the Western Frontier by W. B. (Bat) Masterson: Dover Publications, Inc., 2009

Age of the Gunfighter by Joseph Rosa: University of Oklahoma Press, 1993

Wyatt Earp: A Biography of a Western Lawman by Steve Gatto: San Simon Publishing Co., 1997

Wyatt Earp Speaks by John Stevens: Fern Canyon Press, 1998

The Earp Papers: In a Brother's Image by Don Chaput: Affiliated Writers of America, Inc., 1994

The Truth About Wyatt Earp by Richard Erwin: The O.K. Press, 1993

The Earps Talk by Al Turner: Creative Publishing Co., 1980

Virgil Earp: Western Peace Officer by Don Chaput: Affiliated Writers of America, Inc., 1994

The Earp Brothers of Tombstone (original transcript in Arizona Historical Society) by Frank Waters: University of Nebraska Press, 1976

Travesty: Frank Waters' Earp Agenda Exposed by S. J. Reidhead: Jinglebob Press, 2005

Wyatt Earp: The Untold Story, 1848–1880 by Ed Bartholomew: Frontier Book Co., 1963

ABOUT THE AUTHOR

Mark Warren is a teacher of Native American survival skills. He lives with his wife, Susan, and dog, Sadie, in the Appalachian Mountains of north Georgia. His research into the Earp story has spanned sixty-plus years. Through his travels and studies he has interviewed the storied writers of the Earp saga and trekked with them to sites where the actual events in Earp's life took place.

Warren is the author of *Two Winters in a Tipi*, Lyons Press, 2012, *Secrets of the Forest, Volumes I, II, & III*, Waldenhouse, 2016-18, and *Adobe Moon*, Five Star Publishing, 2017.

The employees of Five Star Publishing hope you have enjoyed this book.

Our Five Star novels explore little-known chapters from America's history, stories told from unique perspectives that will entertain a broad range of readers.

Other Five Star books are available at your local library, bookstore, all major book distributors, and directly from Five Star/Gale.

Connect with Five Star Publishing

Visit us on Facebook:
   https://www.facebook.com/FiveStarCengage

Email:
   FiveStar@cengage.com

For information about titles and placing orders:
   (800) 223-1244
   gale.orders@cengage.com

To share your comments, write to us:
   Five Star Publishing
   Attn: Publisher
   10 Water St., Suite 310
   Waterville, ME 04901